World War One Short Stories

DOVER · THRIFT · EDITIONS

World War One Short Stories

EDITED BY
BOB BLAISDELL

DOVER PUBLICATIONS, INC.
Mineola, New York

DOVER THRIFT EDITIONS

GENERAL EDITOR: MARY CAROLYN WALDREP
EDITOR OF THIS VOLUME: BOB BLAISDELL

ACKNOWLEDGMENTS

Richard Aldington: "Introduction to the Trenches" from *Death of a Hero* by Richard Aldington, copyright 1929 by Richard Aldington, renewed © 1956 by the Estate of Richard Aldington. Used by permission of Penguin, a division of Penguin Group (USA) Inc.

Mary Borden: "Blind" from *The Forbidden Zone* by Mary Borden. Used by permission.

A. P. Herbert: "The Indomitable Tweedy" by A. P. Herbert. Used by permission of A P Watt Ltd on behalf of The Executors of the Estate of Jocelyn Herbert, MT Perkins and Polly MVR Perkins.

Somerset Maugham: "The Traitor" from *Ashenden* by Somerset Maugham. Used by permission of A P Watt Ltd on behalf of The Royal Literary Fund.

Copyright

Bibliographical Note

World War One Short Stories, first published by Dover Publications, Inc., in 2013, is a new anthology of short stories reprinted from standard sources. A new introductory Note has been specially prepared for this edition.

Library of Congress Cataloging-in-Publication Data

World War One short stories / edited by Bob Blaisdell.
    pages cm. — (Dover thrift editions)
  Summary: "This original anthology features tales written mostly by former soldiers and others with firsthand experience of World War I's devastation. Contents include "Introduction to the Trenches" by Richard Aldington, "The Blind Ones," by Isaak Babel, and tales by Ford Madox Ford, John Galsworthy, Rudyard Kipling, Katherine Mansfield, and others"— Provided by publisher.
  Includes bibliographical references.
  ISBN-13: 978-0-486-48503-4 (pbk.) — ISBN-10: 0-486-48503-X
  1. War stories, English. 2. World War, 1914–1918—Fiction. 3. English fiction—20th century. I. Blaisdell, Robert, editor of compilation.
  PR1309.W37W67 2013
  823'.912080358403—dc23

                                                                      2013003546

Manufactured in the United States by Courier Corporation
48503X02   2014
www.doverpublications.com

Contents

NOTE

What treacherous lying is all the heroic poetry of battle!
—H. M. TOMLINSON
"A RAID NIGHT" (SEPTEMBER 17, 1915)

THE SOLDIERS SERVING on the battlefields of Europe during the terrible years of the Great War, 1914–1918, were not composing short stories. Letters and poems, protests and songs, but rarely fiction. The fiction that was eventually created from first-hand experiences usually took several years to crystallize. We also know that in England and Germany there were editors and politicians who did not want their noncombatant citizens to think about or know what was really going on in the trenches of France and Belgium. After thousands and then millions of deaths, there was nothing inspiring about the soldiers continuing to be mown down by bombs, poison gas and machine guns. In "A Raid Night," H. M. Tomlinson's narrator, a journalist who has returned to London after covering the Western Front, blames the mass medium of the time, *newspapers*: ". . . this office was an essential feature of the War; without it, the War might become Peace. It provoked the emotions which assembled civilians in ecstatic support of the sacrifices, just as the staff of a corps headquarters, at some comfortable leagues behind the trenches, maintains its fighting men in the place where gas and shells tend to engender common sense and irresolution."[1]

The suppression of the real news, however, also may have been the result of the soldiers choosing not to make themselves or their loved ones fully conscious of the terrors and mayhem; most of the writers included in this anthology were veterans and spared the homefront the bloodiest details and the most haunting experiences until the war was over. The British artist and author Wyndham Lewis, for example, wrote stories of the war before he enlisted; after serving on the lines,

---

1. H. M. Tomlinson, "A Raid Night." See page 35.

he completely reassessed what his powerful imagination had not been able to appreciate before. Richard Aldington, one of the most prominent of England's literary young men, was able to put into verse his war experiences almost immediately; but he did not publish the autobiographical tales that made up his novel, *Death of a Hero*, until 1929.

The war, which essentially began in June 1914 with the assassination of the Archduke Ferdinand of Austria, and a blustering aggressive Germany daring Europe to call its and Austria-Hungary's military bluff in Serbia, soon drew in countries that wished to save themselves from being run over by Germany as Belgium already had been; Belgium's quiet countryside was devastated by years of trench warfare. Maybe the "Great War" could have been worse for Belgium, but not much. Authors from all the involved countries wrote about this war, which extended its reach from Europe into Africa and the Middle East, but in the main the stories in this anthology come from England, Germany, France, America and Russia. By the end of the war, Russia, which had already lost an estimated million men, had withdrawn in order to fight its own national conflict, a civil war that would kill millions more and lead the country into a decades-long Soviet imprisonment.

While the stories are not, except indirectly, about the politics of the time, one important exception is Somerset Maugham's "The Traitor," one of his series of stories about Ashenden, a British spy. And while most of the writers are men, perhaps one of the deepest impressions will be made by the American nurse Mary Borden's story "Blind": "It was my business to sort out the wounded as they were brought in from the ambulances and to keep them from dying before they got to the operating rooms: it was my business to sort out the nearly dying from the dying. I was there to sort them out and tell how fast life was ebbing in them. Life was leaking away from all of them; but with some there was no hurry, with others it was a case of minutes. It was my business to create a counter-wave of life, to create the flow against the ebb. It was like a tug of war with the tide." Blindness, chronicled as well by the Russian short story master Isaak Babel in "The Blind Ones," was just one of the many disabilities that struck the lucky survivors.

Rather than thematically or by country of origin, I have tried to arrange the stories chronologically—that is, by the events described within the stories. Many dates I can only guess, though the guesses sometimes rely on knowledge of when the author himself was serving. In any case we start with May Sinclair's "Red Tape," about the enthusiasm in 1914 that led hundreds of thousands of British citizens to enlist, and end with Katherine Mansfield's "The Fly," about a businessman wondering at the grief that still has him in its grip six years after the death of his soldier-son.

Two of the newest collections of World War One stories, *The Penguin Book of First World War Stories* (2007) and *Women, Men and the Great War: An Anthology of Stories* (1995), both took the odd strategy of exclusion—presenting mostly English stories and a few by Americans. The very best anthology of stories about World War One was titled in 1930, *Great Short Stories of the War: England, France, Germany, America,* but retitled in 1931 as *Best Short Stories of the War* (they are distinguishable only by typeface and by the author introducing the book); its strength is most easily summed up by its breadth and length, providing sixty-six outstanding stories from England, Germany, France and America. The practically uncredited editor of the volume ("H.C.M.") was Major Humphrey Cotton Minchin (1894–1966), who in the war led the Cameronians and Royal Flying Corps. I have modeled this book after Minchin's, as the inclusion of German, French and now Russian stories show the scope and dynamics of the war not wholly disclosed by British points of views. The eighteen stories reveal the distinctive national experiences as well as the *universally* terrible destructiveness of war that has been dramatized ever since Homer sang of the noble and tragic Trojans and Greeks in *The Iliad.*

—BOB BLAISDELL

SELECTED BIBLIOGRAPHY

Richard Aldington. *Death of a Hero*. London: Chatto & Windus, 1929.

Henri Barbusse. *Under Fire: The Story of a Squad*. Translated from the French by Fitzwater Wray. New York: E. P. Dutton and Company, 1917.

Bartimeus. *The Navy Eternal: Which Is the Navy-That-Floats, the Navy-That-Flies and the Navy-under-the-Sea*. London: Hodder & Stoughton, 1918.

Mary Borden. *The Forbidden Zone*. London: Heinemann, 1929.

Ford Madox Ford. *War Prose*. Manchester: Carcanet Press. 1999. [Ford's story was originally published in the magazine *Land and Water*, 72, May 8, 1919.]

John Galsworthy. *Forsytes, Pendyces and Others*. New York: Scribner, 1936.

Great Short Stories of the War: England, France, Germany, America. Edited by H. C. Minchin. Introduction by Edmund Blunden. London: Eyre & Spottiswoode, 1930. (See also: *Best Short Stories of the War*. Introduction by H. M. Tomlinson. New York: Harper and Brothers, 1931. The second is identical to the first except for formatting and the introduction.)

Rudyard Kipling. *A Diversity of Creatures*. Garden City, New York: Doubleday, Page and Company, 1917.

Somerset Maugham. *Ashenden: Or the British Agent*. London: Heinemann, 1928.

Mikhail Andreevich Osorgin [Michael Ossorgin]. *Quiet Street*. Translated by Nadia Helstein. New York: The Dial Press, 1930.

The Penguin Book of First World War Stories. Barbara Korte, editor. London: Penguin, 2007.

Edward John Moreton Drax Plunkett [Lord Dunsany]. *Tales of War*. Boston: Little, Brown and Company, 1918.

William T. Scanlon. *God Have Mercy on Us!: A Story of 1918*. Boston: Houghton Mifflin Company, 1929.

Henry Major Tomlinson. *Waiting for Daylight*. London: Cassell and Company, 1922.

Women, Men and the Great War. Trudi Tate, editor. Manchester, England: Manchester University Press, 1995.

RED TAPE

by May Sinclair

Sinclair (1863–1946) was a prolific British novelist; in 1914 she cut through the red tape that ties up the heroes of this story and worked for the Red Cross's ambulance corps in Belgium.

[Originally published in *The Queen* magazine on November 14, 1914]

I

THEY WERE GOING. Mr. Starkey had made up his mind from the moment of England's ultimatum to Germany. And Miss Delacheroy had made up hers from the moment when he had faced her with it: "I am going to the front."

There was nowhere else, he said, he *could* go. To which Miss Delacheroy had replied, "If you go I go too."

Nothing in all their long association had drawn such a poignant note from her. But Mr. Starkey was visibly uplifted; so, even more visibly, was Miss Delacheroy.

Uplifted or not uplifted, they knew that there could be no two opinions about their going. It was the only way Mr. Starkey could serve his country. And it was the only way Miss Delacheroy could serve Mr. Starkey. She had to confess that, satisfying as her friendship with Mr. Starkey was, it had lacked hitherto its supreme opportunity.

Of course there had been pretexts and occasions. She found them every day in the office of the Kilburn branch of the United Charities, the scene of their associated labours. But none of them appealed to her imagination; none, in her uplifted moods, gave her sanction and absolution; none counted as supreme. Except (she reminded herself) the first occasion of their meeting, which occurred in the office of the United Charities (Kilburn branch). If it came to that, every hour of their association counted, every minute counted, since the day when

Mr. Starkey, as organising secretary, took over the office and its fittings and Miss Delacheroy.

He had a genius for organisation, and he had begun by organising Miss Delacheroy. She had a genius for being organised. It was his boast that he had trained her; it was hers that she had been trained by him.

More than trained. He took her over as an inconsiderable part of the office furniture—a little machine, shoved aside into its corner, rather the worse for wear and working badly. Under his hands she became a living thing.

That was ten years ago.

He had not always been an organising secretary. Once, in his youth, he had been a medical student. He would have been a medical practitioner now if he had not had the bad luck to fail in his final. Nobody but Mr. Starkey knew how long that was ago. And before Miss Delacheroy became a piece of office furniture she had been a lady of leisure, living in her father the General's house, on his income and his pension. Afterwards she lived in the house on her own pension, the General's income having departed with him. That was in Miss Delacheroy's youth, and nobody knew how long ago that was either.

Certainly Mr. Starkey did not know. Once, when he had taken her over, he had wondered. The little machine had been going then, by its own confession, seven years. Even now, glancing over his glasses at the live woman working competently in her corner, he wondered still. Gazing at the delicate, wistful thing over the cup of tea that she gave him every Sunday afternoon, he wondered more than ever. For every Sunday afternoon towards four o'clock, wistfully, delicately, she bloomed. He repressed his wonderings as unchivalrous; for every Sunday afternoon she gave him tea.

Every Sunday afternoon he went to see her, walking from his rooms in Bayswater to her house in Maida Vale. In ten years he had formed the habit.

Sometimes they took a motor bus to Regent's Park or Primrose Hill and walked there together. Sometimes they walked in the Zoological Gardens and looked at the animals. (They were fond of animals.) Mr. Starkey knew a fellow who knew one of the Fellows, and he could get from him as many Sunday tickets as he wanted, so that they could look at the animals for nothing and with a sense of privilege and intimacy unknown to people who have to plank down their shillings at the gate. From his air of knowing all about it, from his important conversations with the keepers, and from the liberties he took with the King Penguin, Miss Delacheroy thought for some time that Mr. Starkey was a Fellow himself.

She liked to be seen walking with him. He was tall, and, in spite of his deplorably lean flanks, impressive. She knew that he had been young once, and it did not seem to her that it could have been so very long ago. He had one of those lean, white faces that wear well. Pale gold hairs glinted among the others in his eyebrows. His top hat, pressed down and tilted backwards, covered the bleak hinterland above the pale gold fringe. Thick-rimmed glasses accentuated his distinguished scheme of pallor and gold.

Sometimes, when it was fine and warm, they sat in Miss Delacheroy's garden and talked. When it was wet they sat in the drawing-room and talked. They talked about their work. They were up to their necks in it. Long ago the United Charities had opened up and swallowed them up. They were in it for life. Even on a Sunday they had difficulty in emerging. The great thing was that they were in it together. Between them they had brought their organisation to such a pitch that the Kilburn branch surpassed all other branches of the United Charities.

She would say, "It couldn't have been done without you."

And he, "It couldn't have been done without *you*, Miss Delacheroy."

He was necessary to her and she was necessary to him, and they were both necessary to the United Charities. They were in it, they agreed, for life.

There were other things he might have done, other people he might have gone to see, younger women whom he might have known, if he had cared. But Mr. Starkey did not care. He did not get on well with other people, for he was much more serious and earnest than other people were. He was much more serious and earnest than it is good for any man to be. He did not get on very well with young women, for young women made him feel not quite so young. He had not formed the habit of them; whereas he *had* formed the habit of Miss Delacheroy. It was not a dangerous habit; and if sometimes a certain fear came over him, a sneaking and unmanly fear, his chivalry suppressed it as it suppressed his wonder. In his secret heart he knew that he was safe. And so every Sunday of his life he walked from his unspeakably depressing rooms in Bayswater to Miss Delacheroy's little house hidden in a side street off Maida Vale. For it was always peaceful there. And the one thing that Mr. Starkey loved more than his own earnestness was peace.

Their communion was interrupted three times a year by the holidays. Whatever else they did together, they never went away together for the holidays. Mr. Starkey was not prepared to go so far as that, and

Miss Delacheroy had not yet been stirred to her depths; therefore she was still unaware how far she was prepared to go. In the year nineteen-fourteen their holidays were fixed for Friday, Aug. 7.

On Tuesday, Aug. 4, Germany declared war on England, and an extraordinary thing happened to Mr. Starkey and Miss Delacheroy. It happened to them on the morning of the ultimatum. It happened to them together. It was the beginning of still more extraordinary things.

They lost all interest in the United Charities. Together, suddenly and unanimously, they lost it.

At first you would not have known it. The work of the United Charities went on as usual. Cases were registered, Miss Delacheroy was seen dictating letters to her typist. Beyond rushing out bare-headed into Kilburn High-road and buying the special edition of five newspapers whose politics he disapproved of, Mr. Starkey betrayed no sign of aberration. But for all that they were in it the Kilburn branch of the United Charities might have been closed like the Stock Exchange. They, in their innermost essential being, were not there. They were submerged in the ultimatum. They could talk of nothing else, they could think of nothing else. There was nothing beyond the ultimatum that they saw or heard or felt. And yet they were not suffering, like the Stock Exchange, from panic. They were ready for the war. They had expected it any time within the last five years. They had both seen through the Kaiser's protestations. Mr. Starkey had had private information from the War Office. (He was always having private information from important places.) They knew that Germany would not accept the ultimatum.

So it is transparent that they had not lost their heads.

It was the ultimatum. It exalted and possessed them. It filled them—it filled Mr. Starkey and Miss Delacheroy—with the power and glory of the world. All day long the ultimatum sounded in their ears like an incantation. It sank into their nerves and worked there like an exquisite poison; it soared into their brains like a magic and almighty wine.

It made them do things, vehement and orgastic things, that they had never done before. It drove them forth together at six o'clock into England's Bohemia. It compelled them to dine together, fever-ishly, in a low restaurant in Soho. It flung them out under the lamp-light on to the surge of the crowd in Trafalgar-square. It swept them with the crowd down Whitehall to Westminster and back again, up the avenue of the Mall, between the solemn ranks of the plane trees and the long processional lights; it thrust them, wedged in the crowd, through the gilded gates, and held them motionless before the golden white façade of Buckingham Palace.

After that it was the mounted police that kept them moving. The water had ceased playing in the fountain. She wondered why. It was then that he asked her where she was going for her holiday.

She said, "I am not going anywhere. I shall stay in London to protect my cat."

He looked down at the water in the basin. It was green as sea water. The jetsam of the crowd floated there. A miniature Union Jack, dropped from a girl's breast, drifted to the stone curb. He looked at it and smiled. He could still smile.

"And you?" She said it for the sake of saying something, for she knew he was going to Llandudno.

He stared at her.

"I? I am going to the front."

A policeman moved them on. It gave her time to recover.

"Oh, no!" she protested. "No; not to the front."

"Where else," he put it to her, "can I go?"

He reminded her that he had been a medical student. She had forgotten that.

"Well, then—" He left it to her. He laid it down before her and left it there. He couldn't not go.

And she took it up and gave it back to him. "If you go I shall go too."

He said nothing to that, nothing at all. But it stirred in him again, that fear of his, that little creeping and ignoble fear.

It was ten o'clock.

They turned back to the Palace. The crowd had thinned now and was scattered. It moved up and down without rest; it reeled, two-thirds intoxicated; it drifted and returned; it circled round and round the fountain. In the open spaces intoxicated motorcars and taxicabs darted and tore, with the folly of moths and the fury of destroyers. They stung the air with their hooting. Flags, intoxicated flags, hung from their engines. They came flying drunkenly out of the dark, like a trumpeting swarm of enormous insects, irresistibly, incessantly drawn to the lights of the Palace, hypnotised by the golden white façade.

The two stood together, apart, on the edge of the light. They turned their backs on the Palace. They looked into each other's serious, earnest faces. They were disgusted at the folly of the crowd. They were utterly calm, utterly courageous. They were going to the front.

All night long they lay sleepless with ecstasy, he in Bayswater and she in Maida Vale, surrendered to the embraces of their dream. Each tried to think what it would be like. She saw it as one immense, encompassing sheet of shells and bullets that converged on Mr. Starkey in the middle of it. It was there, in the middle of it, that she desired to be. Mr. Starkey saw nothing, absolutely nothing. He felt nothing but the will to go.

II

It was all very well to talk about going to the front. The thing, Mr. Starkey said, was to get there. They would have to take steps.

The first step they took was to notify the United Charities that, having volunteered for active service, they must resign their posts. The United Charities admired and deplored their resolution; it would be difficult to fill their places. Meanwhile, pending the final arrangements, their places would be kept open for them.

The next step was to let everybody know that they were going. They knew it in the office. Mr. Starkey's typist said, "Mr. Starkey is going to the front," and Miss Delacheroy's typist retorted, "And Miss Delacheroy is going, too." All Miss Delacheroy's friends knew. And Mr. Starkey's banker knew it, and his doctor and his solicitor.

A few formalities remained, but the send-off had practically begun. Everybody in the office had congratulated them and bidden them God-speed. Mr. Starkey's banker told him that England had need of men like him. His doctor slapped him on the back, and said he was a lucky fellow to be going. He also overhauled him and passed him medically for nothing. His solicitor gripped him by the hand, and said that Mr. Starkey could rely on him to carry out his instructions to the letter, and that, yes, all legal expenses would be charged to the estate, and that he would await further news with anxiety.

Then Mr. Starkey took the final steps. He called at the War Office, he called at the Admiralty, he called at the headquarters of the White Cross Association, and at the headquarters of the St. George's Ambulance Society. He called at the offices of all their local branches within a radius of five miles. He called at the War Office and the Admiralty a second time. Then, in consequence of certain very serious statements that were made to him there, he found it necessary to call at Scotland Yard. Acting on the advice of Constable D of the Metropolitan Police, he went on to the Home Office. At the instigation of the Home Secretary, he pursued the secretary of the American White Cross Association down Piccadilly and down the Haymarket and down the Strand. And finally ran him to earth in the basement of the Hotel Cecil. Owing mainly to the tense but clear representations of the secretary, he returned up the Strand and up the Haymarket and up Piccadilly to Park-lane, where he looked in at the American Embassy.

After that he called at the Belgian Embassy and the French Embassy and the Japanese Embassy in succession, which, he said, he had very much better have done first as last. For, from the moment of his entrance at the Belgian Embassy, Mr. Starkey's progress became a triumph, an ovation. Nothing could exceed the courtesy and enthusiasm of the foreign officials.

It was Mr. Starkey's reception at the Japanese Embassy that encouraged him to go back, as he did, to the War Office and the Admiralty.

That was the incredible sum of his activities, not counting various minor operations at the centres of the White Cross Association and twenty-seven letters that he wrote, chiefly to the heads of departments.

"And when shall you go?" said Miss Delacheroy.

(They were at Sunday, the 9th.)

"I can't tell you," he said. "It may be to-morrow."

"Oh-h!" she breathed. It was her first sign of dismay. She could not possibly be ready, she said, till the day after.

She had one fear, and one fear only, that he might get there first.

"It's no good my going," she said, "if we can't go together."

He stared at her as he had stared that night when they stood beside the fountain. Then he smiled as a man smiles in fear.

"You don't *go* to the front," he said; "you're sent."

"You mean that you'll be sent and I shan't be?"

"Well—" He broke it to her gently. He had taken steps. So vast was the machinery that he had put in motion, it was impossible that he should not be sent.

She agreed that it was, of course, impossible. But she had taken steps, too; small steps but rapid. The day after war was declared she had had herself inoculated for typhoid. She hoped that he had done the same.

He had not. He had never thought of it.

"You should have thought of it," she said. "They won't look at you if you aren't done."

His attentive face told her she had scored a point.

She followed up her advantage. "You must see about it first thing to-morrow. It takes eight days."

He made a note of it in his memorandum book.

(That gave her five days' start of him.)

And she had ordered in all her medical stores, from quinine to tooth brushes. Her chemist had recommended bone. A celluloid toothbrush, he said, would be almost certain to ignite if it should happen to come in contact with a bomb.

Had he thought of *that*?

He had not. He made another note, and enquired gently if Miss Delacheroy had got her White Cross certificate?

"Because"—he answered her agonised eyes—"they won't look at *you* without it."

"Oh!" (she reproached him) "why didn't you tell me? You knew."

He was shamefaced before her. Of course he knew. And if he had not told her, why, indeed, was it?

He evaded the conscience that accused him.

"I'm telling you now," he pleaded.

And he told her. After all, it was quite simple. She had only got to attend one of the emergency classes round the corner at the Blankmore Institute. There was a course of six lectures with demonstrations. Oh, yes; she would get through all right. Anybody could get through.

She made a calculation. If she got through, it would take her six days.

He would still be a day ahead of her.

If up till now he had not played quite fair—he had not, considering the marches he had stolen on her—there was no doubt of his readiness to redeem his error.

For the large hall of the Blankmore Institute was crammed and running over, and it was owing solely to Mr. Starkey's influence at headquarters that she was pushed and squeezed through some invisible loophole into a non-existing vacancy in the supplementary class in the basement.

In the basement, from 10.30 to 12.30, and from two to four, and from 7.30 to nine, Miss Delacheroy struggled with the secret intricacies of the human frame, with the infinite vagaries and complications of the Esmarch triangular bandage, and the appalling mysteries of first aid.

The White Cross demonstrator destroyed her *morale* at the very beginning. He told her that there was one spot, and one spot only, where digital pressure should be applied to arrest haemorrhage from the subclavian artery, and that if Miss Delacheroy did not find that spot, if she did not put her finger on it, if she put it a hairsbreadth to one side, that artery would go, he said, on its way rejoicing, and she, Miss Delacheroy, would have killed her man more surely than if she had fired a bullet at him. The Germans, said the demonstrator, would *pay* Miss Delacheroy to do what she was doing.

And when it came to bandaging, she had not a chance; for, by a system most just and admirable in itself, the students practised on each other, and the woman next to Miss Delacheroy, whether because she was taller and stronger and more determined, or for some other reason, invariably succeeded in bandaging Miss Delacheroy first, and by the time she had finished with her the demonstrator had gone on to another bandage, so that Miss Delacheroy was always at least three bandages behind.

The struggle lasted till the end of August. Three times Miss Delacheroy went in for her exam, and failed. The first time it was the human frame that dished her; the second time it was the subclavian artery; the third time it was the bandages—there were too many of them.

And all the time Miss Delacheroy's brain was paralysed with anxiety.

For three weeks the movements of Mr. Starkey, like the movements of the Allied Armies, were enveloped in mystery. He had not been to see her for two Sundays. And when she wrote and asked him to tea on the third Sunday, he replied that it was impossible; he was under orders; at any moment he might be sent to the front. Of his whereabouts and of his operations in the meanwhile he gave no account.

She felt that he was keeping something back from her. There followed a brief period of separation, of evasion, of mutual suspicion and hostility. All this was unspeakably painful to Miss Delacheroy.

It was on a Monday that, going late for the first time to her daily bandaging, she came upon him in a place where of all places she had least expected him—in the Blankmore Institute itself. The doors of the large hall were open, and, standing within the towering centre of a dense ring of women, she saw him. He had an Esmarch triangular bandage round his neck, and with another bandage he was doing things to a young woman who had pushed forward (she knew how they *could* push).

And when Mr. Starkey left the large hall at 12.30 he found Miss Delacheroy waiting for him in the vestibule.

"What are you doing *here*?" she said.

He was serious and earnest. "Marking time."

"We seem to be doing the same thing."

He admitted that it did seem so, except that he was giving instruction and she was receiving it.

"Oh—for all I receive! I'm plucked again. It's the third time."

They were walking down Maida Vale together now.

His face was inscrutable, and a terrible suspicion came to her. He was one of them. He did not want her to go with him, and he had kept her back.

They had come to her gate. With the pain of parting madness entered into Miss Delacheroy. She drew him into the garden. The walls sheltered her.

"Were you one of the examiners?"

He was silent.

"I see. You were. It was you who dished me."

He was cold and correct and kind. He paused before he answered her.

"I might have. But I didn't. You must go up again."

"Forgive me."

"There is nothing to forgive."

"You see how it's getting on my nerves. It's all so terrible and mysterious. I know nothing."

She meant that she knew he was keeping something back from her.

"You know," he said, "as much as I do."

"I would, perhaps, if you'd tell me. What are you *doing*? Have you been to the War Office again?"

He had. He owned it.

She was sharp and eager. "Well, what did they say *this* time?"

He looked her squarely in the face. "*This* time I am not at liberty to tell you."

Then she knew that what he was keeping from her was the imminence of his departure.

"What's the use of hiding it?" she said. "They *have* sent for you."

"They will; they will. I'm waiting to hear from Belgium. But it'll be another week."

"Ten days?"

It was more than probable that it would be ten days.

That gave her just time to go up again and wait for the result. There were women who had been up four times, who went again and again till they had got through.

Now, examinations in the Blankmore Institute are held in two rooms on the top floor, and once every ten days the names of successful candidates are posted there.

The building, unfortunately, has no lift.

But four flights of stone stairs were nothing to Miss Delacheroy when she found that she had passed ninth on an interminable list. She would be just in time if she was quick.

She was very quick.

She ran down the first two flights with a clatter of her little heels; she slid, dramatically, down the third; she was hurled down the fourth from the top to the bottom.

Through the well of the staircase on the third landing she had caught sight of Mr. Starkey coming out of the large hall. He had an Esmarch triangular bandage round his neck.

"I'm glad," said Mr. Starkey; "it's a sprained ankle. That's the one I've got all right. You're the fourth I've had a shot at this week."

III

He took her home in a taxicab, and the next evening he went to enquire for her.

She stirred on her couch and gave a little cry when she saw him.

"You haven't gone, then?"

"Not yet."

He said it gently as if to spare her.

She looked at him with humble eyes, a humility incomprehensible to Mr. Starkey.

"This is pretty hard lines," he said, "after you've passed so well."

"Yes. But I couldn't have gone in any case."

"Why not?"

There was a long pause. Then it came from her with the brevity of a supreme confession:

"They won't have me. I'm too old."

He lowered his eyes before it, as if to the very last he spared her.

"It all goes through the War Office, and they won't look at you if you're over forty. That's what they've told me."

"It's what they've told *me*."

"I didn't know," she said, "until this morning."

"I," said Mr. Starkey, "have known it all the time."

And he added something about "the system" and "red tape."

BOMBARDMENT

by Henri Barbusse

Barbusse (1873–1935) wrote Le Feu *(1916), one of the first novels of the war by an active participant. The narrative "we" conveys the experiences of the squad, among them the hard-earned ability to distinguish bombs by their sounds and effects; the literary language communicates the sophisticated narrator's presence. Barbusse was wounded in 1916 and discharged the next year. Born in France, he died in Moscow.*

[From Barbusse's *Under Fire: The Story of a Squad*. Translated from the French by Fitzwater Wray. New York: E. P. Dutton and Co., 1917.]

WE ARE IN the flat country, a vast mistiness, but above it is dark blue. The end of the night is marked by a little falling snow which powders our shoulders and the folds in our sleeves. We are marching in fours, hooded. We seem in the turbid twilight to be the wandering survivors of one Northern district who are trekking to another.

We have followed a road and have crossed the ruins of Ablain-Saint-Nazaire. We have had confused glimpses of its whitish heaps of houses and the dim spider-webs of its suspended roofs. The village is so long that although full night buried us in it we saw its last buildings beginning to pale in the frost of dawn. Through the grating of a cellar on the edge of this petrified ocean's waves, we made out the fire kept going by the custodians of the dead town. We have paddled in swampy fields, lost ourselves in silent places where the mud seized us by the feet, we have dubiously regained our balance and our bearings again on another road, the one which leads from Carency to Souchez. The tall bordering poplars are shivered and their trunks mangled; in one place the road is an enormous colonnade of trees destroyed. Then, marching with us on both sides, we see through the shadows ghostly dwarfs of trees, wide-cloven like spreading palms; botched and jumbled into round blocks or long strips; doubled upon themselves, as if they knelt. From time to time our march is disordered and bustled by the yielding of a swamp. The road becomes a marsh which we cross on our heels, while our feet make the sound of sculling. Planks have been laid in it here and there. Where they have so far sunk in the mud as to proffer their edges to us we slip on them. Sometimes there is enough water to float them, and then under the weight of a man they splash and go under, and the man stumbles or falls, with frenzied imprecations.

It must be five o'clock. The stark and affrighting scene unfolds itself to our eyes, but it is still encircled by a great fantastic ring of mist and of darkness. We go on and on without pause, and come to a place where we can make out a dark hillock, at the foot of which there seems to be some lively movement of human beings.

"Advance by twos," says the leader of the detachment. "Let each team of two take alternately a plank and a hurdle." We load ourselves up. One of the two in each couple assumes the rifle of his partner as well as his own. The other with difficulty shifts and pulls out from the pile a long plank, muddy and slippery, which weighs full eighty pounds, or a hurdle of leafy branches as big as a door, which he can only just keep on his back as he bends forward with his hands aloft and grips its edges.

We resume our march, very slowly and very ponderously, scattered over the now graying road, with complaints and heavy curses which the effort strangles in our throats. After about a hundred yards, the two men of each team exchange loads, so that after two hundred yards, in spite of the bitter blenching breeze of early morning, all but the non-coms are running with sweat.

Suddenly a vivid star expands down yonder in the uncertain direction that we are taking—a rocket. Widely it lights a part of the sky with its milky nimbus, blots out the stars, and then falls gracefully, fairy-like.

There is a swift light opposite us over there; a flash and a detonation. It is a shell! By the flat reflection that the explosion instantaneously spreads over the lower sky we see a ridge clearly outlined in front of us from east to west, perhaps half a mile away.

That ridge is ours—so much of it as we can see from here and up to the top of it, where our troops are. On the other slope, a hundred yards from our first line, is the first German line. The shell fell on the summit, in our lines; it is the others who are firing. Another shell another and yet another plant trees of faintly violet light on the top of the rise, and each of them dully illumines the whole of the horizon.

Soon there is a sparkling of brilliant stars and a sudden jungle of fiery plumes on the hill; and a fairy mirage of blue and white hangs lightly before our eyes in the full gulf of night.

Those among us who must devote the whole buttressed power of their arms and legs to prevent their greasy loads from sliding off their backs and to prevent themselves from sliding to the ground, these neither see nor hear anything. The others, sniffing and shivering with cold, wiping their noses with limp and sodden handkerchiefs, watch and remark, cursing the obstacles in the way with fragments of profanity. "It's like watching fireworks," they say.

And to complete the illusion of a great operatic scene, fairy-like but sinister, before which our bent and black party crawls and splashes, behold a red star, and then a green; then a sheaf of red fire, very much tardier. In our ranks, as the available half of our pairs of eyes watch the display, we cannot help murmuring in idle tones of popular admiration, "Ah, a red one!"—"Look, a green one!" It is the Germans who are sending up signals, and our men as well who are asking for artillery support.

Our road turns and climbs again as the day at last decides to appear. Everything looks dirty. A layer of stickiness, pearl-gray and white, covers the road, and around it the real world makes a mournful appearance. Behind us we leave ruined Souchez, whose houses are only flat heaps of rubbish and her trees but humps of bramble-like slivers. We plunge into a hole on our left, the entrance to the communication trench. We let our loads fall in a circular enclosure prepared for them, and both hot and frozen we settled in the trench and wait, our hands abraded, wet, and stiff with cramp.

Buried in our holes up to the chin, our chests heaving against the solid bulk of the ground that protects us, we watch the dazzling and deepening drama develop. The bombardment is redoubled. The trees of light on the ridge have melted into hazy parachutes in the pallor of dawn, sickly heads of Medusae with points of fire; then, more sharply defined as the day expands, they become bunches of smoke-feathers, ostrich feathers white and gray, which come suddenly to life on the jumbled and melancholy soil of Hill 119, five or six hundred yards in front of us, and then slowly fade away. They are truly the pillar of fire and the pillar of cloud, circling as one and thundering together. On the flank of the hill we see a party of men running to earth. One by one they disappear, swallowed up in the adjoining anthills.

Now, one can better make out the form of our "guests." At each shot a tuft of sulphurous white underlined in black forms sixty yards up in the air, unfolds and mottles itself, and we catch in the explosion the whistling of the charge of bullets that the yellow cloud hurls angrily to the ground. It bursts in six-fold squalls, one after another—bang, bang, bang, bang, bang, bang. It is the 77 mm. gun.

We disdain the 77 mm. shrapnel, in spite of the fact that Blesbois was killed by one of them three days ago. They nearly always burst too high. Barque explains it to us, although we know it well: "One's chamber-pot protects one's nut well enough against the bullets. So they can destroy your shoulder and damn well knock you down, but they don't spread you about. Naturally, you've got to be fly, all the same. Got to be careful you don't lift your neb in the air as long as they're buzzing about, nor put your hand out to see if it's raining. Now, our 75 mm.—"

"There aren't only the 77's," Mesnil André broke in, "there's all damned sorts. Spell *those* out for me—" *Those* are shrill and cutting whistles, trembling or rattling; and clouds of all shapes gather on the slopes yonder whose vastness shows through them, slopes where our men are in the depths of the dug-outs. Gigantic plumes of faint fire mingle with huge tassels of steam, tufts that throw out straight filaments, smoky feathers that expand as they fall—quite white or greenish-gray, black or copper with gleams of gold, or as if blotched with ink.

The two last explosions are quite near. Above the battered ground they take shape like vast balls of black and tawny dust; and as they deploy and leisurely depart at the wind's will, having finished their task, they have the outline of fabled dragons.

Our line of faces on the level of the ground turns that way, and we follow them with our eyes from the bottom of the trench in the middle of this country peopled by blazing and ferocious apparitions, these fields that the sky has crushed.

"Those, they're the 150 mm. howitzers."—"They're the 210's, calf-head."—"There go the regular guns, too; the hogs! Look at that one!" It was a shell that burst on the ground and threw up earth and debris in a fan-shaped cloud of darkness. Across the cloven land it looked like the frightful spitting of some volcano, piled up in the bowels of the earth.

A diabolical uproar surrounds us. We are conscious of a sustained crescendo, an incessant multiplication of the universal frenzy. A hurricane of hoarse and hollow banging, of raging clamor, of piercing and beast-like screams, fastens furiously with tatters of smoke upon the earth where we are buried up to our necks, and the wind of the shells seems to set it heaving and pitching.

"Look at that," bawls Barque, "and me that said they were short of munitions!"

"Oh, la, la! We know all about that! That and the other fudge the newspapers squirt all over us!"

A dull crackle makes itself audible amidst the babel of noise. That slow rattle is of all the sounds of war the one that most quickens the heart.

"The coffee-mill![1] One of ours, listen. The shots come regularly, while the Boches' haven't got the same length of time between the shots; they go crack—crack-crack-crack—crack-crack—crack—"

"Don't cod yourself, crack-pate; it isn't an unsewing-machine at all; it's a motor-cycle on the road to 31 dug-out, away yonder."

"Well, *I* think it's a chap up aloft there, having a look round from his broomstick," chuckles Pépin, as he raises his nose and sweeps the firmament in search of an aeroplane.

A discussion arises, but one cannot say what the noise is, and that's all. One tries in vain to become familiar with all those diverse disturbances. It even happened the other day in the wood that a whole section mistook for the hoarse howl of a shell the first notes of a neighboring mule as he began his whinnying bray.

"I say, there's a good show of sausages in the air this morning," says Lamuse. Lifting our eyes, we count them.

"There are eight sausages on our side and eight on the Boches'," says Cocon, who has already counted them.

There are, in fact, at regular intervals along the horizon, opposite the distance-dwindled group of captive enemy balloons, the eight long hovering eyes of the army, buoyant and sensitive, and joined to the various headquarters by living threads.

"They see us as we see them. How the devil can one escape from that row of God Almighties up there?"

There's our reply!

Suddenly, behind our backs, there bursts the sharp and deafening stridor of the 75's. Their increasing crackling thunder arouses and elates us. We shout with our guns, and look at each other without hearing our shouts—except for the curiously piercing voice that comes from Barque's great mouth—amid the rolling of that fantastic drum whose every note is the report of a cannon.

Then we turn our eyes ahead and outstretch our necks, and on the top of the hill we see the still higher silhouette of a row of black infernal trees whose terrible roots are striking down into the invisible slope where the enemy cowers.

While the "75" battery continues its barking a hundred yards behind us—the sharp anvil-blows of a huge hammer, followed by a dizzy scream of force and fury—a gigantic gurgling dominates the devilish oratorio; that, also, is coming from our side. "It's a gran'pa, that one!"

---

1. Military slang for machine-gun.—Translator.

The shell cleaves the air at perhaps a thousand yards above us; the voice of its gun covers all as with a pavilion of resonance. The sound of its travel is sluggish, and one divines a projectile bigger-bowelled, more enormous than the others. We can hear it passing and declining in front with the ponderous and increasing vibration of a train that enters a station under brakes; then, its heavy whine sounds fainter. We watch the hill opposite, and after several seconds it is covered by a salmon-pink cloud that the wind spreads over one-half of the horizon. "It's a 220 mm."

"One can see them," declares Volpatte, "those shells, when they come out of the gun. If you're in the right line, you can even see them a good long away from the gun."

Another follows: "There! Look, look! Did you see that one? You didn't look quick enough, you missed it. Get a move on! Look, another! Did you see it?"

"I did not see it."—"Ass! Got to be a bedstead for you to see it! Look, quick, that one, there! Did you see it, unlucky good-for-nothing?"—"I saw it; is that all?"

Some have made out a small black object, slender and pointed as a blackbird with folded wings, pricking a wide curve down from the zenith.

"That weighs 240 pounds, that one, my old bug," says Volpatte proudly, "and when that drops on a funk-hole it kills everybody inside it. Those that aren't picked off by the explosion are struck dead by the wind of it, or they're gas-poisoned before they can say 'ouf!'"

"The 270 mm. shell can be seen very well, too—talk about a bit of iron—when the howitzer sends it up—*allez*, off you go!"

"And the 155 Rimailho, too; but you can't see that one because it goes too straight and too far; the more you look for it the more it vanishes before your eyes."

In a stench of sulfur and black powder, of burned stuffs and calcined earth which roams in sheets about the country, all the menagerie is let loose and gives battle. Bellowings, roarings, growlings, strange and savage; feline caterwaulings that fiercely rend your ears and search your belly, or the long-drawn piercing hoot like the siren of a ship in distress. At times, even, something like shouts cross each other in the air-currents, with curious variation of tone that make the sound human. The country is bodily lifted in places and falls back again. From one end of the horizon to the other it seems to us that the earth itself is raging with storm and tempest.

And the greatest guns, far away and still farther, diffuse growls much subdued and smothered, but you know the strength of them by the displacement of air which comes and raps you on the ear.

Now, behold a heavy mass of woolly green which expands and hovers over the bombarded region and draws out in every direction. This touch of strangely incongruous color in the picture summons attention, and all we encaged prisoners turn our faces towards the hideous outcrop.

"Gas, probably. Let's have our masks ready."—"The hogs!"

"They're unfair tricks, those," says Farfadet.

"They're what?" asks Barque jeeringly.

"Why, yes, they're dirty dodges, those gases—"

"You make me tired," retorts Barque, "with your fair ways and your unfair ways. When you've seen men squashed, cut in two, or divided from top to bottom, blown into showers by an ordinary shell, bellies turned inside out and scattered anyhow, skulls forced bodily into the chest as if by a blow with a club, and in place of the head a bit of neck, oozing currant jam of brains all over the chest and back—you've seen that and yet you can say 'There are *clean* ways!'"

"Doesn't alter the fact that the shell is allowed, it's recognized—"

"Ah, la, la! I'll tell you what—you make me blubber just as much as you make me laugh!" And he turns his back.

"Hey, look out, boys!"

We strain our eyes, and one of us has thrown himself flat on the ground; others look instinctively and frowning towards the shelter that we have not time to reach. And during these two seconds each one bends his head. It is a grating noise as of huge scissors which comes near and nearer to us, and ends at last with a ringing crash of unloaded iron.

That one fell not far from us—two hundred yards away, perhaps. We crouch in the bottom of the trench and remain doubled up while the place where we are is lashed by a shower of little fragments.

"Don't want this in my tummy, even from that distance," says Paradis, extracting from the earth of the trench wall a morsel that has just lodged there. It is like a bit of coke, bristling with edged and pointed facets, and he dances it in his hand so as not to burn himself.

There is a hissing noise. Paradis sharply bows his head and we follow suit. "The fuse!—it has gone over." The shrapnel fuse goes up and then comes down vertically; but that of the percussion shell detaches itself from the broken mass after the explosion and usually abides buried at the point of contact, but at other times it flies off at random like a big red-hot pebble. One must beware of it. It may hurl itself on you a very long time after the detonation and by incredible paths, passing over the embankment and plunging into the cavities.

"Nothing so piggish as a fuse. It happened to me once—"

"There's worse things," broke in Bags of the 11th, "The Austrian shells, the 130's and the 74's. I'm afraid of them. They're nickel-plated, they say, but what I do know, seeing I've been there, is they come so quick you can't do anything to dodge them. You no sooner hear 'em snoring than they burst on you."

"The German 105's, neither, you haven't hardly the time to flatten yourself. I once got the gunners to tell me all about them."

"I tell you, the shells from the naval guns, you haven't the time to hear 'em. Got to pack yourself up before they come."

"And there's that new shell, a dirty devil, that breaks wind after it's dodged into the earth and out of it again two or three times in the space of six yards. When I know there's one of them about, I want to go round the corner. I remember one time——"

"That's all nothing, my lads," said the new sergeant, stopping on his way past, "you ought to see what they chucked us at Verdun, where I've come from. Nothing but whoppers, 380's and 420's and 244's. When you've been shelled down there you know all about it—the woods are sliced down like cornfields, the dug-outs marked and burst in even when they've three thicknesses of beams, all the road-crossings sprinkled, the roads blown into the air and changed into long heaps of smashed convoys and wrecked guns, corpses twisted together as though shoveled up. You could see thirty chaps laid out by one shot at the cross-roads; you could see fellows whirling around as they went up, always about fifteen yards, and bits of trousers caught and stuck on the tops of the trees that were left. You could see one of these 380's go into a house at Verdun by the roof, bore through two or three floors, and burst at the bottom, and all the damn lot's got to go aloft; and in the fields whole battalions would scatter and lie flat under the shower like poor little defenseless rabbits. At every step on the ground in the fields you'd got lumps as thick as your arm and as wide as *that*, and it'd take four poilus to lift the lump of iron. The fields looked as if they were full of rocks. And that went on without a halt for months on end, months on end!" the sergeant repeated as he passed on, no doubt to tell again the story of his souvenirs somewhere else.

"Look, look, corporal, those chaps over there—are they soft in the head?" On the bombarded position we saw dots of human beings emerge hurriedly and run towards the explosions.

"They're gunners," said Bertrand; "as soon as a shell's burst they sprint and rummage for the fuse in the hole, for the position of the fuse gives the direction of its battery, you see, by the way it's dug itself in; and as for the distance, you've only got to read it—it's shown on the range-figures cut on the time-fuse which is set just before firing."

"No matter—they're off their onions to go out under such shelling."

"Gunners, my boy," says a man of another company who was strolling in the trench, "are either quite good or quite bad. Either they're trumps or they're trash. I tell you—"

"That's true of all privates, what you're saying."

"Possibly; but I'm not talking to you about all privates; I'm talking to you about gunners, and I tell you too that—"

"Hey, my lads! Better find a hole to dump yourselves in, before you get one on the snitch!"

The strolling stranger carried his story away, and Cocon, who was in a perverse mood, declared: "We can be doing our hair in the dugout, seeing it's rather boring outside."

"Look, they're sending torpedoes over there!" said Paradis, pointing. Torpedoes go straight up, or very nearly so, like larks, fluttering and rustling; then they stop, hesitate, and come straight down again, heralding their fall in its last seconds by a "baby-cry" that we know well. From here, the inhabitants of the ridge seem like invisible players, lined up for a game with a ball.

"In the Argonne," says Lamuse, "my brother says in a letter that they get turtle-doves, as he calls them. They're big heavy things, fired off very close. They come in cooing, really they do, he says, and when they break wind they don't half make a shindy, he says."

"There's nothing worse than the mortar-toad, that seems to chase after you and jump over the top of you, and it bursts in the very trench, just scraping over the bank."

"*Tiens, tiens,* did you hear it?" A whistling was approaching us when suddenly it ceased. The contrivance has not burst. "It's a shell that cried off," Paradis asserts. And we strain our ears for the satisfaction of hearing—or of not hearing—others.

Lamuse says: "All the fields and the roads and the villages about here, they're covered with dud shells of all sizes—ours as well, to say truth. The ground must be full of 'em, that you can't see. I wonder how they'll go on, later, when the time comes to say, 'That's enough of it, let's start work again.'"

And all the time, in a monotony of madness, the avalanche of fire and iron goes on; shrapnel with its whistling explosion and its overcharged heart of furious metal, and the great percussion shells, whose thunder is that of the railway engine which crashes suddenly into a wall, the thunder of loaded rails or steel beams, toppling down a declivity. The air is now glutted and viewless, it is crossed and recrossed by heavy blasts, and the murder of the earth continues all around, deeply and more deeply, to the limit of completion.

There are even other guns which now join in—they are ours. Their report is like that of the 75's, but louder, and it has a prolonged and resounding echo, like thunder reverberating among mountains.

"They're the long 120's. They're on the edge of the wood half a mile away. Fine guns, old man, like gray-hounds. They're slender and fine-nosed, those guns—you want to call them 'Madame.' They're not like the 220's—they're all snout, like coal-scuttles, and spit their shells out from the bottom upwards. The 120's get there just the same, but among the teams of artillery they look like kids in bassinettes."

Conversation languishes; here and there are yawns. The dimensions and weight of this outbreak of the guns fatigue the mind. Our voices flounder in it and are drowned.

"I've never seen anything like this for a bombardment," shouts Barque.

"We always say that," replies Paradis.

"Just so," bawls Volpatte. "There's been talk of an attack lately; I should say this is the beginning of something."

The others say simply, "Ah!"

Volpatte displays an intention of snatching a wink of sleep. He settles himself on the ground with his back against one wall of the trench and his feet buttressed against the other wall.

We converse together on divers subjects. Biquet tells the story of a rat he has seen: "He was cheeky and comical, you know. I'd taken off my trotter-cases, and that rat, he chewed all the edge of the uppers into embroidery. Of course, I'd greased 'em."

Volpatte, who is now definitely out of action, moves and says, "I can't get to sleep for your gabbling."

"You can't make me believe, old fraud," says Marthereau, "that you can raise a single snore with a shindy like this all round you."

Volpatte replies with one.

Fall in! March!

We are changing our spot. Where are they taking us to? We have no idea. The most we know is that we are in reserve, and that they may take us round to strengthen certain points in succession, or to clear the communication trenches, in which the regulation of passing troops is as complicated a job, if blocks and collisions are to be avoided, as it is of the trains in a busy station. It is impossible to make out the meaning of the immense maneuver in which the rolling of our regiment is only that of a little wheel, nor what is going on in all the huge area of the sector. But, lost in the network of deeps where we go and come without end, weary, harassed and stiff-jointed by prolonged halts, stupefied by noise and delay, poisoned by smoke, we make out that our artillery is becoming more and more active; the offensive seems to have changed places.

Halt! A fire of intense and incredible fury was threshing the parapets of the trench where we were halted at the moment: "Fritz is going it strong; he's afraid of an attack, he's going dotty. Ah, *isn't* he letting fly!"

A heavy hail was pouring over us, hacking terribly at atmosphere and sky, scraping and skimming all the plain.

I looked through a loophole and saw a swift and strange vision. In front of us, a dozen yards away at most, there were motionless forms outstretched side by side—a row of mown-down soldiers—and the countless projectiles that hurtled from all sides were riddling this rank of the dead!

The bullets that flayed the soil in straight streaks and raised slender stems of cloud were perforating and ripping the bodies so rigidly close to the ground, breaking the stiffened limbs, plunging into the wan and vacant faces, bursting and bespattering the liquefied eyes; and even did that file of corpses stir and budge out of line under the avalanche.

We could hear the blunt sound of the dizzy copper points as they pierced cloth and flesh, the sound of a furious stroke with a knife, the harsh blow of a stick upon clothing. Above us rushed jets of shrill whistling, with the declining and far more serious hum of ricochets. And we bent our heads under the enormous flight of noises and voices.

"Trench must be cleared—Gee up!" We leave this most infamous corner of the battlefield where even the dead are torn, wounded, and slain anew.

We turn towards the right and towards the rear. The communication trench rises, and at the top of the gully we pass in front of a telephone station and a group of artillery officers and gunners. Here there is a further halt. We mark time, and hear the artillery observer shout his commands, which the telephonist buried beside him picks up and repeats: "First gun, same sight; two-tenths to left; three a minute!"

Some of us have risked our heads over the edge of the bank and have glimpsed for the space of the lightning's flash all the field of battle round which our company has uncertainly wandered since the morning. I saw a limitless gray plain, across whose width the wind seemed to be driving faint and thin waves of dust, pierced in places by a more pointed billow of smoke.

Where the sun and the clouds trail patches of black and of white, the immense space sparkles dully from point to point where our batteries are firing, and I saw it one moment entirely spangled with short-lived flashes. Another minute, part of the field grew dark under a steamy and whitish film, a sort of hurricane of snow.

Afar, on the evil, endless, and half-ruined fields, caverned like cemeteries, we see the slender skeleton of a church, like a bit of torn paper; and from one margin of the picture to the other, dim rows of vertical marks, close together and underlined, like the straight strokes of a written page—these are the roads and their trees. Delicate meandering lines streak the plain backward and forward and rule it in squares, and these windings are stippled with men.

We can make out some fragments of lines made up of these human points who have emerged from the hollowed streaks and are moving on the plain in the horrible face of the flying firmament. It is difficult to believe that each of those tiny spots is a living thing with fragile and quivering flesh, infinitely unarmed in space, full of deep thoughts, full of far memories and crowded pictures. One is fascinated by this scattered dust of men as small as the stars in the sky.

Poor unknowns, poor fellow-men, it is your turn to give battle. Another time it will be ours. Perhaps tomorrow it will be ours to feel the heavens burst over our heads or the earth open under our feet, to be assailed by the prodigious plague of projectiles, to be swept away by the blasts of a tornado a hundred thousand times stronger than the tornado.

They urge us into the rearward shelters. For our eyes the field of death vanishes. To our ears the thunder is deadened on the great anvil of the clouds. The sound of universal destruction is still. The squad surrounds itself with the familiar noises of life, and sinks into the fondling littleness of the dug-outs.

THE FRENCH POODLE

by Wyndham Lewis

One of the outstanding artists of the early twentieth century, Lewis (1882–1957) was born in Canada, raised in England, and served on the Western Front from 1916 to 1917.

[First published in the magazine *The Egoist* in March 1916.]

I WAS REMINDED of another man's fate when I saw Peter yesterday, in khaki, with his dog. The dog appeared rather confused by Peter's newly resumed uniform. It fell in behind other people in khaki: even when keeping in orderly proximity to its master, it followed a certain indifference or contempt.—Peter's destiny had nothing sultry in its lines: his dog was a suburban appendage. It was the khaki and the dog brought me to the other story.

It appears the following things happened to a man called Rob Cairn, during a long sick-leave. The time was between July and October 1915. I can tell the story with genuine completeness: for James Fraser, the man he saw most of then, told it to me with a great wealth of friendly savagery.

Rob Cairn was drifting about London in mufti, by no means well, and full of anxiety, the result of his ill-health and the shock he had received at finding himself blown into the air and painted yellow by the unavoidable shell. His tenure on earth seemed insecure, and he could not accustom himself to the idea of insecurity. When the shell came he had not bounded gracefully and coldly up, but with a clumsy dismay. His spirit, that spirit that should have been winged for the life of a soldier, and ready fiercely to take flight into the unknown, strong for other lives, was also grubbily attached to the earth. It, like his body, was not graceful in its fearlessness, nor resilient, nor young. All the minutiæ of existence mesmerised it. It could not disport itself genially in independence of surrounding objects and ideas. Even as a

24

boy he had never been able to learn to dive: hardly to swim. Yet he was a big red-headed chap that those who measure men by redness and by size would have considered fairly imposing as a physical specimen. It requires almost a professional colour-matcher, as a matter of fact, to discriminate between the different reds: and then the various constitutional conditions they imply is a separate discovery.

Cairn, then, was arrested in a vague but troublesome maze of discomfort and ill-health: his sick leave, after he had left the hospital, lasted some time. As an officer, therefore more responsible, he had more latitude. He was an architect. He went to his office every day for an hour or two. But he was haunted by the necessity to return once more to the trench-life with which he had been for some weeks mesmerically disconnected, and which he felt was another element, with which he had only become acquainted in a sudden dream. This element of malignant and monotonous missiles, which worried less or more, sleeplessness and misery, now appeared to him in its true colours. They were hard, poisonous and flamboyant. A fatiguing sonority, an empty and pretentious energy: something about it all like the rhetoric of a former age, revolted him. It all seemed incredibly old and superannuated. Should he go back and get killed it would be as though the dead of a century ago were striking him down. Cairn must have been a fairly brave man, considering all things, before his tossing. It was now with him rather sullen neurasthenia at the thought of recommencing, than anything else: renewed monotonous actions and events, and fear not of death but of being played with too much.

James Fraser, his partner, who because of heart-trouble had been unable to join the Army, heard all this from his friend, and cursed "the whole business" of bloodshed in sympathy with the recriminating soldier.

"I'm sure there's something wrong, Rob. How do you feel exactly; physically, I mean? What can happen to a man inside who is blown up in the air? What do the doctors exactly say?"

"They can find nothing. I don't believe there is anything. But I don't feel at all well. It's something in my brain, rather, that's dislocated: cracked, I think, sometimes. I shall never be any good out there again."

He read a great deal, chiefly Natural History. The lives of animals seemed to have a great fascination for his stolid, faithful thoughts. When he got an idea he stuck to it with unconscious devotion. He was a good friend to his ideas.

One of the principal notions to which he became attached at this time was that human beings suffered in every way from the absence of animal life around them. Pigs, horses, buffalos, snakes, birds, goats:

the majority of men living in towns were deprived of this rich animal neighbourhood. The sanity of direct animal processes: the example suggested constantly by the equilibrium of these various cousins of ours, with their snouts and their wings: the steady and soothing brotherhood of their bodies; this environment appeared necessary to human beings.

"Few men and many animals!" as he said to Fraser, blinking dogmatically and heavily, light red eyelashes falling with a look of modesty at the base of eyes always seeming a little dazzled by the reds all round them. "That's what I should like; rather than *men* and nothing else. It is bad for men to beat and kill each other. When there are no patient backs of beasts to receive their blows men turn them more towards their fellows. Irruptions of the hunting instinct are common in cities. Irruptions of all instincts are common and inevitable in modern life, among human swarms. Men have taken to the air; they are fighting there almost before they can fly. Man is losing his significance."

Fraser had an objection to make.

"You suggest the absence of animals.—Did not men in every time kill and beat one another?"

Cairn twisted as it were archly in his chair.

"Men loved each other better formerly; and—they at least killed other animals as well. I have never killed any animal; never a bird; not a mouse; not knowingly an insect; but I have killed men."

He said this staring hard at his friend, as though he might be able to discover the meaning of this fact in his face.

"And I did not mind killing men," he proceeded. "I hardly knew what killing meant."

"You do now?" his delighted partner asked him.

Rob looked at him with suspicion.

"No; possibly because I have never killed anyone I could see properly."

"Yes; your gunner's scalps are very abstract. But, again, I do not see what you mean. Do you think that a butcher, because of his familiarity with the shambles, would have more compunction in killing a man?"

"No. But it would do him no harm to kill a man or anything else, of course. Then he's a professional murderer."

"But why did you never kill birds?" Fraser asked him with uninterested persistence.

"I should have if I'd lived among them.—Do you think men would eat each other if there were no succulent animals left?"

"Very likely." Fraser laughed in accordance with the notion. "They might possibly at all events eat all the ugly women!"

Rob Cairn discussed these things with a persistent and often mildly indignant solemnity. The trenches had scarred his mind. Swarms of minute self-preservative and active thoughts moved in the furrows. Little bombs of irritable logic appeared whirling up from these grave clefts and exploded around his uneasy partner. Fraser wondered if Cairn would be able to take up his place in the business again, if nothing happened to him, as usefully as he had occupied it before the war. He seemed queer and was not able at the office to concentrate his mind on anything for more than a few minutes.

As to the war, his ideas appeared quite confusedly stagnant. He wondered, arguing along the same lines of the incompleteness of modern life, whether the savagery we arrive at were better than the savagery we came from.

"Since we must be savage, is not a real savage better than a sham one?"

"Must we be savage?" Fraser would ask.

"This 'great war' is the beginning of a period, far from being a war-that-will-end-war, take my word for it."

So Cairn was a tired man, and his fancy set out on a pilgrimage to some patriarchal plain. He had done his eight months' sprint, and was exhausted. His bounce into the air had shaken him out of his dream. He was awake and harshly anxious and reflective.

It was at this point that he bought his French poodle.

In an answer to an advertisement in two papers for a fairly large dog, a lady at Guildford answered that she had such an animal to sell. The lady brought the dog to his flat in a street off Theobalds Road, and he immediately bought it. He was very shy with it at first. He was conscious of not being its first love, and attempted to bribe it into forgetfulness of its former master by giving it a great deal to eat. It shortly vomited in his sitting-room. It howled a great deal at first.

But the dog soon settled down to novel life. Cairn became excessively fond of it. He abused a man in the street who insulted it. It was a large fat and placid brute that received Rob's caresses with obedient steadiness, occasionally darting friendship back at him. As he held it against his legs Cairn felt a deep attachment for this warm bag of blood and bone, whose love was undiluted habit and an uncomplicated magnetism. It recognised his friendliness in spasms of servile good nature, as absent-minded as its instincts.

Cairn noted all the modes of its nature with a delighted care. Its hunger enthralled him; its ramping gruff enthusiasm at the prospect of the streets filled him with an almost Slavic lyricism and glee. He was calm in the midst of its hysteria; but there was a contented pathos in his quietness. Its adventures with other dogs he followed with indulgence. The amazing physical catholicism of its taste he felt was a just reproach to his fastidiousness and maturity. It would have approached a rhinoceros with amorous proposals, were it not for elementary prudence.

He called his dog Carp. He loved him like a brother. But it is not at all sure that in the end Carp did not take the place that some lady should have occupied in his heart, as many of the attachments of men for girls seem a sentiment sprung up in the absence of a dog. Cairn had had one sweetheart; but after several years of going about together she had seemed so funny to him—she had seemed settling down like an old barge into some obscure and too personal human groove—that he had jerked himself away. The war had put the finishing touch to their estrangement.

"Dolly's lurch is becoming more pronounced," was his Monday morning's bulletin at the office. She appeared to remain an incredible time on each foot, while her body swung round. In following her out of the restaurant he felt that she was doing a sort of lugubrious cakewalk. He could hardly help getting into step. She became more dogmatic every minute: and rheumatism made her knuckles like so many dull and obstinate little faces.

"You're getting tired of her at last." Fraser advised him to take advantage of his mood and to say good-bye to her.

He had done so and had regretted it ever since. He felt superstitious about this parting: he regarded her in this conjuncture, as a mascot abandoned. He blamed his partner and the war for this. Somehow his partner and the war were closely connected. In many ways he found them identified—a confused target for his resentment. When he found himself cursing the war he found himself disliking his partner so much the *next* minute that it seemed the *same* minute. Fraser did not approve of Carp, either: although Carp appeared to like Fraser better than he did his own master. Cairn noticed this, and his humour did not improve. Towards the end they did not see him so much at the office as formerly. Once or twice a week he put in an appearance, rather primed with criticism of the conduct of the business in his absence. Then he turned up one day in khaki again: he was going back to the Front in a couple of days. Fraser and he got on better than they had done of late. He was much more open and good-humoured, and had seemingly recovered his old personality entirely. This may have been due somewhat to his friend's sentimental spurt of pleasantness under the circumstances.

"What are you going to do with Carp?"

When Fraser asked him this he seemed confused.

"I hadn't thought about that—."

They did not say anything, and there was the illusion of sudden groping out of sight.

"Are you going to take him to the Front?" Fraser suggested, and laughed impatiently.

"No, he might get shot there," Cairn replied, screwing up his nose, and recovering his good humour, apparently. "I must give him away."

Fraser knew how fond he was of the dog, and attributed his awkwardness to his dislike at the notion of parting from it.

"Let me keep it for you," he said, generously.

"No, thanks. I'll get rid of it."

Fraser saw his partner on the following day at their office. The next thing that he heard was that Cairn was ill in bed, and that his return to France would have to be again postponed. On going to his friend's flat he crossed at the door two men carrying out a small box. The charwoman was very mysterious. He asked what the box was.

"It's the dog," she replied.

"Is he sold then?" Fraser asked.

"No. 'E's dead."

He looked at her melodramatically unconcerned and bloated face for a moment.

Rob Cairn was alone in his bedroom. He was very exhausted, and faintly bad-tempered.

"What's up? Have you had a relapse?"

"Yes—something: I'm not well."

"Can I do anything for you?"

Cairn was lying on his back and hardly looked at his visitor.

"No, thanks. Listen." He turned towards Fraser, and his face became long and dulled with excitement. "Listen to this. You know Carp, the dog? I killed it yesterday.—I shot it with a revolver; but I aimed too low. It nearly screamed the place down.—Poor brute!— You know—"

He suddenly lurched round, face downwards, flattened in his arm, and sobbed in a deep howling way, that reminded Fraser of a dog.

When he looked up his face was a scared and bitter mask.

"What a coward I am! Poor beast! Poor—. How could I—"

"Nonsense, Rob! You're not yourself. You know you're not yourself! Have you seen a doctor? Don't worry about this—."

"I'm only glad of one thing. I *know* I shall pay for it. That thought is the only one that quiets me. I know as surely as I am lying here that my hour is fixed! I have killed my best living luck. Not that I wanted the luck! God, no! I care little enough what happens to me! But that poor beast!—"

"Damn you and your mascots! You are the slave of any poodle—!"

Fraser remembered his detestable lady-love, and the perpetual threat of an idiotic marriage.

The doctor came into the room.—He told me that he fancied more had happened between Cairn and Carp, at the dog's death, than his friend had cared to tell him. Cairn was another fortnight in London, then went to France. Two weeks after that he was killed. He understood the mechanism of his destiny better than his partner.

THE PORT LOOKOUT

by "Bartimeus"

Bartimeus (1883–?) was the penname of the British writer Lewis Anselm da Costa Ricci (or Ritchie), about whom little is known. Bartimeus's jaunty stories of the war treat serious issues in a somewhat amused manner. "The Port Lookout" describes a would-be desertion by a sailor on leave in London.

[From Bartimeus's *The Navy Eternal: Which Is the Navy-That-Floats, the Navy-That-Flies and the Navy-under-the-Sea.* Hodder & Stoughton, 1918.]

THERE IS A tendency among some people to regard war as a morally uplifting pursuit. Because a man fights in the cause of right and freedom, it is believed by quite a large section of those who don't fight that he goes about the business in a completely regenerate spirit, unhampered by any of the human failings that were apt to beset him in pre-war days. Be that as it may, Able-Seaman Pettigrew, wearer of no good conduct badges and incorrigible leave-breaker in peacetime, remained in war merely Able-Seaman Pettigrew, leave-breaker, and still minus good conduct badges.

He stood at the door of a London public-house, contemplating the night distastefully. The wind howled down the muddy street, and the few lamps, casting smears of yellow light at intervals along the thoroughfare, only served to illuminate the driving rain. His leave expired at 7 a.m. the following morning, and he had just time to catch the last train to Portsmouth that night. To do Mr. Pettigrew justice, he had completed the first stage of his journey— the steps of the public-house—with that laudable end in view. Here, however, he faltered, and as he faltered he remembered a certain hospitable lady of his acquaintance who lived south of the river.

"To 'ell!" said Mr. Pettigrew recklessly, and swung himself into a passing bus. As he climbed the steps he noted that it passed Waterloo Station, and for an instant the flame of good intent, temporarily dowsed, flickered into life again. His ship, he remembered, was under sailing orders. He found himself alone on top of the bus, and walked forward to the left-hand seat. For a moment he stood there, gripping the rail and peering ahead through the stinging rain while the bus lurched and skidded on its way through deserted streets. Then his imagination, quickened somewhat by hot whisky and water, obliterated the impulse of conscience. He saw himself twenty-four hours later, standing thus as port lookout on board his destroyer, peering ahead through the drenching spray, gripping the rail with numbed hands. . . .

"Oh, to 'ell!" said Mr. Pettigrew again, and, sitting down, gave himself up sullenly to amorous anticipation.

He was interrupted by a girl's voice at his elbow.

"Fare, please."

He turned his head, and saw it was the conductress, a slim, compact figure swaying easily to the lurch of the vehicle. Her fingers touched his as she handed him the ticket, and they were bitterly cold.

"Nice night, ain't it?" said Mr. Pettigrew.

"Not 'arf," said the girl philosophically. "But there! it ain't so bad for us 's what it is for them boys in the trenches."

"Ah!" said Mr. Pettigrew archly. "Them boys—'*im*, you means."

The girl shook her head swiftly. Seen in the gleam of a passing lamp, her face was pretty and glistening with rain. "Not me," she said. "There was two—my brothers—but they went West. There's only me left . . . carryin' on." The bus lurched violently, causing the little conductress to lose her balance, and her weight rested momentarily against Mr. Pettigrew's shoulder. She recovered her equilibrium instantly without self-consciousness, and stood looking absently ahead into the darkness.

"That's what we've all got to do, ain't it?" she said—"do our bit. . . ."

She jingled the coppers in her bag and turned abruptly.

Mr. Pettigrew watched the trim, self-respecting little figure till it vanished down the steps.

"Oh, 'ell!" he groaned, as imperious flesh and immortal spirit awoke to renew the unending combat.

Five minutes later the conductress reappeared at Mr. Pettigrew's shoulder.

"Waterloo," she said. "That's where all you boys gets off, ain't it. . . ? You're for Portsmouth, I s'pose?"

"That's right," said Mr. Pettigrew. He jerked to his feet, gripping his bundle, and made for the steps with averted head. " 'Night," he said brusquely. The bus slowed and stopped.

"Good luck," said the girl.

The port lookout gripped the bridge-rail to steady himself, and stared out through the driving spray and the darkness as the destroyer thrashed her way down Channel. He was chosen for the trick because of his eyesight. "I gotter eye like a adjective 'awk," Mr. Pettigrew was wont to admit in his more expansive moments, and none gainsaid him the length and breadth of the destroyer's mess-deck. None gainsaid him on the bridge that night when suddenly he wheeled inboard and bawled at the full strength of his lungs:

"Objec' on the port bow, sir!"

There was an instant's pause, a confused shouting of orders, a vision of the coxswain struggling at the kicking wheel as the helm went over, and a man's clear voice saying: "By God, we've got her!"

Then came the stunning shock of the impact, the grinding crash of blunt metal shearing metal, more shouts, faces seen white for an instant against the dark waters, something scraping past the side of the forecastle, and finally a dull explosion aft.

"Rammed a submarine and sunk the perisher!" shouted the yeoman in Mr. Pettigrew's ear. "Wake up! What the 'ell's up? Are ye dazed?"

Mr. Pettigrew was considerably more dazed when he was sent for the following day in harbour by his Captain. From force of custom on obeying such summonses, the ship's black sheep removed his cap.[1]

"Put your damned cap on!" said the Lieutenant-Commander. Mr. Pettigrew replaced his cap. "Now shake hands." Mr. Pettigrew shook hands. "Now go on leave." Mr. Pettigrew obeyed.

For forty minutes the policeman on duty outside Waterloo Station had been keeping under observation a rather dejected-looking blue-jacket carrying a bundle, who stood at the corner scrutinising the buses as they passed. Finally, with deliberate measured tread he approached the man of the sea.

"What bus do you want, mate?"

Mr. Pettigrew enlightened him as to the number.

"There's been four of that number gone past while you was standin' 'ere," said the policeman, not without suspicion in his tones.

---

1. By the ancient custom of the Navy a defaulter removes his cap when his case is investigated by the Captain.

"I'm very partickler about buses," said Mr. Pettigrew coldly.

"Well," said the constable, "'ere's another one."

The sailor waited till it slowed up abreast of them. His blue eyes were cocked on the rear end.

"An' *this* 'ere's the right one," said Mr. Pettigrew.

He stepped briskly into the roadway, ran half a dozen paces, and swung himself on to the footboard beside the conductress.

A RAID NIGHT

by H. M. (Henry Major) Tomlinson

Tomlinson (1873–1958), a British journalist who covered the war in France, introduced the fine anthology Best Short Stories of the War *(1931). This story of a journalist who has returned to London describes the destructive arrival of a German zeppelin over the dark city.*

[From Tomlinson's *Waiting for Daylight*. London: Cassell and Company, 1922.]

SEPTEMBER 17, 1915. I had crossed from France to Fleet Street, and was thankful at first to have about me the things I had proved, with their suggestion of intimacy, their look of security; but I found the once familiar editorial rooms of that daily paper a little more than estranged. I thought them worse, if anything, than Ypres. Ypres is within the region where, when soldiers enter it, they abandon hope, because they have become sane at last, and their minds have a temperature a little below normal. In Ypres, whatever may have been their heroic and exalted dreams, they awake, see the world is mad, and surrender to the doom from which they know a world bereft will give them no reprieve.

There was a way in which the office of that daily paper was familiar. I had not expected it, and it came with a shock. Not only the compulsion, but the bewildering inconsequence of war was suggested by its activities. Reason was not there. It was ruled by a blind and fixed idea. The glaring artificial light, the headlong haste of the telegraph instruments, the wild litter on the floor, the rapt attention of the men scanning the news, their abrupt movements and speed when they had to cross the room, still with their gaze fixed, their expression that of those who dreaded something worse to happen; the suggestion of tension, as though the Last Trump were expected at any moment, filled me with vague alarm. The only place where that incipient panic is not usual is the front line, because there the enemy is within hail and is known to be another unlucky fool. But I allayed my anxiety. I leaned over one of the still figures, and scanned the fateful document which had given its reader the aspect of one who was staring at what the Moving Finger had done. Its message was no more than the excited whisper of a witness who had just left a keyhole. But I realized in that moment of surprise that this office was an essential feature of the War; without it, the War might become Peace. It provoked the emotions which assembled civilians in ecstatic support of the sacrifices, just as the staff of a corps headquarters, at some comfortable leagues behind the trenches, maintains its fighting men in the place where gas and shells tend to engender common sense and irresolution.

I left the glare of that office, its heat and half-hysterical activity, and went into the coolness and quiet of the darkened street, and there the dread left me that it could be a duty of mine to keep hot pace with patriots in full stampede. The stars were wonderful. It is such a tran-quillizing surprise to discover there are stars over London. Until this War, when the street illuminations were doused, we never knew it. It strengthens one's faith to discover the Pleiades over London; it is not true that their delicate glimmer has been put out by the remark-able incandescent energy of our power stations. As I crossed London Bridge the City was as silent as though it had come to the end of its days, and the shapes I could just make out under the stars were no more substantial than the shadows of its past. Even the Thames was a noiseless ghost. London at night gave me the illusion that I was really hidden from the monstrous trouble of Europe, and, at least for one sleep, had got out of the War. I felt that my suburban street, secluded in trees and unimportance, was as remote from the evil I knew of as though it were in Alaska. When I came to that street I could not see my neighbors' homes. It was with some doubt that I found my own. And there, with three hours to go to midnight, and a book, and some circumstances that certainly had not changed, I had retired thankfully into a fragment of that world I had feared we had completely lost.

"What a strange moaning the birds in the shrubbery are making!" my companion said once. I listened to it, and thought it was strange. There was a long silence, and then she looked up sharply. "What's that?" she asked. "Listen!"

I listened. My hearing is not good.

"Nothing!" I assured her.

"There it is again." She put down her book with decision, and rose, I thought, in some alarm.

"Trains," I suggested. "The gas bubbling. The dog next door. Your imagination." Then I listened to the dogs. It was curious, but they all seemed awake and excited.

"What is the noise like?" I asked, surrendering my book on the antiquity of man.

She twisted her mouth in a comical way most seriously, and tried to mimic a deep and solemn note.

"Guns," I said to myself, and went to the front door.

Beyond the vague opposite shadows of some elms, lights twinkled in the sky, incontinent sparks, as though glow lamps on an invisible pattern of wires were being switched on and off by an idle child. That was shrapnel. I walked along the empty street a little to get a view between and beyond the villas. I turned to say something to my companion, and saw then my silent neighbors, shadowy groups about me, as though they had not approached but had materialized where they stood. We watched those infernal sparks. A shadow lit its pipe and offered me its match. I heard the guns easily enough now, but they were miles away.

A slender finger of brilliant light moved slowly across the sky, checked, and remained pointing, firmly accusatory, at something it had found in the heavens. A Zeppelin!

There it was, at first a wraith, a suggestion on the point of vanishing, and then illuminated and embodied, a celestial maggot stuck to the round of a cloud like a caterpillar to the edge of a leaf. We gazed at it silently, I cannot say for how long. The beam of light might have pinned the bright larva to the sky for the inspection of interested Londoners. Then somebody spoke: "I think it is coming our way."

I thought so too. I went indoors, calling out to the boy as I passed his room upstairs, and went to where the girls were asleep. Three miles, three minutes! It appears to be harder to waken children when a Zeppelin is coming your way. I got the elder girl awake, lifted her, and sat her on the bed, for she had become heavier, I noticed. Then I put her small sister over my shoulder, as limp and indifferent as a half-filled bag. By this time the elder one had snuggled into the foot of her bed, resigned to that place if the other end were disputed, and was asleep again. I think I became annoyed, and spoke sharply. We were in a hurry. The boy was waiting for us at the top of the stairs.

"What's up?" he asked with merry interest, hoisting his slacks.

"Come on down," I said.

We went into a central room, put coats round them, answering eager and innocent questions with inconsequence, had the cellar door and a light ready, and then went out to inspect affairs. There were more searchlights at work. Bright diagonals made a living network on the overhead dark. It was remarkable that those rigid beams should not rest on the roof of night, but that their ends should glide noiselessly about the invisible dome. The nearest of them was followed, when in the zenith, by a faint oval of light. Sometimes it discovered and broke on delicate films of high fair-weather clouds. The shells were still twinkling brilliantly, and the guns were making a rhythmless baying in the distance, like a number of alert and indignant hounds. But the Zeppelin had gone. The firing diminished and stopped.

They went to bed again, and as I had become acutely depressed, and the book now had no value, I turned in myself, assuring everyone, with the usual confidence of the military expert, that the affair was over for the night. But once in bed I found I could see there only the progress humanity had made in its movement heavenwards. That is the way with us; never to be concerned with the newest clever trick of our enterprising fellow-men till a sudden turn of affairs shows us, by the immediate threat to our own existence, that that cleverness has added to the peril of civilized society, whose house has been built on the verge of the pit. War now would be not only between soldiers. In future wars the place of honor would be occupied by the infants, in their cradles. For war is not murder. Starving children is war, and it is not murder. What treacherous lying is all the heroic poetry of battle! Men will now creep up after dark, ambushed in safety behind the celestial curtains, and drop bombs on sleepers beneath, for the greater glory of some fine figment or other. It filled me, not with wrath at the work of Kaisers and Kings, for we know what is possible with them, but with dismay at the discovery that one's fellows are so docile and credulous that they will obey any order, however abominable. The very heavens had been fouled by this obscene and pallid worm, crawling over those eternal verities to which eyes had been lifted for light when night and trouble were over-dark. God was dethroned by science. One looked startled at humanity, seeing not the accustomed countenance, but, for a moment, glimpsing instead the baleful lidless stare of the evil of the slime, the unmentionable of a nightmare . . .

A deafening crash brought us out of bed in one movement. I must have been dozing. Someone cried, "My children!" Another rending uproar interrupted my effort to shepherd the flock to a lower floor. There was a raucous avalanche of glass. We muddled down somehow—I forget how. I could not find the matches. Then in the dark we lost the youngest for some eternal seconds while yet another explosion shook the house. We got to the cellar stairs, and at last there they all were, their backs to the coals, sitting on lumber.

A candle was on the floor. There were more explosions, somewhat muffled. The candle-flame showed a little tremulous excitement, as if it were one of the party. It reached upwards curiously in a long intent flame, and then shrank flat with what it had learned. We were accompanied by grotesque shadows. They stood about us on the white and unfamiliar walls. We waited. Even the shadows seemed to listen with us; they hardly moved, except when the candle-flame was nervous. Then the shadows wavered slightly. We waited. I caught the boy's eye, and winked. He winked back. The youngest, still with sleepy eyes, was trembling, though not with cold, and this her sister noticed, and put her arms about her. His mother had her hand on her boy's shoulder.

There was no more noise outside. It was time, perhaps, to go up to see what had happened. I put a raincoat over my pajamas, and went into the street. Some of my neighbors, who were special constables, hurried by. The enigmatic night, for a time, for five minutes, or five seconds (I do not know how long it was), was remarkably still and usual. It might have been pretending that we were all mistaken. It was as though we had been merely dreaming our recent excitements. Then, across a field, a villa began to blaze. Perhaps it had been stunned till then, and had suddenly jumped into a panic of flames. It was wholly involved in one roll of fire and smoke, a sudden furnace so consuming that, when it as suddenly ceased, giving one or two dying spasms, I had but an impression of flames rolling out of windows and doors to persuade me that what I had seen was real. The night engulfed what may have been an illusion, for till then I had never noticed a house at that point.

Whispers began to pass of tragedies that were incredible in their incidence and craziness. Three children were dead in the rubble of one near villa. The ambulance that was passing was taking their father to the hospital. A woman had been blown from her bed into the street. She was unhurt, but she was insane. A long row of humbler dwellings, over which the dust was still hanging in a faint mist, had been demolished, and one could only hope the stories about that place were far from true. We were turned away when we would have assisted; all the help that was wanted was there. A stranger offered me his tobacco pouch, and it was then I found my rainproof was a lady's, and therefore had no pipe in its pocket.

The sky was suspect, and we watched it, but saw only vacuity till one long beam shot into it, searching slowly and deliberately the whole mysterious ceiling, yet hesitating sometimes, and going back on its path as though intelligently suspicious of a matter which it had passed over too quickly. It peered into the immense caverns of a cloud to which it had returned, illuminating to us unsuspected and horrifying possibilities of hiding-places above us. We expected to see the discovered enemy boldly emerge then. Nothing came out. Other beams by now had joined the pioneer, and the night became bewildering with a dazzling mesh of light. Shells joined the wandering beams, those sparks of orange and red. A world of fantastic chimney-pots and black rounds of trees leaped into being between us and the sudden expansion of a fan of yellow flame. A bomb! We just felt, but hardly heard, the shock of it. A furious succession of such bursts of light followed, a convulsive opening and shutting of night. We saw that when midnight is cleft asunder it has a fiery inside.

The eruptions ceased. Idle and questioning, not knowing we had heard the last gun and bomb of the affair, a little stunned by the maniacal rapidity and violence of this attack, we found ourselves gazing at the familiar and shadowy peace of our suburb as we have always known it. It had returned to that aspect. But something had gone from it for ever. It was not, and never could be again, as once we had known it. The security of our own place had been based on the goodwill or indifference of our fellow-creatures everywhere. Tonight, over that obscure and unimportant street, we had seen a celestial portent illuminate briefly a little of the future of mankind.

A TRADE REPORT ONLY

by C. E. (Charles Edward) Montague

Montague (1867–1928) was Anglo-Irish and served in the trenches as full sergeant with the Royal Fusiliers before joining the British Military Intelligence office. This story, about an incident in northern France on the Western Front, is told by an aggressive and haunted platoon sergeant, whose frustration boils over: "But you were not there. So you cannot feel how the cursed place had tried to shake itself free of its curse, and had failed and fallen rigid again, dreeing its weird, and poor Billy with it."

[First published in *Blackwood's Magazine*, September 1921.]

No ONE HAS said what was wrong with The Garden, nor even why it was called by that name: whether because it had apples in it, and also a devil, like Eden; or after Gethsemane and the agonies there; or, again, from Proserpine's garden, because of the hush filling the foreground. All the air near you seemed like so much held breath, with the long rumble of far-away guns stretching out beyond it like some dreamful line of low hills in the distance of a landscape.

The rest of the Western Front has been well written up much too well. The Garden alone—the Holy Terror, as some of the men used to call it has not. It is under some sort of taboo. I think I know why. If you never were in the line there before the smash came and made it like everywhere else, you could not know how it would work on the nerves when it was still its own elvish self. And if you were there and did know, then you knew also that it was no good to try to tell people. They only said, "Oh, so you all had the wind up?" We had. But who could say why? How is a horse to say what it is that bedevils one empty place more than another? He has to prick up his ears when he gets there. Then he starts sweating. That's all he knows, and it was the same story with us in The Garden. All I can do is to tell you, just roughly, the make of the place, the way that the few honest solids and liquids were fixed that came into it. They were the least part of it, really.

It was only an orchard, to look at: all ancient apples, dead straight in the stem, with fat wet grass underneath, a little unhealthy in colour for want of more sun. Six feet above ground, the lowest apple boughs all struck out level, and kept so; some beasts, gone in our time, must have eaten every leaf that tried to grow lower. So the under side of the boughs made a sort of flat awning or roof. We called the layer of air between it and the ground "The Six-Foot Seam," as we were mostly miners. The light in this seam always appeared to have had something done to it: sifted through branches, refracted, messed about somehow, it was not at all the stuff you wanted just at that time. You see the like of it in an eclipse, when the sun gives a queer wink at the earth round the edge of a black mask. Very nice, too, in its place; but the war itself was quite enough out of the common—just then falling skies all over the place, and half your dead certainties shaken.

We and the Germans were both in The Garden, and knew it. But nobody showed. Everywhere else on the Front somebody showed up at last; somebody fired. But here nothing was seen or heard ever. You found you were whispering and walking on tiptoe, expecting you didn't know what. Have you been in a great crypt at twilight under a church, nothing round you but endless thin pillars, holding up a low roof? Suppose there's a wolf at the far end of the crypt and you alone at the other, staring and staring into the thick of the pillars, and wondering, wondering round which of the pillars will that grey nose come rubbing?

Why not smash up the silly old spell, you may say—let a good yell, loose a shot, do any sane thing to break out? That's what I said till I got there. Our unit took over the place from the French. A French platoon sergeant, my opposite number, showed me the quarters and posts and the like, and I asked the usual question, "How's the old Boche?"

"Mais assez gentil," he pattered. That Gaul was not waiting to chat. While he showed me the bomb-store, he muttered something low, hurried, and blurred— *"Le bon Dieu Boche,"* I think it was, had created the orchard. The Germans themselves were "bons bourgeois" enough, for all he had seen or heard of them—"Not a shot in three weeks. *Seulement,"* he grinned, half-shamefaced and half-confidential, as sergeant to sergeant, *"ne faut pas les embeter."*

I knew all about that. French sergeants were always like that: dervishes in a fight when it came, but dead set, at all other times, on living *paisiblement,* smoking their pipes. *Paisiblement*—they love the very feel of the word in their mouths. Our men were no warrior race, but they all hugged the belief that they really were marksmen, not yet found out by the world. They would be shooting all night at clods, heads of posts, at anything that might pass for a head. Oh, I knew. Or I thought so.

But no. Not a shot all the night. Nor on any other night either. We were just sucked into the hush of The Garden, the way your voice drops in a church—when you go in at the door you become part of the system. I tried to think why. Did nobody fire just because in that place it was so easy for anybody to kill? No trench could be dug; it would have filled in an hour with water filtering through from the full stream flanking. The Garden. Sentries stood out among the fruit trees, behind little breastworks of sods, like the things you use to shoot grouse. These screens were merely a form; they would scarcely have slowed down a bullet. They were not defenses, only symbols of things that were real elsewhere. Everything else in the place was on queer terms with reality; so were they.

Our first event was the shriek. It was absolutely detached, unrelated to anything seen or heard before or soon after, just like the sudden fall of a great tree on a still windless day. At three o'clock on a late autumn morning, a calm moonless night, the depths of The Garden in front of our posts yielded a long wailing scream. I was making a round of our posts at the time, and the scream made me think of a kind of dream I had had twice or thrice: not a story dream, but a portrait dream; just a vivid rending vision of the face of some friend with a look on it that made me feel the brute I must have been to have never seen how he or she had suffered, and how little I had known or tried to know. I could not have fancied before that one yell could tell such a lot about anyone. Where it came from there must be some kind of hell going on that went beyond all the hells now in the books, like one of the stars that are still out of sight because the world has not lived long enough to give time for the first ray of light from their blaze to get through to our eyes.

I found the sentries jumpy. "What is it, sergeant?" one of them almost demanded of me, as if I were the fellow in charge of the devils. "There's no one on earth," he said, "could live in that misery." Toomey himself, the redheaded gamekeeper out of the County Fermanagh, betrayed some perturbation. He hinted that "Thim Wans" were in it. "Who?" I asked. "Ach, the Good People," he said, with a trace of reluctance. Then I remembered, from old days at school, that the Greeks too had been careful; they called their Furies "The Well-disposed Ladies."

All the rest of the night there was not a sound but the owls. The sunless day that followed was quiet till 2:30 P.M., when the Hellhound appeared. He came trotting briskly out of the orchard, rounding stem after stem of the fruit trees, leapt our little formal pretence of barbed wire, and made straight for Toomey, as any dog would. It was a young male black-and-tan. It adored Toomey till three, when he was relieved. Then it came capering around him in ecstasy, back to the big living cellar, a hundred yards to the rear. At the door it heard voices within and let down its tail, ready to plead lowliness and contrition before any tribunal less divine than Toomey.

The men, or most of them, were not obtrusively divine just then. They were out to take anything ill that might come. All the hushed days had first drawn their nerves tight, and then the scream had cut some of them. All bawled or squeaked in the cellar, to try to feel natural after the furtive business outside.

"Gawd a'mighty!" Looker shrilled at the entry of Toomey, "if Fritz ain't sold 'im a pup!"

Jeers flew from all parts of the smoky half-darkness.

"Where's licence, Toomey?"

"Sure 'e's clean in th' 'ouse?"

"'Tain't no Dogs 'Ome 'ere. Over the way!" Corporal Mullen, the ever-friendly, said to Toomey, more mildly, "Wot! Goin' soft?"

"A daycent dog, Corp," said Toomey. "He's bruk wi' the Kaiser. An' I'll engage he's through the distemper. Like as not, he'll be an Alsatian." Toomey retailed these commendations slowly, with pauses between, to let them sink in.

"What'll you feed him?" asked Mullen, inspecting the points of the beast with charity.

"Feed 'im!" Looker squealed. "Feed 'im into th' incinerator!"

Toomey turned on him. "Aye, an' be et be the rats!"

"Fat lot o' talk 'bout rats," growled Brunt, the White Hope, the company's only prize-fighter. "Tha'd think rats were struttin' down fairway, shovin' folk off duck-board."

"Ah!" Looker agreed. "An' roostin' up yer armpit."

"Thot's reet, Filthy," said Brunt. We all called Looker "Filthy," without offence meant or taken.

"I'll bet 'arf a dollar," said Looker, eyeing the Hellhound malignantly, "the 'Uns 'ave loaded 'im up with plague fleas. Sent 'im acrorse. Wiv instructions."

Toomey protested. "Can't ye see the dog has been hit, ye blind man?" In fact, the immigrant kept his tail licking expressively under his belly except when it lifted under the sunshine of Toomey's regard.

Brunt rumbled out slow gloomy prophecies from the gloom of his corner. "'E'll be tearin' 'imsel' t'bits wi' t'mange in a fortneet. Rat for breakfas', rat for dinner, rat for tea; bit o' rat las' thing at neet, 'fore 'e'll stretch down to 't."

"An' that's the first sinse ye've talked," Toomey conceded. "A rotten diet-sheet is ut. An' dirt! An' no kennel the time the roof'll start drippin'. A dog's life for a man, an' God knows what for a dog."

We felt the force of that. We all had dogs at home. The Hellhound perhaps felt our ruth in the air like a rise of temperature, for at this point he made a couple of revolutions on his wheel base to get the pampas grass of his imagination comfortable about him, and then collapsed in a curve and lay at rest with his nose to the ground and two soft enigmatic gleams from his eyes raking the twilight recesses of our dwelling. For the moment he was relieved of the post of nucleus-in-chief for the vapours of fractiousness to condense upon.

He had a distinguished successor. The Company Sergeant-Major, no less, came round about five minutes after with a word from the Colonel. Some mischief, all our hearts told us at once. They were right too. The Corps had sent word—just what it would, we inwardly groaned. The Corps had sent word that G.H.Q.—Old G.H.Q.! At it again! we savagely thought. We knew what was coming. Yes, G.H.Q. wanted to know what German unit was opposite to us. That meant a raid, of course. The Colonel couldn't help it. Like all sane men below Brigade staffs, he hated raids. But orders were orders. He did all he could. He sent word that if anyone brought in a German, dead or alive, on his own, by this time tomorrow, he, the Colonel, would give him a fiver. Of course nobody could, but it was an offer, meant decently.

Darkness and gnashing of teeth, grunts and snarls of disgust, filled the cellar the moment the C.S.M. had departed. "Gawd 'elp us!" "A ride! In The Gawden!" "'Oo says Gawd made gawdens?" "Ow! Everythink in The Gawden is lovely!" "Come into The Gawden, Maud!" You see, the wit of most of us was not a weapon of precision. Looker came nearest, perhaps, to the point. "As if we 'ad a chawnce," he said, "to gow aht rattin' Germans, wiv a sack!"

"We gotten dog for't ahl reet," said Brunt. This was the only audible trace of good humor. Toomey looked at Brunt quickly.

Toomey was destined to trouble that afternoon; one thing came after another. At 3:25 I sent him and Brunt, with a clean sack apiece, to the Sergeant-Major's dugout for the rations. They came back in ten minutes. As Toomey gave me his sack, I feared that I saw a thin train of mixed black and white dust trending across the powdered mortar floor to the door. Then I saw Looker, rage in his face, take a candle and follow this trail, stooping down, and once tasting the stuff on a wet fingertip.

And then the third storm burst. "Christ!" Looker yelled. "If he ain't put the tea in the sack with the 'ole in it!"

We all knew that leak in a bottom corner of that special sack as we knew every very small thing in our life of small things—the cracked dixie-lid, the brazier's short leg, the way that Mynns had of clearing his throat, and Brunt of working his jaws before spitting. Of course, the sack was all right for loaves and the tinned stuff. But tea!—loose tea mixed with powdered sugar! It was like loading a patent seed-sowing machine with your fortune in gold-dust. There was a general groan of "God help us!" with extras. In this report I leave out, all along, a great many extras. Print and paper are dear.

Looker was past swearing. "Plyin' a piper-chise!" he ejaculated with venom. "All owver Frawnce! Wiv our grub!"

Toomey was sorely distressed. He, deep in whose heart was lodged the darling vision of Toomey the managing head, the contriver, the "ould lad that was in ut," had bungled a job fit for babes. "Ah, then, who could be givin' his mind to the tea," he almost moaned, "an' he with a gran' thought in ut?"

At any other time and place the platoon would have settled down, purring, under those words. "A gran' thought," "a great idaya"—when Toomey in happier days had owned to being in labor with one of those heirs of his invention, some uncovenanted mercy had nearly always accrued before long to his friends—a stew of young rabbits, two brace of fat pheasants, once a mighty wild goose. The tactician, we understood in a general way, had "put the comether upon" them. Now even those delicious memories were turned to gall. "Always the sime!"

Looker snarled at the fallen worker of wonders. "Always the sime! Ye cawn't 'ave a bit o' wire sived up for pipe-cleanin' without 'e'll loan it off yer to go snarin' 'ares." Looker paused for a moment, gathering all the resources of wrath, and then he swiftly scaled the high top-gallant of ungraciousness: "'E wiv the 'ole platoon workin' awaye for 'im, pluckin' pawtridge an' snipes, the 'ole wye up from the sea! Top end o' Frawnce is all a muck o' feathers wiv 'im!"

All were good men; Looker, like Toomey, a very good man. It was only their nerves that had gone, and the jolly power of gay and easy relentment after a jar. However they tried, they could not cease yapping. I went out for a drink of clean air. If you are to go on loving mankind, you must take a rest from it sometimes. As I went up the steps from the cellar the rasping jangle from below did not cease; it only sank on my ears as I went. "Ow, give us 'Owm Rule for England, Gord's sike!" "Sye there ain't no towds in Irelan', do they?" "Filthy, I've tould ye I'm sorry an'—" "Garn, both on yer! Ol' gas projectors!" "Begob, if ye want an eye knocked from ye then—!" I nearly went back, but then I heard Corporal Mullen, paternal and firm, like Neptune rebuking the winds, "Now, then, we don't none of us want to go losing our heads about nothing." No need to trouble. Mullen would see to the children.

I went east, into The Garden. Ungathered apples were going to loss on its trees. I stood looking at one of them for a time, and then it suddenly detached itself and fell to the ground with a little thud and a splash of squashed brown rottenness, as if my eye had plucked it. After that sound the stillness set in again: stillness of autumn, stillness of vigilant fear, and now the stillness of oncoming evening, the nun, to make it more cloistral. No silence so deep but that it can be deepened? As minutes passed, infinitesimal whispers—I think from mere wisps of eddies, twisted round snags in the stream—began to lift into hearing. Deepening silence is only the rise into clearness of this or that more confidential utterance.

I must have been sucking that confidence in for a good twenty minutes before I turned with a start. I had to, I did not know why. It seemed as if some sense, which I did not know I had got, told me that someone was stealing up behind me. No one there; nothing but Arras, the vacuous city, indistinct among her motionless trees. She always seemed to be listening and frightened. It was as if the haggard creature had stirred.

I looked to my front again, rather ashamed. Was I losing hold too, I wondered, as I gazed level out into the Seam and watched the mist deepening. Each evening, that autumn, a quilt of very white mist would come out of the soaked soil of The Garden, lay itself out, flat and dense, but shallow at first, over the grass, and then deepen upward as twilight advanced, first submerging the tips of the grass and the purple snake-headed flowers, and then thickening steadily up till the whole Six-Foot Seam was packed with milky opaqueness.

Sixty yards out from our front a heron was standing, immobilized, in the stream, staring down—for a last bit of fishing, no doubt. As I watched him, his long head came suddenly round and half up. He listened. He stood like that, warily, for a minute, then seemed to decide it was no place for him, hoisted himself off the ground, and winged slowly away with great flaps. I felt cold, and thought, "What a time I've been loafing round here!" But I found it was four o'clock only. I thought I would go on and visit my sentries, the three-o'clock men who would come off duty at five. It would warm me; and one or two of the young ones were apt to be creepy about sundown.

Schofield, the lad in one of our most advanced posts, was waist-deep in the mist when I reached him.

"Owt, boy?" I whispered. He was a North-country man.

"Nowt, Sergeant," he whispered, "barrin'—" He checked. He was one of the stout ones you couldn't trust to yell out for help if the devil were at them.

"What's wrong?" I asked pretty sharply.

"Nobbut t'way," he said slowly, "they deucks doan't seem t'be gettin' down to it to-neet." My eye followed his through the boughs to the pallid sky. A flight of wild-duck were whirling and counter-whirling aloft in some wild *pas d'inquietude*. Yes; no doubt our own duck that had come during the war, with the herons and snipe, to live in The Garden, the untrodden marsh, where, between the two lines of rifles never unloaded, no shot was ever heard, and snipe were safe from all snipers. A good lad, Schofield; he always took notice of things. But what possessed the creatures? What terror infested their quarters tonight?

I looked Schofield over. He was as near to dead white as a tanned man can come—that is, a bad yellow. But he could be left. A man that keeps on taking notice of things he can see, instead of imagining ones that he can't, is a match for the terror that walketh by twilight. I stole on to our most advanced post of all. There I was not so sure of my man. He was Mynns. We called him Billy Wisdom, because he was a schoolmaster in civil life—some Council School at Hoggerston. "What cheer, Billy?" I whispered. "Anything to report?"

The mist was armpit deep on him now, but the air quite clear above that; so that from three feet off I saw his head and shoulders well, and his bayonet; nothing else at all. He did not turn when I spoke, nor unfix his eyes from the point he had got them set on, in front of his post and a little below their own level. "All—quiet—and—correct—Sergeant," he said, as if each word were a full load and had to be hauled by itself. I had once seen a man drop his rifle and bolt back overland from his post, to trial and execution and anything rather than that everlasting wait for a bayonet's point to come lunging up out of thick mist in front and a little below him, into the gullet, under the chin. Billy was near bolting-point, I could tell by more senses than one. He was losing hold on one bodily function after another, but still hanging on hard to something, some grip of the spirit that held from second to second after muscle had mutinied and nerve was gone.

He had hardly spoken before a new torment wrung him. The whole landscape suddenly gave a quick shiver. The single poplar, down the stream, just perceptibly shuddered and rustled, and then was dead still again. A bed of rushes, nearer us, swayed for an instant, and stood taut again. Absurd, you will say. And, of course, it was only a faint breath of wind, the only stir in the air all that day. But you were not there. So you cannot feel how the cursed place had tried to shake itself free of its curse, and had failed, and fallen rigid again, dree-ing its weird, and poor Billy with it. His hold on his tongue was what he lost now. He began to wail, under his breath, "Christ, pity me! Oh, suffering Christ, pity me!" He was still staring hard to his front, but I had got a hand ready to grab at his belt when, from somewhere out in the mist before us, there came, short and crisp, the crack of a dead branch heavily trodden upon.

Billy was better that instant. Better an audible enemy, one with a body, one that could trample on twigs, than that horrible infestation of life with impalpable sinisterness. Billy turned with a grin ghastly enough, but a grin.

"Hold your fire," I said in his ear, "till I order." I made certain dispositions of bombs on a little shelf. Then we waited, listening, second by second. I think both our ears must have flicked like a mule's. But the marvel came in at the eye. We both saw the vision at just the same instant. It was some fifty yards from us, straight to our front. It sat on the top of the mist as though mist were ice and would bear. It was a dog of the very same breed as the Hellhound, sitting upright like one of the beasts that support coats-of-arms; all proper, too, as the heralds would say, with the black-and-tan as in life. The image gazed at us fixedly. How long? Say, twenty seconds. Then it about-turned without any visible use of its limbs, and receded some ten or twelve yards, still sitting up and now rhythmically rising and falling as though the mist it rode upon were undulating. Then it clean vanished. I thought it sank, as if the mist had ceased to bear. Billy thought the beast just melted into the air radially, all round, as rings made of smoke do.

You know the crazy coolness, a sort of false presence of mind, that will come in and fool you a little bit further at these moments of stag-gering dislocation of cause and effect. One of these waves of mad rationalism broke on me now. I turned quickly round to detect the cinema lantern behind us which must have projected the dog's moving figure upon the white sheet of mist. None there, of course. Only the terrified city, still there, aghast, with held breath.

Then all my anchors gave together. I was adrift; there was nothing left certain. I thought, "What if all we are sure of be just a mistake, and our sureness about it conceit, and we no better than puppies ourselves to wonder that dogs should be taking their ease in mid-air and an empty orchard be shrieking?" While I was drifting, I happened to notice the sleepy old grumble of guns from the rest of the front, and I envied those places. Sane, normal places; happy all who were there; only their earthworks were tumbling, not the last few certain-ties that we men think we have got hold of.

All of this, of course, had to go on in my own mind behind a shut face. For Billy was one of the nerve specialists; he might get a V.C. or be shot in a walled yard at dawn, according to how he was handled. So I was pulling my wits together a little to dish out some patter fit for his case—you know, the "bright, breezy, brotherly" bilge— when the next marvel came. A sound this time—a voice, too; no shriek, not even loud, but tranquil, articulate, slow, and so distant that only the deathly stillness which gave high relief to every bubble that burst with a plop, out in the marsh, could bring the words to us at all. "Has annywan here lost a dog? Annywan lost a good dog? *Hoond? Goot hoond?* Anny wan lost a *goot hoond?*"

You never can tell how things will take you. I swear I was right out of that hellish place for a minute or more, alive and free and back at home among the lost delights of Epsom Downs, between the races; the dear old smelly crowd all over the course, and the merchant who carries a tray crying, "'Oo'll 'ave a good cigar, gents? Two pence! 'Oo wants a good cigar? 'Oo says a good smoke?" And the sun shining good on all the bookies and crooks by the rails, the just and unjust, all jolly and natural. Better than Lear's blasted heath and your mind running down!

You could see the relief settle on Mynns like oil going on to a burn on your hand. Have you seen an easy death in bed?—the yielding sigh of peace and the sinking inwards, the weary job over? It was like that. He breathed, "That Irish swine!" in a voice that made it a blessing. I felt the same, but more uneasily. One of my best was out there in the wide world, having God knew what truck with the enemy. Any Brass Hat that came loafing round might think, in his blinded soul, that Toomey was fraternizing; whereas Toomey was dead or prisoner by now, or as good, unless delivered by some miracle of gumption surpassing all his previous practices against the brute creation. We could do nothing, could not even guess where he was in the fog. It had risen right up to the boughs; the whole Seam was packed with it, tight. No one but he who had put his head into the mouth of the tiger could pull it out now.

We listened on, with pricked ears. Voices we certainly heard; yes, more than one; but not a word clear. And voices were not what I harked for; it was for the shot that would be the finish of Toomey. I remembered during the next twenty minutes quite a lot of good points about Toomey. I found that I had never had a sulky word from him, for one. At the end of the twenty minutes the voices finally stopped. But no shot came. A prisoner, then?

The next ten minutes were bad. Towards the end of the two hours for which they lasted, I could have fancied the spook symptoms were starting again. For out of the mist before us there came something that was not seen, or heard, or felt; no one sense could fasten upon it; only a mystic consciousness came of some approaching displacement of the fog. The blind, I believe, feel the same when they come near a lamp-post. Slowly this undefined source of impressions drew near, from out the uncharted spaces beyond, to the frontiers of hearing and sight, slipped across them and took form, at first as the queerest tangle of two sets of limbs, and then as Toomey bearing on one shoulder a large corpse, already stiff, clothed in field-grey.

"May I come in, Sergeant?" said Toomey, "an' bring me sheaves wid me?" The pride of 'cuteness shone from his eyes like a lamp through the fog; his voice had the urbanely affected humility of the consciously great.

"You may," said I, "if you've given nothing away."

"I have not," said he. "I'm an importer entirely. Me exports are nil." He rounded the flank of the breastwork and laid the body tenderly down, as a collector would handle a Strad. "There wasn't the means of an identification about me. Me shoulder titles, me badge, me pay-book, me small-book, me disc, an' me howl correspondence—I left all beyant in the cellar. They'd not have got value that tuk me." Toomey's face was all one wink. To value himself on his courage would never enter his head. It was a sense of the giant intellect within that filled him with triumph.

I inspected the bulging eyes of the dead. "Did you strangle him sitting?" I asked.

"Not at all. Amn't I just after tradin' the dog for him?" Then, in the proper whisper, Toomey made his report:

"Ye'll remember the whillabalooin' there was at meself in the cellar. Leppin' they were, at the loss of the tea. The ind of it was that 'I'm goin' out now,' I said, 'to speak to a man,' said I, 'about a dog,' an' I quitted the place, an' the dog with me, knockin' his nose against every lift of me heel. I'd a gran' thought in me head, to make them whisht thinkin' bad of me. Very near where the lad Schofiel' is, I set out for Germ'ny, stoopin' low, to get all the use of the fog. Did you notus me, Sergeant?"

"Breaking the firewood?" I said.

"Aye, I med sure that ye would. So I signaled."

Now I perceived. Toomey went on. "I knew, when I hild up the dog on the palm of me hand, ye'd see where I was, an' where going. Then I wint on, deep into th' East. Their wire is nothin' at all; it's the very spit of our own. I halted among ut, an' gev out a notus, in English and German, kapin' down well in the fog to rejuice me losses. They didn't fire—ye'll have heard that. They sint for the man with the

English. An', by the will of God, he was the same man that belonged to the dog."

"'Hans,' says I, courcheous but firrum, 'the dog is well off where he is. Will you come to him quietly?'

"I can't just give ye his words, but the sinse of them only. 'What are ye doin' at all,' he says, 'askin' a man to desert!'

"There was trouble in that fellow's voice. It med me ashamed. But I wint on, an' only put double strenth in me temptin's. 'Me Colonel,' I told him, 'is offerin' five pounds for a prisoner. Come back with me now an' ye'll have fifty francs when I get the reward. Think over ut well. Fifty francs down. There's a gran' lot of spendin' in that. An' ye'll be with the dog.' As I offered him each injuicement, I lifted the tirrier clear of the mist for two sicconds or three, to keep the man famished wid longin'. Ye have to be crool in a war. Aich time that I lowered the dog I lep two paces north, under the fog, to bedivil their aim if they'd fire.

"'Ach, to hell wi' your francs an' your pounds!' says he in his ag'ny. 'Give me the dog or I'll shoot. I see where ye are.'

"'I'm not there at all,' says I, 'an' the dog's in front of me bosom.'

"Ye'll understan', Sergeant," Toomey said to me gravely, "that las' was a roose. I'd not do the like o' that to a dog, anny more than yourself.

"The poor divil sckewed in his juice for a while, very quiet. Then he out with an offer. 'Will ye take sivinty francs for the dog? It's the whole of me property. An' it only comes short be five francs of th' entire net profuts ye'd make on the fiver, an' I comin' wid you.'

"'I will not,' says I, faint and low. It was tormint, refusin' the cash.

"'Won't *annythin'* do ye,' says he in despair, 'but a live wan?'

"'Depinds,' says I pensively, playin' me fish. I hild up the dog for a siccond again, to kape his sowl workin'.

"He plunged at the sight of the creature. 'Couldn't ye do with a body?' he says very low.

"'Depinds,' says I, marvellin' was ut a human sacrifice he was for makin', the like of the Druids, to get back the dog.

"'Not fourteen hours back,' says he, 'he died on us.'

"'Was he wan of yourselves?' says I. 'A nice fool I'd look if I came shankin' back from the fair wid a bit of the wrong unit.'

"'He was,' says he, 'an' the best of us all.' An' then he went on, wid me puttin' in a word now and then, or a glimpse of the dog, to kape him desirous an' gabbin'. There's no use in cheapenin' your wares. He let on how this fellow he spoke of had niver joyed since they came to that place, an' gone mad at the finish, wi' not gettin' his sleep without he'd be seein' Thim Wans in a dream an' hearin' the

Banshies; the way he bruk out at three in the mornin' that day, apt to cut anny in two that would offer to hold him. 'Here's out of ut all,' he appeared to have said; 'I've lived through ivery room in hell: how long, O Lord, how long, but it's glory an' victory now,' an' off an' away wid him West, through The Garden. 'Ye'll not have seen him at all?' said me friend. We hadn't notussed, I told him. 'We were right, then,' says he; 'he'll have died on the way. For he let a scream in the night that a man couldn't give an' live after. If he'd fetched up at your end,' says he, 'you'd have known, for he was as brave as a lion.'

"'A livin' dog's better,' says I, 'than anny dead lion. It's a Jew's bargain you're makin'. Where's the deceased?'

"'Pass me the dog,' says he, 'an' I'll give ye his route out from here to where he'll have dropped. It's his point of deparchure I stand at.'

"'I'll come to ye there,' says I, 'an' ye'll give me his bearin's, an' when I've sot eyes on me man I'll come back an' han' ye the dog, an' not sooner.'

"He was spaichless a moment. 'Come now,' says I, from me lair in the fog, 'wan of the two of us has to be trustful. I'll not let ye down.'

"'Ye'll swear to come back?' says he in great anguish.

"I said, 'Tubbe sure.'

"'Come on wid ye, then,' he answered.

"I went stoopin' along to within six feet of his voice, the way ye'd swim under water, an' then I came to the surface. His clayey-white face an' the top of his body showed over a breas'-work the moral of ours. An', be cripes, ut was all right. The red figures were plain on his shoulder-strap—wan-eighty-six. Another breas'-work, the fellow to his, was not thirty yards south. There was jus' the light left me to see that the sintry there was wan-eighty-six too. I'd inspicted the goods in bulk now, an' had only to see to me sample, and off home wid it."

Toomey looked benedictively down at the long stiff frame with its Iron Cross ribbon and red worsted "186." "An ould storm-trooper!" Toomey commendingly said. "His friend gev me the line to him. Then he got anxious. 'Ye'll bury him fair?' he said. 'Is he a Prod'stant?' said I, 'or a Cath'lic?' 'A good Cath'lic,' says he; 'we're Bavarians here.' 'Good,' says I; 'I'll speak to Father Moloney meself.' 'An' yell come back,' says he, 'wi' the dog?' 'I will not,' says I, 'I shall hand him ye now. Ye're a straight man not to ha' shot me before. Besides, ye're a Cath'lic?' So I passed him the an'mal, and off on me journey. Not the least trouble at all, findin' the body. The birds was all but pointin' to ut. They hated ut. Begob, that fellow had seen the quare things." Toomey looked down again, at the monstrously starting eyes of his capture, bursting with agonies more fantastic, I thought, than any that stare from the bayoneted dead in a trench.

"The man wi' the dog," Toomey said, "may go the same road. His teeth were all knockin' together. A match for your own, Billy." In trenches you did not pretend not to know all about one another, the best and the worst. In that screenless life friendship frankly condoled with weak nerves or an ugly face or black temper.

"Sergeant," said Toomey, "ye'll help me indent for the fiver? A smart drop of drink it'll be for the whole of the boys."

I nodded. "Bring him along," I said, "now."

"Well, God ha' mercy on his sowl," said Toomey, hoisting the load up on to his back.

"And of all Christian souls, I pray God." I did not say it. Only Ophelia's echo, crossing my mind. How long would Mynns last? Till I could wangle his transfer to the Divisional laundry or gaff?

I brought Toomey along to claim the fruit of his guile. We had to pass Schofield. He looked more at ease in his mind than before. I asked the routine question. "All correct, Sergeant," he answered. "Deucks is coom dahn. Birds is all stretchin' dahn to it, proper."

Its own mephitic mock-peace was refilling The Garden. But no one can paint a miasma. Anyhow, I am not trying to. This is a trade report only.

THE TRAITOR

by Somerset Maugham

Maugham (1874–1965) began his service in the war as an ambulance driver; in 1915 he became an agent for the British Secret Service. In Switzerland, far from the trenches, Ashenden, the hero of the novel in which this story appears, is a member of the British Secret Service whose job is to lure a British citizen who has been spying for the Germans back to England. The story gives us a glimpse into Maugham's own creative impulse, which led to his several books and famous novels: "The little incident offered a key to their whole lives, and from it Ashenden began to reconstruct their histories, circumstances, and characters . . ."

[First published in Maugham's *Ashenden: Or the British Agent*. London: Heinemann, 1928]

Note.—Ashenden, a British Secret Service Agent, has received orders to go into Switzerland on a mission from his chief R.

HAVING TAKEN A room at the hotel at which he had been instructed to stay, Ashenden went out; it was a lovely day, early in August, and the sun shone in an unclouded sky. He had not been to Lucerne since he was a boy, and but vaguely remembered a covered bridge, a great stone lion, and a church in which he had sat, bored yet impressed, while they played an organ; and now, wandering along a shady quay (and the lake looked just as tawdry and unreal as it looked on the picture postcards), he tried not so much to find his way about a half-forgotten scene as to reform in his mind some recollection of the shy and eager lad, so impatient for life (which he saw not in the present of his adolescence but only in the future of his manhood), who so long ago had wandered there. But it seemed to him that the most vivid of his memories was not of himself but of the crowd; he seemed to remember sun and heat and people; the train was crowded and so was the hotel; the lake steamers were packed, and on the quays and in the streets you threaded your way among the throng of holiday

55

makers. They were fat and old and ugly and odd, and they stank. Now, in war-time, Lucerne was as deserted as it must have been before the world at large discovered that Switzerland was the playground of Europe. Most of the hotels were closed, the streets were empty, the rowing boats for hire rocked idly at the water's edge and there was none to take them, and in the avenues by the lake the only persons to be seen were serious Swiss taking their neutrality, like a dachshund, for a walk with them. Ashenden felt exhilarated by the solitude, and, sitting down on a bench that faced the water, surrendered himself deliberately to the sensation. It was true that the lake was absurd, the water was too blue, the mountains too snowy, and its beauty, hitting you in the face, exasperated rather than thrilled; but all the same, there was something pleasing in the prospect, an artless candour, like one of Mendelssohn's "Songs Without Words," that made Ashenden smile with complacency. Lucerne reminded him of wax flowers under glass cases and cuckoo clocks and fancy work in Berlin wool. So long, at all events, as the fine weather lasted he was prepared to enjoy himself. He did not see why he should not at least try to combine pleasure to himself with profit to his country. He was travelling with a brand-new passport in his pocket, under a borrowed name, and this gave him an agreeable sense of owning a new personality. He was often slightly tired of himself, and it diverted him for a while to be merely a creature of R.'s facile invention. The experience he had just enjoyed appealed to his acute sense of the absurd. R., it is true, had not seen the fun of it: what humour R. possessed was of a sardonic turn, and he had no facility for taking in good part a joke at his own expense. To do that you must be able to look at yourself from the outside and be at the same time spectator and actor in the pleasant comedy of life. R. was a soldier, and regarded introspection as unhealthy, un-English, and unpatriotic.

Ashenden got up and strolled slowly to his hotel. It was a small German hotel of the second class, spotlessly clean, and his bedroom had a nice view; it was furnished with brightly varnished pitch-pine, and though on a cold, wet day it would have been wretched, in that warm and sunny weather it was gay and pleasant. There were tables in the hall, and he sat down at one of these and ordered a bottle of beer. The landlady was curious to know why in that dead season he had come to stay, and he was glad to satisfy her curiosity. He told her that he had recently recovered from an attack of typhoid, and had come to Lucerne to get back his strength. He was employed in the Censorship Department, and was taking the opportunity to brush up his rusty German. He asked her if she could recommend to him a German teacher. The landlady was a blond and blowsy Swiss, good humoured and talkative, so that Ashenden felt pretty sure that she would repeat in the proper quarter the information he gave her. It was his turn now to ask a few questions. She was voluble on the subject of the War, on account of which the hotel, in that month so full that rooms had to be found for visitors in neighbouring houses, was nearly empty. A few people came in from outside to eat their meals *en pension*, but she had only two lots of resident guests. One was an old Irish couple who lived in Vevey and passed their summers in Lucerne, and the other was an Englishman and his wife. She was a German, and they were obliged on that account to live in a neutral country. Ashenden took care to show little curiosity about them—he recognised in the description Grantley Caypor—but of her own accord she told him that they spent most of the day walking about the mountains. Herr Caypor was a botanist and much interested in the flora of the country. His lady was a very nice woman, and she felt her position keenly. Ah, well, the War could not last for ever. The land-lady bustled away and Ashenden went upstairs.

Dinner was at seven, and, wishing to be in the dining-room before anyone else, so that he could take stock of his fellow-guests as they entered, he went down as soon as he heard the bell. It was a very plain, stiff, whitewashed room, with chairs of the same shiny pitch-pine as in his bedroom, and on the walls were oleographs of Swiss lakes. On each little table was a bunch of flowers. It was all neat and clean and presaged a bad dinner. Ashenden would have liked to make up for it by ordering a bottle of the best Rhine wine to be found in the hotel, but did not venture to draw attention to himself by extrava-gance (he saw on two or three tables half-empty bottles of table hock, which made him surmise that his fellow-guests drank thriftily), and so contented himself with ordering a pint of lager. Presently one or two persons came in, single men with some occupation in Lucerne and obviously Swiss, and sat down each at his little table and untied the napkins that at the end of luncheon they had neatly tied up. They propped newspapers against their water-jugs and read while they somewhat noisily ate their soup. Then entered a very tall, bent man, with white hair and a drooping white moustache, accompanied by a little old white-haired lady in black. These were certainly the Irish Colonel and his wife of whom the landlady had spoken. They took their seats, and the Colonel poured out a thimbleful of wine for his wife and a thimbleful for himself. They waited in silence for their dinner to be served to them by the buxom, hearty maid.

At last the persons arrived for whom Ashenden had been waiting. He was doing his best to read a German book, and it was only by an exercise of self-control that he allowed himself only for one instant to raise his eyes as they came in. His glance showed him a man of about forty-five with short, dark hair, somewhat grizzled, of middle height but corpulent, with a broad, red, clean-shaven face. He wore a shirt open at the neck, with a wide collar and a grey suit. He walked ahead of his wife, and of her Ashenden only caught the impression of a German woman, self-effaced and dusty. Grantley Caypor sat down and began in a loud voice explaining to the waitress that they had taken an immense walk. They had been up some mountain the name of which meant nothing to Ashenden, but which excited in the maid expressions of astonishment and enthusiasm. Then Caypor, still in fluent German, but with a marked English accent, said that they were so late they had not even gone up to wash, but had just rinsed their hands outside. He had a resonant voice and a jovial manner.

"Serve me quick; we're starving with hunger, and bring beer— bring three bottles. *Lieber Gott*, what a thirst I have!"

He seemed to be a man of exuberant vitality. He brought into that dull, over-clean dining-room the breath of life, and everyone in it appeared on a sudden more alert. He began to talk to his wife in English, and everything he said could be heard by all; but presently she interrupted him with a remark made in an undertone. Caypor stopped, and Ashenden felt that his eyes were turned in his direction. Mrs. Caypor had noticed the arrival of a stranger and had drawn her husband's attention to it. Ashenden turned the page of the book he was pretending to read, but he felt that Caypor's gaze was fixed intently upon him. When he addressed his wife again it was in so low a tone that Ashenden could not even tell what language he used; but when the maid brought them their soup Caypor, his voice still low, asked her a question. It was plain that he was enquiring who Ashenden was. Ashenden could catch of the maid's reply but the one word *lander*.

One or two people finished their dinner and went out picking their teeth. The old Irish Colonel and his old wife rose from their table, and he stood aside to let her pass. They had eaten their meal without exchanging a word. She walked slowly to the door; but the Colonel stopped to say a word to a Swiss who might have been a local attorney, and when she reached it she stood there, bowed and with a sheep-like look, patiently waiting for her husband to come and open it for her. Ashenden realised that she had never opened a door herself. She did not know how to. In a minute the Colonel, with his old, old gait, came to the door and opened it; she passed out and he followed. The little incident offered a key to their whole lives, and from it Ashenden began to reconstruct their histories, circumstances, and characters; but he pulled himself up: he could not allow himself the luxury of creation. He finished his dinner.

When he went into the hall he saw tied to the leg of a table a bull-terrier, and, in passing, mechanically put down his hand to fondle the dog's drooping, soft ears. The landlady was standing at the foot of the stairs.

"Whose is this lovely beast?" asked Ashenden.

"He belongs to Herr Caypor. Fritzi he is called. Herr Caypor says he has a longer pedigree than the King of England."

Fritzi rubbed himself against Ashenden's leg, and with his nose sought the palm of his hand. Ashenden went upstairs to fetch his hat, and when he came down saw Caypor standing at the entrance of the hotel talking with the landlady. From the sudden silence and their constrained manner he guessed that Caypor had been making inquiries about him. When he passed between them into the street, out of the corner of his eye he saw Caypor give him a suspicious stare. That frank, jovial red face bore then a look of shifty cunning.

Ashenden strolled along till he found a tavern where he could have his coffee in the open, and, to compensate himself for the bottle of beer that his sense of duty had urged him to drink at dinner, ordered the best brandy the house provided. He was pleased at last to have come face to face with the man of whom he had heard so much, and in a day or two hoped to become acquainted with him. It is never very difficult to get to know anyone who has a dog. But he was in no hurry; he would let things take their course. With the object he had in view he could not afford to be hasty.

Ashenden reviewed the circumstances. Grantley Caypor was an Englishman, born, according to his passport, in Birmingham, and he was forty-two years of age. His wife, to whom he had been married for eleven years, was of German birth and parentage. That was public knowledge. Information about his antecedents was contained in a private document. He had started life, according to this, in a lawyer's office in Birmingham and then had drifted into journalism. He had been connected with an English paper in Cairo and with another in Shanghai. There he got into trouble for attempting to get money by false pretences and was sentenced to a short term of imprisonment. All trace of him was lost for two years after his release, when he reappeared in a shipping office in Marseilles. From there, still in the shipping business, he went to Hamburg, where he married, and to London. In London he set up for himself in the export business, but after some time failed and was made a bankrupt. He returned to journalism. At the outbreak of war he was once more in the shipping business, and in August, 1914, was living quietly with his German wife at Southampton. In the beginning of the following year he told his employers that owing to the nationality of his wife his position was intolerable; they had no fault to find with him, and, recognising that he was in an awkward fix, granted his request that he should be transferred to Genoa. Here he remained till Italy entered the War, but then gave notice, and with his papers in perfect order crossed the border and took up his residence in Switzerland.

All this indicated a man of doubtful honesty and unsettled disposition, with no background and of no financial standing; but the facts were of no importance to anyone till it was discovered that Caypor, certainly from the beginning of the War and perhaps sooner, was in the service of the German Intelligence Department. He had a salary of forty pounds a month. But, though dangerous and wily, no steps would have been taken to deal with him if he had contented himself with transmitting such news as he was able to get in Switzerland. He could do no great harm there, and it might even be possible to make use of him to convey information that it was desirable to let the enemy have. He had no notion that anything was known of him. His letters, and he received a good many, were closely censored; there were few codes that the people who dealt with such matters could not in the end decipher, and it might be that sooner or later through him it would be possible to lay hands on the organisation that still flourished in England. But then he did something that drew R.'s attention to him. Had he known it, none could have blamed him for shaking in his shoes: R. was not a very nice man to get on the wrong side of. Caypor scraped acquaintance in Zürich with a young Spaniard, Gomez by name, who had lately entered the British Secret Service, by his nationality inspired him with confidence, and managed to worm out of him the fact that he was engaged in espionage. Probably the Spaniard, with a very human desire to seem important, had done no more than talk mysteriously; but on Caypor's information he was watched when he went to Germany, and one day caught just as he was posting a letter in a code that was eventually deciphered. He was tried, convicted, and shot. It was bad enough to lose a useful and disinterested agent, but it entailed besides the changing of a safe and simple code. R. was not pleased. But R. was not the man to let any desire of revenge stand in the way of his main object, and it occurred to him that if Caypor was merely betraying his country for money it might be possible to get him to take more money to betray his employers. The fact that he had succeeded in delivering into their hands an agent of the Allies must seem to them an earnest of his good faith. He might be very useful. But R. had no notion what kind of man Caypor was; he had lived his shabby, furtive life obscurely, and the only photograph that existed of him was one taken for a passport. Ashenden's instructions were to get acquainted with Caypor and see whether there was any chance that he would work honestly for the British. If he thought there was, he was entitled to sound him, and if his suggestions were met with favour to make certain propositions. It was a task that needed tact and a knowledge of men. If, on the other hand, Ashenden came to the conclusion that Caypor could not be bought, he was to watch and report his movements. The information he had obtained from Gustav was vague but important; there was only one point in it that was interesting, and this was that the head of the German Intelligence Department in Berne was growing restive at Caypor's lack of activity. Caypor was asking for a higher salary, and Major von P. had told him that he must earn it. It might be that he was urging him to go to England. If he could be induced to cross the frontier Ashenden's work was done.

"How the devil do you expect *me* to persuade him to put his head in a noose?" asked Ashenden.

"It won't be a noose, it'll be a firing squad," said R.

"Caypor's clever."

"Well, be cleverer, damn your eyes!"

Ashenden made up his mind that he would take no steps to make Caypor's acquaintance, but allow the first advances to be made by him. If he was being pressed for results it must surely occur to him that it would be worth while to get into conversation with an Englishman who was employed in the Censorship Department. Ashenden was prepared with a supply of information that it could not in the least benefit the Central Powers to possess. With a false name and a false passport he had little fear that Caypor would guess that he was a British agent.

Ashenden did not have to wait long. Next day he was sitting in the doorway of the hotel, drinking a cup of coffee and already half asleep after a substantial *mittagessen*, when the Caypors came out of the dining-room. Mrs. Caypor went upstairs and Caypor released his dog. The dog bounded along and in a friendly fashion leaped up against Ashenden.

"Come here, Fritzi," cried Caypor, and then to Ashenden: "I'm so sorry. But he's quite gentle."

"Oh, that's all right. He won't hurt me."

Caypor stopped at the doorway.

"He's a bull-terrier. You don't often see them on the Continent." He seemed while he spoke to be taking Ashenden's measure; he called to the maid: "A coffee, please, fräulein. You've just arrived, haven't you?"

"Yes, I came yesterday."

"Really? I didn't see you in the dining-room last night. Are you making a stay?"

"I don't know. I've been ill; and I've come here to recuperate."

The maid came with the coffee, and, seeing Caypor talking to Ashenden, put the tray on the table at which he was sitting. Caypor gave a laugh of faint embarrassment.

"I don't want to force myself upon you. I don't know why the maid put my coffee on your table."

"Please sit down," said Ashenden.

"It's very good of you. I've lived so long on the Continent that I'm always forgetting that my countrymen are apt to look upon it as confounded cheek if you talk to them. Are you English, by the way, or American?"

"English," said Ashenden.

Ashenden was by nature a very shy person, and he had in vain tried to cure himself of a failing that at his age was unseemly, but on occasion he knew how to make effective use of it. He explained now, in a hesitating and awkward manner, the facts that he had the day before told the landlady and that he was convinced she had already passed on to Caypor.

"You couldn't have come to a better place than Lucerne. It's an oasis of peace in this war-weary world. When you're here you might almost forget that there is such a thing as a war going on. That is why I've come here. I'm a journalist by profession."

"I couldn't help wondering if you wrote," said Ashenden, with an eagerly timid smile.

It was clear that he had not learnt that "oasis of peace in a war-weary world" at the shipping office.

"You see, I married a German lady," said Caypor gravely.

"Oh, really?"

"I don't think anyone could be more patriotic than I am. I'm English through and through, and I don't mind telling you that in my opinion the British Empire is the greatest instrument for good that the world has ever seen; but having a German wife I naturally see a good deal of the reverse of the medal. You don't have to tell me that the Germans have faults, but, frankly, I'm not prepared to admit that they're devils incarnate. At the beginning of the War my poor wife had a very rough time in England, and I for one couldn't have blamed her if she'd felt rather bitter about it. Everyone thought she was a spy. It'll make you laugh when you know her. She's the typical German *hausfrau*, who cares for nothing but her house and her husband and our only child Fritzi." Caypor fondled his dog and gave a little laugh. "Yes, Fritzi, you are our child, aren't you? Naturally, it made my position very awkward. I was connected with some very important papers, and my editors weren't quite comfortable about it. Well, to cut a long story short I thought the most dignified course was to resign and come to a neutral country till the storm blew over. My wife and I never discuss the War, though I'm bound to tell you that it's more on my account than hers. She's much more tolerant than I am, and she's more willing to look upon this terrible business from my point of view than I am from hers."

"That is strange," said Ashenden. "As a rule women are so much more rabid than men."

"My wife is a very remarkable person. I should like to introduce you to her. By the way, I don't know if you know my name. Grantley Caypor."

"My name is Somerville," said Ashenden.

He told him then of the work he had been doing in the Censorship Department, and he fancied that into Caypor's eyes came a certain intentness. Presently he told him that he was looking for someone to give him conversation lessons in German, so that he might rub up his rusty knowledge of the language; and as he spoke a notion flashed across his mind. He gave Caypor a look, and saw that the same notion had come to him. It had occurred to them at the same instant that it would be a very good plan for Ashenden's teacher to be Mrs. Caypor.

"I asked our landlady if she could find me someone, and she said she thought she could. I must ask her again. It ought not to be very hard to find a man who is prepared to come and talk German to me for an hour a day."

"I wouldn't take anyone on the landlady's recommendation," said Caypor. "After all, you want someone with a good North-German accent, and she only talks Swiss. I'll ask my wife if she knows anyone. My wife's a very highly educated woman, and you could trust her recommendation."

"That's very kind of you."

Ashenden observed Grantley Caypor at his ease. He noticed how the small, grey-green eyes, which last night he had not been able to see, contradicted the red, good-humoured frankness of the face. They were quick and shifty, but when the mind behind them was seized by an unexpected notion they were suddenly still. It gave one a peculiar feeling of the working of the brain. They were not eyes that inspired confidence; Caypor did that with his jolly, good-natured smile, the openness of his broad, weather-beaten face, his comfortable obesity, and the cheeriness of his loud, deep voice. He was doing his best now to be agreeable. While Ashenden talked to him, a little shyly still but gaining confidence from that breezy, cordial manner, capable of

putting anyone at his ease, it intrigued him to remember that the man
was a common spy. It gave a tang to his conversation to reflect that
he had been ready to sell his country for no more than forty pounds
a month. Ashenden had known Gomez, the young Spaniard, whom
Caypor had betrayed. He was a high-spirited youth, with a love of
adventure, and he had undertaken his dangerous mission not for the
money he earned by it but from a passion for romance. It amused him
to outwit the clumsy German, and it appealed to his sense of the
absurd to play a part in a shilling shocker. It was not very nice to think
of him now, six feet underground in a prison yard. He was young and
he had a certain grace of gesture. Ashenden wondered whether
Caypor had felt a qualm when he delivered him up to destruction.

"I suppose you know a little German?" asked Caypor, interested in
the stranger.

"Oh yes, I was a student in Germany, and I used to talk it flu-
ently; but that is long ago, and I have forgotten. I can still read it
comfortably."

"Oh yes, I noticed you were reading a German book last night."

Fool! It was only a little while since he had told Ashenden that he
had not seen him at dinner. He wondered whether Caypor had
observed the slip. How difficult it was never to make one! Ashenden
must be on his guard; the thing that made him most nervous was the
thought that he might not answer readily enough to his assumed
name of Somerville. Of course, there was always the chance that
Caypor had made the slip on purpose to see by Ashenden's face
whether he noticed anything. Caypor got up.

"There is my wife. We go for a walk up one of the mountains
every afternoon. I can tell you some charming walks. The flowers
even now are lovely."

"I'm afraid I must wait till I'm a bit stronger," said Ashenden with
a little sigh.

He had naturally a pale face and never looked as robust as he was.
Mrs. Caypor came downstairs and her husband joined her. They
walked down the road, Fritzi bounding round them, and Ashenden
saw that Caypor immediately began to speak with volubility. He was
evidently telling his wife the results of his interview with Ashenden.
Ashenden looked at the sun shining so gaily on the lake; the shadow
of a breeze fluttered the green leaves of the trees; everything invited
to a stroll. He got up, went to his room, and, throwing himself on his
bed, had a very pleasant sleep.

He went into dinner that evening as the Caypors were finishing,
for he had wandered melancholy about Lucerne in the hope of
finding a cocktail that would enable him to face the potato salad that

he foresaw, and on their way out of the dining-room Caypor stopped and asked him if he would drink coffee with them. When Ashenden joined them in the hall, Caypor got up and introduced him to his wife. She bowed stiffly, and no answering smile came to her face to respond to Ashenden's civil greeting. It was not hard to see that her attitude was definitely hostile. It put Ashenden at his ease. She was a plainish woman, nearing forty, with a muddy skin and vague features; her drab hair was arranged in a plait round her head like that of Napoleon's Queen of Prussia, and she was squarely built, plump rather than fat, and solid. But she did not look stupid; she looked, on the contrary, a woman of character, and Ashenden, who had lived enough in Germany to recognise the type, was ready to believe that though capable of doing the housework, cooking the dinner, and climbing a mountain, she might be also prodigiously well informed. She wore a white blouse that showed a sunburned neck, a black skirt, and heavy walking boots. Caypor, addressing her in English, told her in his jovial way, as though she did not know it already, what Ashenden had told him about himself. She listened grimly.

"I think you told me you understood German," said Caypor, his big red face wreathed in polite smiles but his little eyes darting about restlessly.

"Yes, I was for some time a student in Heidelberg."

"Really?" said Mrs. Caypor in English, an expression of faint interest for a moment chasing away the sullenness from her face. "I know Heidelberg very well. I was at school there for one year."

Her English was correct but throaty, and the mouthing emphasis she gave her words was disagreeable. Ashenden was diffuse in praise of the old university town and the beauty of the neighbourhood. She heard him, from the standpoint of her Teutonic superiority, with toleration rather than with enthusiasm.

"It is well known that the valley of the Neckar is one of the beauty places of the whole world," she said.

"I have not told you, my dear," said Caypor then, "that Mr. Somerville is looking for someone to give him conversation lessons while he is here. I told him that perhaps you could suggest a teacher."

"No, I know no one whom I could conscientiously recommend," she answered. "The Swiss accent is hateful beyond words. It could do Mr. Somerville only harm to converse with a Swiss."

"If I were in your place, Mr. Somerville, I would try and persuade my wife to give you lessons. She is, if I may say so, a very cultivated and highly educated woman."

"*Ach*, Grantley, I have not the time. I have my own work to do."

Ashenden saw that he was being given his opportunity. The trap was prepared, and all he had to do was fall in. He turned to Mrs. Caypor with a manner that he tried to make shy, deprecating, and modest.

"Of course, it would be too wonderful if you would give me lessons. I should look upon it as a real privilege. Naturally, I wouldn't want to interfere with your work. I am just here to get well, with nothing in the world to do, and I would suit my time entirely to your convenience."

He felt a flash of satisfaction pass from one to the other, and in Mrs. Caypor's blue eyes he fancied that he saw a dark glow.

"Of course, it would be a purely business arrangement," said Caypor. "There's no reason that my good wife shouldn't earn a little pin-money. Would you think ten francs an hour too much?"

"No," said Ashenden, "I should think myself lucky to get a first-rate teacher for that."

"What do you say, my dear? Surely you can spare an hour, and you would be doing this gentleman a kindness. He would learn that all Germans are not the devilish fiends that they think them in England."

On Mrs. Caypor's brow was an uneasy frown, and Ashenden could not but think with apprehension of that hour's conversation a day that he was going to exchange with her. Heaven only knew how he would have to rack his brain for subjects of discourse with that heavy and morose woman. Now she made a visible effort.

"I shall be very pleased to give Mr. Somerville conversation lessons."

"I congratulate you, Mr. Somerville," said Caypor noisily. "You're in for a treat. When will you start—to-morrow at eleven?"

"That would suit me very well if it suits Mrs. Caypor."

"Yes, that is as good an hour as another," she answered.

Ashenden left them to discuss the happy outcome of their diplomacy. But when, punctually at eleven the next morning, he heard a knock at his door (for it had been arranged that Mrs. Caypor should give him his lesson in his room), it was not without trepidation that he opened it. It behoved him to be frank, a trifle indiscreet, but obviously wary of a German woman, sufficiently intelligent and impulsive. Mrs. Caypor's face was dark and sulky. She plainly hated having anything to do with him. But they sat down, and she began, somewhat peremptorily, to ask him questions about his knowledge of German literature. She corrected his mistakes with exactness, and when he put before her some difficulty in German construction explained it with clearness and precision. It was obvious that though she hated giving him a lesson she meant to give it conscientiously.

She seemed to have not only an aptitude for teaching but a love of it, and as the hour went on she began to speak with greater earnestness. It was already only by an effort that she remembered that he was a brutal Englishman. Ashenden, noticing the unconscious struggle within her, found himself not a little entertained; and it was with truth that, when later in the day Caypor asked him how the lesson had gone, he answered that it was highly satisfactory. Mrs. Caypor was an excellent teacher and a most interesting person.

"I told you so. She's the most remarkable woman I know."

And Ashenden had a feeling that when in his hearty, laughing way Caypor said this he was for the first time entirely sincere.

In a day or two Ashenden guessed that Mrs. Caypor was giving him lessons only in order to enable Caypor to arrive at a closer intimacy with him, for she confined herself strictly to matters of literature, music, and painting; and when Ashenden, by way of experiment, brought the conversation round to the War, she cut him short.

"I think that is a topic that we had better avoid, Herr Somerville," she said.

She continued to give her lessons with the greatest thoroughness, and he had his money's worth; but every day she came with the same sullen face, and it was only in the interest of teaching that she lost for a moment her instinctive dislike of him. Ashenden exercised in turn, but in vain, all his wiles. He was ingratiating, ingenious, humble, grateful, flattering, simple, and timid. She remained coldly hostile. She was a fanatic. Her patriotism was aggressive but disinterested, and, obsessed with the notion of the superiority of all things German, she loathed England with a virulent hatred because in that country she saw the chief obstacle to their diffusion. Her ideal was a German world, in which the rest of the nations, under a hegemony greater than that of Rome, should enjoy the benefits of German science and German art and German culture. There was in the conception a magnificent impudence that appealed to Ashenden's sense of humour. She was no fool. She had read much in several languages, and she could talk of the books she had read with good sense. She had a knowledge of modern painting and modern music that not a little impressed Ashenden. It was amusing once to hear her before luncheon play one of those silvery little pieces of Debussy; she played it disdainfully because it was French and so light, but with an angry appreciation of its grace and gaiety. When Ashenden congratulated her she shrugged her shoulders.

"The decadent music of a decadent nation," she said. Then, with powerful hands, she struck the first resounding chords of a sonata by Beethoven; but she stopped. "I cannot play, I am out of practice; and you English, what do you know of music? You have not produced a composer since Purcell."

"What do you think of that statement?" Ashenden asked Caypor, who was standing near.

"I confess its truth. The little I know of music my wife taught me. I wish you could hear her play when she is in practice." He put his fat hand, with its square, stumpy fingers on her shoulder. "She can wring your heart-strings with pure beauty."

"*Dummer Kerl* (Stupid fellow)," she said in a soft voice; and Ashenden saw her mouth for a moment quiver, but she quickly recovered. "You English, you cannot paint, you cannot model, you cannot write music."

"Some of us can at times write pleasing verses," said Ashenden with good humour, for it was not his business to be put out, and—he did not know why—two lines occurring to him, he said them:

> "Whither, O splendid ship, thy white sails crowding,
> Leaning across the bosom of the urgent West?"

"Yes," said Mrs. Caypor, with a strange gesture, "you can write poetry. I wonder why?"

And to Ashenden's surprise she went on, in her guttural English, to recite the next two lines of the poem he had quoted.

"Come, Grantley, *mittagessen* is ready; let us go into the dining-room."

They left Ashenden reflective.

Ashenden admired goodness, but was not outraged by wickedness. People sometimes thought him heartless because he was more often interested in others than attached to them, and even in the few to whom he was attached his eyes saw with equal clearness the merits and the defects. When he liked people it was not because he was blind to their faults—he did not mind their faults—but accepted them with a tolerant shrug of the shoulders, or because he ascribed to them excellencies that they did not possess; and since he judged his friends with candour they never disappointed him, and he seldom lost one. He asked from none more than he could give. He was able to pursue his study of the Caypors without prejudice and without passion. Mrs. Caypor seemed to him more of a piece, and therefore the easier of the two to understand; she obviously detested him. Though it was so necessary for her to be civil to him her antipathy was strong enough to wring from her now and then an expression of rudeness; and had she been safely able to do so she would have killed him without a qualm. But in the pressure of Caypor's chubby hand on his wife's shoulder and in the fugitive trembling of her lips Ashenden had divined that this unprepossessing woman and that mean, fat man were joined together by a deep and sincere love. It was touching. Ashenden assembled the observations that he had been making for the past few days, and little things that he had noticed but to which he had attached no significance returned to him. It seemed to him that Mrs. Caypor loved her husband because she was of a stronger character than he and because she felt his dependence on her; she loved him for his admiration of her, and you might guess that till she met him this dumpy, plain woman with her dulness, good sense, and want of humour could not have much enjoyed the admiration of men. She enjoyed his heartiness and his noisy jokes, and his high spirits stirred her sluggish blood; he was a great big bouncing boy, and he would never be anything else, and she felt like a mother towards him. She had made him what he was, and he was her man and she was his woman, and she loved him, notwithstanding his weakness (for with her clear head she must always have been conscious of that); she loved him, *ach, was*, as Isolde loved Tristan. But then there was the espionage. Even Ashenden, with all his tolerance for human frailty, could not but feel that to betray your country for money is not a very pretty proceeding. Of course, she knew of it—indeed, it was probably through her that Caypor had first been approached; he would never have undertaken such work if she had not urged him to it. She loved him, and she was an honest and upright woman. By what devious means had she persuaded herself to force her husband to adopt so base and dishonourable a calling? Ashenden lost himself in a labyrinth of conjecture as he tried to piece together the actions of her mind.

Grantley Caypor was another story. There was little to admire in him, but at that moment Ashenden was not looking for an object of admiration; but there was much that was singular and much that was unexpected in that gross and vulgar fellow. Ashenden watched with entertainment the suave manner in which the spy tried to inveigle him in his toils. It was a couple of days after his first lesson that Caypor after dinner, his wife having gone upstairs, threw himself heavily into a chair by Ashenden's side. His faithful Fritzi came up to him and put his long muzzle with its black nose on his knee.

"He has no brain," said Caypor, "but a heart of gold. Look at those little pink eyes. Did you ever see anything so stupid? And what an ugly face, but what incredible charm!"

"Have you had him long?" asked Ashenden.

"I got him in 1914, just before the outbreak of war. By the way, what do you think of the news to-day? Of course, my wife and I never discuss the War. You can't think what a relief to me it is to find a fellow-countryman to whom I can open my heart."

He handed Ashenden a cheap Swiss cigar, and Ashenden making a rueful sacrifice to duty, accepted it.

"Of course, they haven't got a chance, the Germans," said Caypor— "not a dog's chance. I knew they were beaten the moment we came in."

His manner was earnest, sincere, and confidential. Ashenden made a commonplace rejoinder.

"It's the greatest grief of my life that, owing to my wife's nationality, I was unable to do any war work. I tried to enlist the day war broke out, but they wouldn't have me on account of my age; but I don't mind telling you, if the War goes on much longer, wife or no wife, I'm going to do something. With my knowledge of languages I ought to be of some service in the Censorship Department. That's where you were, wasn't it?"

That was the mark at which he had been aiming, and in answer now to his well-directed questions Ashenden gave him the information that he had already prepared. Caypor drew his chair a little nearer and dropped his voice.

"I'm sure you wouldn't tell me anything that anyone shouldn't know, but after all, these Swiss are absolutely pro-German, and we don't want to give anyone the chance of overhearing."

Then he went on another tack. He told Ashenden a number of things that were of a certain secrecy.

"I wouldn't tell this to anybody else, you know, but I have one or two friends who are in pretty influential positions, and they know they can trust me."

Thus encouraged, Ashenden was a little more deliberately indiscreet, and when they parted both had reason to be satisfied. Ashenden guessed that Caypor's typewriter would be kept busy next morning and that that extremely energetic Major in Berne would shortly receive a most interesting report.

One evening, going upstairs after dinner, Ashenden passed an open bath-room. He caught sight of the Caypors.

"Come in," cried Caypor in his cordial way. "We're washing our Fritzi."

The bull-terrier was constantly getting himself very dirty, and it was Caypor's pride to see him clean and white. Ashenden went in. Mrs. Caypor, with her sleeves turned up and a large white apron, was standing at one end of the bath, while Caypor, in a pair of trousers and a singlet, his fat, freckled arms bare, was soaping the wretched hound.

"We have to do it at night," he said, "because the Fitzgeralds use this bath, and they'd have a fit if they knew we washed the dog in it. We wait till they go to bed. Come along, Fritzi; show the gentleman how beautifully you behave when you have your face scrubbed."

The poor brute, woebegone but faintly wagging his tail to show that however foul was this operation performed on him he bore no malice to the god who did it, was standing in the middle of the bath in six inches of water. He was soaped all over, and Caypor, talking the while, shampooed him with his great fat hands.

"Oh, what a beautiful dog he's going to be when he's as white as the driven snow! His master will be as proud as Punch to walk out with him, and all the little lady dogs will say: 'Good gracious! who's that beautiful aristocratic-looking bull-terrier, walking as though he owned the whole of Switzerland?' Now stand still while you have your ears washed. You couldn't bear to go out into the street with dirty ears, could you? Like a nasty little Swiss school-boy? *Noblesse oblige*. Now the black nose. Oh, and all the soap is going into his little pink eyes and they'll smart."

Mrs. Caypor listened to this nonsense with a good-humoured, sluggish smile on her broad, plain face, and presently gravely took a towel.

"Now he's going to have a ducking. Upsie-daisy."

Caypor seized the dog by the fore-legs and ducked him once and ducked him twice. There was a struggle, a flurry, and a splashing. Caypor lifted him out of the bath.

"Now go to mother and she'll dry you."

Mrs. Caypor sat down and, taking the dog between her strong legs, rubbed him till the sweat poured off her forehead. And Fritzi a little shaken and breathless, but happy it was all over, with his sweet, stupid face, white and shining.

"Blood will tell," cried Caypor exultantly. "He knows the names of no less than sixty-four of his ancestors, and they were all nobly born."

Ashenden was faintly troubled. He shivered a little as he walked upstairs.

Then, one Sunday, Caypor told him that he and his wife were going on an excursion and would eat their luncheon at some little mountain restaurant; and he suggested that Ashenden, each paying his share, should come with them. After three weeks at Lucerne, Ashenden thought that his strength would permit him to venture the exertion. They started early, Mrs. Caypor businesslike in her walking boots and Tyrolese hat and alpenstock, and Caypor in stockings and plus-fours, looking very British. The situation amused Ashenden, and he was prepared to enjoy his day. But he meant to keep his eyes open; it was not inconceivable that the Caypors had discovered what he was, and it would not do to go too near a precipice. Mrs. Caypor would not hesitate to give him a push, and Caypor, for all his jolliness, was an ugly customer. But on the face of it there was nothing to mar Ashenden's pleasure in the golden morning. The air was fragrant. Caypor was full of conversation. He told funny stories. He was gay and jovial. The sweat rolled off his great red face, and he laughed at himself because he was so fat. To Ashenden's astonishment he showed a peculiar knowledge of the mountain flowers. Once he went out of the way to pick one he saw a little distance from the path and brought it back to his wife. He looked at it tenderly.

"Isn't it lovely?" he cried, and his shifty, grey-green eyes for a moment were as candid as a child's. "It's like a poem by Walter Savage Landor."

"Botany is my husband's favourite science," said Mrs. Caypor. "I laugh at him sometimes. He is devoted to flowers. Often when we have hardly had enough money to pay the butcher he has spent everything in his pocket to bring me a bunch of roses."

"*Qui fleurit sa maison fleurit son cœur*," said Grantley Caypor.

Ashenden had once or twice seen Caypor, coming in from a walk, offer Mrs. Fitzgerald a nosegay of mountain flowers with an elephantine courtesy that was not entirely displeasing; and what he had just learned added a certain significance to the pretty little action. His passion for flowers was genuine, and when he gave them to the old Irish lady he gave her something he valued. It showed a real kindness of heart. Ashenden had always thought botany a tedious science, but Caypor, talking exuberantly as they walked along, was able to impart to it life and interest. He must have given it a good deal of study.

"I've never written a book," he said. "There are too many books already, and any desire to write I have is satisfied by the more immediately profitable and quite ephemeral composition of an article for a daily paper. But if I stay here much longer I have half a mind to write a book about the wild flowers of Switzerland. Oh, I wish you'd been here a little earlier. They were marvellous. But one wants to be a poet for that, and I'm only a poor newspaper man."

It was curious to observe how he was able to combine real emotion with false fact.

When they reached the inn, with its view of the mountains and the lake, it was good to see the sensual pleasure with which he poured down his throat a bottle of ice-cold beer. You could not but feel sympathy for a man who took so much delight in simple things. They lunched deliciously off scrambled eggs and mountain trout. Even

Mrs. Caypor was moved to an unwonted gentleness by her surroundings—the inn was in an agreeably rural spot; it looked like a picture of a Swiss châlet in a book of early nineteenth-century travels—and she treated Ashenden with something less than her usual hostility. When they arrived she had burst into loud German exclamations on the beauty of the scene, and now, softened perhaps, too, by food and drink, her eyes, dwelling on the grandeur before her, filled with tears. She stretched out her hand.

"It is dreadful and I am ashamed; notwithstanding this horrible and unjust war I can feel in my heart at the moment nothing but happiness and gratitude."

Caypor took her by the hand and pressed it, and, an unusual thing with him, addressing her in German, called her little pet-names. It was absurd, but touching. Ashenden, leaving them to their emotions, strolled through the garden and sat down on a bench that had been prepared for the comfort of the tourist. The view was, of course, spectacular, but it captured you; it was like a piece of music that was obvious and meretricious, but for the moment shattered your self-control.

And as Ashenden lingered idly in that spot he pondered over the mystery of Grantley Caypor's treachery. If he liked strange people he had found in him one who was strange beyond belief. It would be foolish to deny that he had amiable traits. His joviality was not assumed, he was without pretence a hearty fellow, and he had real good nature. He was always ready to do a kindness. Ashenden had often watched him with the old Irish Colonel and his wife, who were the only other residents of the hotel; he would listen good-humouredly to the old man's tedious stories of the Egyptian war, and he was charming with her. Now that Ashenden had arrived at terms of some familiarity with Caypor he found that he regarded him less with repulsion than with curiosity. He did not think that he had become a spy merely for the money; he was a man of modest tastes, and what he had earned in a shipping office must have sufficed to so good a manager as Mrs. Caypor, and after war was declared there was no lack of remunerative work for men over the military age. It might be that he was one of those men who prefer devious ways to straight for some intricate pleasure they get in fooling their fellows; and that he had turned spy, not from hatred of the country that had imprisoned him, not even from love of his wife, but from a desire to score off the bigwigs who never even knew of his existence. It might be that it was vanity that impelled him, a feeling that his talents had not received the recognition they merited, or just a puckish, impish desire to do mischief. He was a crook. It is true that only two cases of dishonesty had been brought home to him, but if he had been caught twice it might be surmised that he had often been dishonest without being caught. What did Mrs. Caypor think of this? They were so united that she must be aware of it. Did it make her ashamed, for her own uprightness surely none could doubt, or did she accept it as an inevitable kink in the man she loved? Did she do all she could to prevent it or did she close her eyes to something she could not help?

How much easier life would be if people were all black or all white, and how much simpler it would be to act in regard to them! Was Caypor a good man who loved evil, or a bad man who loved good? And how could such unreconcilable elements exist side by side and in harmony within the same heart? For one thing was clear: Caypor was disturbed by no gnawing of conscience; he did his mean and despicable work with gusto. He was a traitor who enjoyed his treachery. Though Ashenden had been studying human nature more or less consciously all his life, it seemed to him that he knew as little about it now in middle age as he had done when he was a child. Of course, R. would have said to him: "Why the devil do you waste your time with such nonsense? The man's a dangerous spy, and your business is to lay him by the heels."

That was true enough. Ashenden had decided that it would be useless to attempt to make any arrangement with Caypor. Though doubtless he would have no feeling about betraying his employers, he could certainly not be trusted. His wife's influence was too strong. Besides, notwithstanding what he had from time to time told Ashenden, he was in his heart convinced that the Central Powers must win the War, and he meant to be on the winning side. Well, then Caypor must be laid by the heels, but how he was to effect that Ashenden had no notion. Suddenly he heard a voice.

"There you are. We've been wondering where you had hidden yourself."

He looked round and saw the Caypors strolling towards him. They were walking hand-in-hand.

"So this is what has kept you quiet," said Caypor as his eyes fell on the view. "What a spot!"

Mrs. Caypor clasped her hands.

"*Ach Gott, wie schön!*" she cried. "*Wie schön.* When I look at that blue lake and those snowy mountains I feel inclined, like Goethe's Faust, to cry to the passing moment: Tarry."

"This is better than being in England with the excursions and alarums of war, isn't it?" said Caypor.

"Much," said Ashenden.

"By the way, did you have any difficulty in getting out?"

"No, not the smallest."

"I'm told they make rather a nuisance of themselves at the frontier nowadays."

"I came through without the smallest difficulty. I don't fancy they bother much about the English. I thought the examination of passports was quite perfunctory."

A fleeting glance passed between Caypor and his wife. Ashenden wondered what it meant. It would be strange if Caypor's thoughts were occupied with the chances of a journey to England at the very moment when he was himself reflecting on its possibility. In a little while Mrs. Caypor suggested that they had better be starting back, and they wandered together in the shade of the trees down the mountain paths.

Ashenden was watchful. He could do nothing (and his inactivity irked him) but wait with his eyes open to seize the opportunity that might present itself. A couple of days later an incident occurred that made him certain something was in the wind. In the course of his morning lesson Mrs. Caypor remarked:

"My husband has gone to Geneva to-day. He had some business to do there."

"Oh," said Ashenden, "will he be gone long?"

"No, only two days."

It is not everyone who can tell a lie, and Ashenden had the feeling, he hardly knew why, that Mrs. Caypor was telling one then. Her manner, perhaps, was not quite as indifferent as you would have expected when she was mentioning a fact that could be of no interest to Ashenden. It flashed across his mind that Caypor had been summoned to Berne to see the redoubtable head of the German Secret Service. When he had the chance he said casually to the waitress:

"A little less work for you to do, fräulein. I hear that Herr Caypor has gone to Berne."

"Yes. But he'll be back to-morrow."

That proved nothing, but it was something to go upon. Ashenden knew in Lucerne a Swiss who was willing on emergency to do odd jobs, and, looking him up, asked him to take a letter to Berne. It might be possible to pick up Caypor and trace his movements. Next day Caypor appeared once more with his wife at the dinner-table, but merely nodded to Ashenden, and afterwards both went straight upstairs. They looked troubled. Caypor, as a rule so animated, walked with bowed shoulders, and looked neither to the right nor to the left. Next morning Ashenden received a reply to his letter. Caypor had seen Major von P. It was possible to guess what the Major had said to him. Ashenden well knew how rough he could be; he was a hard man and brutal, clever, and unscrupulous, and he was not accustomed to mince his words. They were tired of paying Caypor a salary to sit still in Lucerne and do nothing; the time was come for him to go to England. Guesswork? Of course it was guesswork, but in that trade it mostly was: you had to deduce the animal from its jaw-bone. Ashenden knew from Gustav that the Germans wanted to send someone to England. He drew a long breath; if Caypor went he would have to get busy.

When Mrs. Caypor came in to give him his lesson she was dull and listless. She looked tired, and her mouth was set obstinately. It occurred to Ashenden that the Caypors had spent most of the night talking. He wished he knew what they had said. Did she urge him to go or did she try to dissuade him? Ashenden watched them again at luncheon. Something was the matter, for they hardly spoke to one another, and as a rule they found plenty to talk about. They left the room early, but when Ashenden went out he saw Caypor sitting in the hall by himself.

"Hulloa!" he cried jovially, but surely the effort was patent, "how are you getting on? I've been to Geneva."

"So I heard," said Ashenden.

"Come and have your coffee with me. My poor wife's got a head-ache. I told her she'd better go and lie down."

In his shifty green eyes was an expression that Ashenden could not read. "The fact is, she's rather worried, poor dear; I'm thinking of going to England."

Ashenden's heart gave a sudden leap against his ribs, but his face remained impassive.

"Oh, are you going for long? We shall miss you."

"To tell you the truth, I'm fed up with doing nothing. The War looks as though it were going on for years, and I can't sit here indefi-nitely. Besides, I can't afford it. I've got to earn my living. I may have a German wife, but I am an Englishman, hang it all! and I want to do my bit. I could never face my friends again if I just stayed here in ease and comfort till the end of the War and never attempted to do a thing to help the country. My wife takes her German point of view, and I don't mind telling you that she's a bit upset. You know what women are."

Now Ashenden knew what it was that he saw in Caypor's eyes. Fear. It gave him a nasty turn. Caypor didn't want to go to England, he wanted to stay safely in Switzerland; Ashenden knew now what the Major had said to him when he went to see him in Berne. He had got to go or lose his salary. What was it that his wife had said when he told her what had happened? He had wanted her to press him to stay, but it was plain she hadn't done that; perhaps he had not dared to tell her how frightened he was. To her he had always been gay, bold, adventurous, and devil-may-care; and now, the prisoner of his own lies, he had not found it in him to confess himself the mean and sneaking coward he was.

"Are you going to take your wife with you?" asked Ashenden.

"No, she'll stay here."

It had been arranged very neatly. Mrs. Caypor would receive his letters and forward the information they contained to Berne.

"I've been out of England so long that I don't quite know how to set about getting war work. What would you do in my place?"

"I don't know; what sort of work are you thinking of?"

"Well, you know, I imagine I could do the same thing as you did. I wonder if there's anyone in the Censorship Department that you could give me a letter of introduction to."

It was only by a miracle that Ashenden saved himself from showing by a smothered cry or by a broken gesture how startled he was; but not by Caypor's request, by what had just dawned upon him. What an idiot he had been! He had been disturbed by the thought that he was wasting his time at Lucerne; he was doing nothing, and though, in fact, as it turned out, Caypor was going to England, it was due to no cleverness of his. He could take to himself no credit for the result. And now he saw that he had been put in Lucerne, told how to describe himself and given the proper information, so that what actually had occurred should occur. It would be a wonderful thing for the German Secret Service to get an agent into the Censorship Department; and by a happy accident there was Grantley Caypor, the very man for the job, on friendly terms with someone who had worked there. What a bit of luck! Major von P. was a man of culture and, rubbing his hands, he must surely have murmured: *stultum facit fortuna quem vult perdere*. It was a trap of that devilish R., and the grim Major at Berne had fallen into it. Ashenden had done his work just by sitting still and doing nothing. He almost laughed as he thought what a fool R. had made of him.

"I was on very good terms with the chief of my department. I could give you a note to him if you liked."

"That would be just the thing."

"But, of course, I must give the facts. I must say I've met you here and only known you a fortnight."

"Of course. But you'll say what else you can for me, won't you?"

"Oh, certainly."

"I don't know yet if I can get a visa. I'm told they're rather fussy."

"I don't see why. I shall be very sick if they refuse me one when I want to go back."

"I'll go and see how my wife is getting on," said Caypor suddenly, getting up. "When will you let me have that letter?"

"Whenever you like. Are you going at once?"

"As soon as possible."

Caypor left him. Ashenden waited in the hall for a quarter of an hour so that there should appear in him no sign of hurry. Then he went upstairs and prepared various communications. In one he informed R. that Caypor was going to England; in another he made arrangements through Berne that wherever Caypor applied for a visa it should be granted to him without question; and these he despatched forthwith. When he went down to dinner he handed to Caypor a cordial letter of introduction.

Next day but one Caypor left Lucerne.

Ashenden waited. He continued to have his hour's lesson with Mrs. Caypor, and under her conscientious tuition began now to speak German with ease. They talked of Goethe and Winckelmann, of art and life and travel. Fritzi sat quietly by her chair.

"He misses his master," she said, pulling his ears. "He only really cares for him, he suffers me only as belonging to him."

After his lesson Ashenden went every morning to Cook's to ask for his letters. It was here that all communications were addressed to him. He could not move till he received instructions, but R. could be trusted not to leave him idle long; and meanwhile there was nothing for him to do but have patience. Presently he received a letter from the consul in Geneva to say that Caypor had there applied for his visa and had set out for France. Having read this, Ashenden went on for a little stroll by the lake, and on his way back happened to see Mrs. Caypor coming out of Cook's office. He guessed that she was having her letters addressed there too. He went up to her.

"Have you had news of Herr Caypor?" he asked her.

"No," she said. "I suppose I could hardly expect to yet."

He walked along by her side. She was disappointed, but not yet anxious; she knew how irregular was the post. But next day during the lesson he could not but see that she was impatient to have done with it. The post was delivered at noon, and at five minutes to she looked at her watch and him. Though Ashenden knew very well that no letter would ever come for her, he had not the heart to keep her on tenterhooks.

"Don't you think that's enough for the day? I'm sure you want to go down to Cook's," he said.

"Thank you. That is very amiable of you."

When a little later he went there himself he found her standing in the middle of the office. Her face was distraught. She addressed him wildly:

"My husband promised to write from Paris. I am sure there is a letter for me, but these stupid people say there's nothing. They're so careless; it's a scandal."

Ashenden did not know what to say. While the clerk was looking through the bundle to see if there was anything for him she came up to the desk again.

"When does the next post come in from France?" she asked.

"Sometimes there are letters about five."

"I'll come then."

She turned and walked rapidly away. Fritzi followed her with his tail between his legs. There was no doubt of it; already the fear had seized her that something was wrong. Next morning she looked dreadful; she could not have closed her eyes all night; and in the lesson she started up from her chair.

"You must excuse me, Herr Somerville, I cannot give you a lesson to-day. I am not feeling well."

Before Ashenden could say anything she had flung herself nervously from the room, and in the evening he got a note from her to say that she regretted that she must discontinue giving him conversation lessons. She gave no reason. Then Ashenden saw no more of her; she ceased coming in to meals; except to go morning and afternoon to Cook's she spent apparently the whole day in her room. Ashenden thought of her sitting there hour after hour with that hideous fear gnawing at her heart. Who could help feeling sorry for her? The time hung heavy on his hands too. He read a good deal and wrote a little, he hired a canoe and went for long leisurely paddles on the lake; and at last one morning the clerk at Cook's handed him a letter. It was from R. It had all the appearance of a business communication, but between the lines he read a good deal.

"DEAR SIR (it began),

"The goods, with accompanying letter, despatched by you from Lucerne have been duly delivered. We are obliged to you for executing our instructions with such promptness."

It went on in this strain. R. was exultant. Ashenden guessed that Caypor had been arrested, and by now had paid the penalty of his crime. He shuddered. He remembered a dreadful scene. Dawn. A cold, grey dawn, with a drizzling rain falling. A man, blindfolded, standing against a wall, an officer, very pale, giving an order, a volley, and then a young soldier, one of the firing-party, turning round and holding on to his gun for support, vomiting. The officer turned paler still, and he, Ashenden, feeling dreadfully faint. How terrified Caypor must have been! It was awful when the tears ran down their faces. Ashenden shook himself. He went to the ticket-office and, obedient to his orders, bought himself a ticket for Geneva.

As he was waiting for his change Mrs. Caypor came in. He was shocked at the sight of her. She was blowsy and dishevelled, and there were heavy rings round her eyes. She was deathly pale. She staggered up to the desk and asked for a letter. The clerk shook his head.

"I'm sorry, madam, there's nothing yet."

"But look, look! Are you sure? Please look again."

The misery in her voice was heartrending. The clerk, with a shrug of the shoulders, took out the letters from a pigeon-hole and sorted them once more.

"No, there's nothing, madam."

She gave a hoarse cry of despair, and her face was distorted with anguish.

"Oh, God! oh, God!" she moaned.

She turned away, the tears streaming from her weary eyes, and for a moment she stood there like a blind man groping and not knowing which way to go. Then a fearful thing happened. Fritzi, the bull-terrier, sat down on his haunches and threw back his head and gave a long, long melancholy howl. Mrs. Caypor looked at him with terror; her eyes seemed really to start from her head. The doubt, the gnawing doubt that had tortured her during those dreadful days of suspense, was a doubt no longer. She knew. She staggered blindly into the street.

THE FIFTH CARD[1]

by Mikhail Andreevich Osorgin
(Michael Ossorgin)

After the Russian Civil War, Osorgin (1878–1942), a nobleman by birth, left and settled in Paris in 1922. In this self-contained episode from Osorgin's novel Quiet Street, *a card game breaks out in the Russian trenches in a dugout on the Eastern Front: "The whole world was cut off from the players by a curtain of smoke."*

[First published in Russian in Paris in 1929; published in English, translated by Nadia Helstein, in *Quiet Street*, New York: The Dial Press, 1930.]

STOLNIKOV FELT WITH his foot for the step that had been hollowed out of the ground, and went down into the officers' common dugout, protected by a bomb-proof shelter. It was stuffy inside and the air was thick with smoke. On the bench nearest the entrance the doctor was playing chess with a young ensign; and there was a group of officers at the table, continuing the game that had been begun after lunch. Stolnikov went up to the table and slipped in among the players.

"You've got to pass twice, Sasha. You mean to play?"

"Yes. I know."

When his turn came he felt in his pocket for his paper money and said:

"All that's left. How much here?"

"A hundred and thirty for you and the card."

"Hand over."

The players' eyes, as though at a command, shifted from the banker's cards to Stolnikov's.

"Well, give me one," he said.

"Nothing for you, and nothing for us. Two points."

---

1. The game played is a variation of baccara.

"Three," said Stolnikov, and stretched his hand for the stake.

The cards were passed on to the next player.

The war stopped short. Everything vanished save the surface of the table, the money passing from hand to hand and the thumb-marked packs of cards. It was as though Stolnikov had never been a student, nor danced at Tanyusha's party, nor changed from a fresh little officer to a war-bitten captain with the Cross of St. George; as though he had not been to the opera the day before and was not returning to Moscow. The whole world was cut off from the players by a curtain of smoke. He, too, lit a cigarette.

"Your bank now, Sasha."

"Well, here you are. I'm putting down the whole of my winnings. To begin with . . . a nine. I'm going on. Three for you; for me . . . again a nine. Three hundred and sixty roubles in the bank. Half for you, and a hundred for you. What's left for you, Ignatov? I ought to get another nine. . . . Your turn . . . there, take it."

Stolnikov handed over the "gadget"—an adapted cigarette-box—with the cards.

There were ten of them playing, so that now he would have to wait some time. All eyes turned to the hand of his neighbour on the left and all ears listened:

"Rotten luck—curse it! Six? No, we've only got seven. I'm taking up half. Whatever are you risking all your fortune for? There, not once the third card! I didn't even get a second. . . . Must break the luck."

They did so, railing at the run of bad luck, tried passing two banks and placed notes in various pockets "in case the worst came to the worst." Then the fourth card came, and growing noble and generous, and altogether a finer being, the lucky player consented to give credit to some of the other players; after which his money dribbled away at three big stakes, and he nervously fingered the note he had put aside in case the worst came to the worst.

The ensign at the end of the table passed twice. He was no longer even called upon to play.

"Gone broke?"

"Clean broke."

"That happens, my lad. The luck's cycle."

"I never have any other."

Nevertheless, he did not go away; he watched, as if luck might fall from the skies upon the head of a non-player; or thinking perhaps that somebody might get rich and offer a loan of his own accord—for he didn't want to ask.

Stolnikov was having a run of good luck.

"This is the second day I'm in luck: yesterday in action, to-day in cards."

At the words "in action" all wakened for an instant to reality, but only for an instant. No other life should exist beyond the one they were living.

A soldier entered, saying:

"There's a droning, your honour."

"A German? All right, I'm coming. Curse it! Just before my turn for the bank!"

"Give him hell, Ossipov!"

The artilleryman went out, and nobody followed him with his eyes. As he crossed the threshold there came from without the old familiar noise of a distant engine in the sky. A few minutes later the guns were rumbling.

"Ossipov's going at it for all he's worth. What are the Germans flying at night for?"

A crash—the German airman's answer. But Ossipov had already got his finger on the enemy in the sky, and one could hear the rapping of the machine-guns.

Another crash; nearer this time. All raised their heads.

"Curse him! Hand over the cards. . . . Seven. Better sell the bank, or they'll break it after the seven. . . . Very well, then, give me a card."

A tremendous crash quite close to the dug-out. The candle was overturned, but did not go out. The officers leaped from their seats, gathering up the money. Some earth fell through the beams that supported the ceiling.

"Curse it, he nearly gave us one on the head. We must go out and have a look."

"Remember the bank's mine," said Stolnikov, raising his voice. "My turn isn't yet over."

The officers streamed out into the open. A searchlight illumined the sky almost above their very heads, but the streak of light was already slanting. The anti-aircraft guns were rumbling and the machine-guns rapping away unceasingly.

"Don't stand about in groups, gentlemen," said a senior officer; "you shouldn't do that."

"He's already gone, sir."

"He may return and open fire."

The shell-hole was just beside them. Fortunately there were no victims. The German had merely scared them.

Stolnikov remembered that he had no cigarettes left, and went along to his own dug-out. When he reached it he paused. The sky was marvellously clear. The searchlight was piercing into the depths, calling back the enemy, no larger now than a faintly luminous speck on the dark background. Then there came yet another crash—the giant of the skies had placed his first cast-iron foot upon the earth. Somewhere in the neighbourhood there dropped the empty shell-case of the answering discharge.

"Why doesn't it put the wind up me, I wonder?" thought Stolnikov. "And yet it might quite easily kill me! In action, yes—one does get scared, but there's never any time to think then. But as for these toys from the skies . . ."

Then he recollected that the bank was his. "I've taken four cards. I'll leave everything in. If only I could take the fifth. That would make a jolly good stake."

And he saw himself uncovering a nine. Involuntarily he smiled.

When the German's last gift struck the ground the officers instinctively rushed to the bomb-proof shelter. They stood about at the doors listening to the roar of the engine diminishing in the distance and to the dying down of the machine-guns; then, when everything was quiet again, they returned to the table. The German had apparently located the position of the stores fairly accurately, though he had succeeded only in scaring the raw recruits.

"Ossipov will come back. How is he ever to bring down such a bird as that?"

"It was flying too high."

"Let's sit down, shall we? Whose bank?"

"Stolnikov's. He took four cards."

"But where is he? Are we going to wait for him?"

"We ought to wait."

"He went to fetch some cigarettes," someone said. "He'll be back in a moment."

An orderly came running into the dug-out—for the doctor.

"Captain Stolnikov has been wounded, your honour."

And lowering his hand from the peak of his cap, he added in an undertone to the first man to leave the dug-out: "His legs have been shot clean away, your honour! A German bomb it was that did it. . . ."

TOLD BY THE SCHOOLMASTER

by John Galsworthy

The renowned author (1867–1933) of The Forsyte Saga, *like the narrator of this story (who was also "nearly fifty"), did not serve in the war; instead, one of his pupils, a farm-boy, enlists—eagerly and fatefully.*

[From Galsworthy's *Forsytes, Pendyces and Others*. New York: Scribner, 1936. It appeared first in *The Forum*, vol. 76, December 1926, then in *Argosy* in May 1927.]

WE ALL REMEMBER still, I suppose, the singular beauty of the summer when the war broke out. I was then schoolmaster in a village on the Thames. Nearly fifty, with a game shoulder and extremely deficient sight, there was no question of my fitness for military service, and this, as with many other sensitive people, induced in me, I suppose, a mood abnormally receptive. The perfect weather, that glowing countryside, with corn harvest just beginning and the apples already ripening, the quiet nights trembling with moonlight and shadow and, in it all, this great horror launched and growing, the weazening of Europe deliberately undertaken, the death-warrant of millions of young men signed—Such summer loveliness walking hand in hand with murder thus magnified beyond conception was too piercingly ironical!

One of those evenings, towards the end of August, when the news of Mons was coming through, I left my house at the end of the village street and walked up towards the downs. I have never known anything more entrancing than the beauty of that night. All was still and coloured like the bloom of dark grapes; so warm, so tremulous. A rush of stars was yielding to the moon fast riding up, and from the corn-stooks of that early harvest the shadows were stealing out. We had no daylight-saving then, and it was perhaps half past nine when I passed two of my former scholars, a boy and a girl, standing silently at the edge of an old gravel pit opposite a beech clump. They looked up and gave me good evening. Passing

85

on over the crest, I could see the unhedged fields to either hand; the corn stooked and the corn standing, just gilded under the moon; the swelling downs of a blue-grey; and the beech clump I had passed dark-cut against the brightening sky. The moon itself was almost golden, as if it would be warm to the touch, and from it came a rain of glamour over sky and fields, woods, downs, farm-houses and the river down below. All seemed in a conspiracy of unreality to one obsessed, like me, by visions of the stark and trampling carnage going on out there. Refuging from that grim comparison, I remember thinking that Jim Beckett and Betty Roofe were absurdly young to be sweethearting, if indeed they were, for they hadn't altogether looked like it. They could hardly be sixteen yet, for they had only left school last year. Betty Roofe had been head of the girls; an interesting child, alert, self-contained, with a well-shaped, dark-eyed little face and a head set on very straight. She was the daughter of the village laundress, and I used to think too good for washing clothes, but she was already at it and, as things went in that village, would probably go on doing it till she married. Jim Beckett was working on Carver's farm down there below me and the gravel pit was about half-way between their homes. A good boy, Jim, freckled, reddish in the hair and rather too small in the head; with blue eyes that looked at you very straight, and a short nose; a well-grown boy, very big for his age, and impulsive in spite of the careful stodginess of all young rustics; a curious vein of the sensitive in him, but a great deal of obstinacy, too—altogether an interesting blend!

I was still standing there when up he came on his way to Carver's and I look back to that next moment with as much regret as to any in my life.

He held out his hand.

"Good-bye, sir, in case I don't see you again."

"Why, where are you off to, Jim?"

"Joinin' up."

"Joining up? But, my dear boy, you're two years under age, at least."

He grinned. "I'm sixteen this month, but I bet I can make out to be eighteen. They ain't particular, I'm told."

I looked him up and down. It was true, he could pass for eighteen well enough, with military needs what they were. And possessed, as everyone was just then, by patriotism and anxiety at the news, all I said was:

"I don't think you ought, Jim; but I admire your spirit."

He stood there silent, sheepish at my words. Then:

"Well, good-bye, sir. I'm goin' to —ford to-morrow."

I gave his hand a good hard squeeze. He grinned again, and without looking back, ran off down the hill towards Carver's farm, leaving me alone once more with the unearthly glamour of that night. God! what a crime was war! From this hushed moonlit peace boys were hurrying off to that business of man-made death as if there were not Nature's deaths galore to fight against. And we—we could only admire them for it! Well! I have never ceased to curse the sentiment which stopped me from informing the recruiting authorities of that boy's real age.

Crossing back over the crest of the hill towards home I came on the child Betty, at the edge of the gravel pit where I had left her.

"Well, Betty, was Jim telling you?"

"Yes, sir; he's going to join up."

"What did you say to him?"

"I said he was a fool, but he's so headstrong, Jim!" Her voice was even enough, but she was quivering all over.

"It's very plucky of him, Betty."

"M'm! Jim just gets things into his head. I don't see that he has any call to go and—and leave me."

I couldn't help a smile. She saw it, and said sullenly:

"Yes, I'm young, and so's Jim; but he's my boy, for all that!"

And then, ashamed or startled at such expansiveness, she tossed her head, swerved into the beech clump like a shying foal, and ran off among the trees. I stood a few minutes, listening to the owls, then went home and read myself into forgetfulness on Scott's first Polar book.

So Jim went and we knew him no more for a whole year. And Betty continued with her mother washing for the village.

In September, 1915, just after term had begun again, I was standing one afternoon in the village schoolroom pinning up on the wall a pictorial piece of imperial information for the benefit of my scholars, and thinking, as usual, of the war, and its lingering deadlock. The sunlight slanted through on to my dusty forms and desks, and under the pollard lime-trees on the far side of the street I could see a soldier standing with a girl. Suddenly he crossed over to the school, and there in the doorway was young Jim Beckett in his absurd short-tailed khaki jacket, square and tanned to the colour of his freckles, looking, indeed, quite a man.

"How d'you do, sir?"

"And you, Jim?"

"Oh, I'm fine! I thought I'd like to see you. Just got our marching orders. Off to France tomorrow; been havin' my leave."

I felt the catch at my throat that we all felt when youngsters whom we knew were going out for the first time.

"Was that Betty with you out there?"

"Yes—fact is, I've got something to tell you, sir. She and I were spliced last week at —mouth. We been stayin' there since, and I brought her home to-day, as I got to go to-night."

I was staring hard, and he went on hurriedly:

"She just went off there and I joined her for my leave. We didn't want any fuss, you see, because of our bein' too young."

"Young!"

The blankness of my tone took the grin off his face.

"Well, I was seventeen a week ago and she'll be seventeen next month."

"Married? Honest Injun, Jim?"

He went to the door and whistled. In came Betty, dressed in dark blue, very neat and self-contained; only the flush on her round young face marked any disturbance.

"Show him your lines, Betty, and your ring."

The girl held out the official slip and from it I read that a registrar had married them at —mouth, under right names and wrong ages.

Then she slipped a glove off and held up her left hand—there was the magic hoop! Well! the folly was committed; no use in crabbing it!

"Very good of you to tell me, Jim," I said at last. "Am I the first to know?"

"Yes, sir. You see, I've got to go at once, and like as not her mother won't want it to get about till she's a bit older. I thought I'd like to tell *you*, in case they said it wasn't all straight and proper."

"Nothing I say will alter the fact that you've falsified your ages."

Jim grinned again.

"That's all right," he said. "I got it from a lawyer's clerk in my platoon. It's a marriage all the same."

"Yes; I believe that's so."

"Well, sir, there she is till I come back." Suddenly his face changed; he looked for all the world as if he were going to cry; and they stood gazing at each other exactly as if they were alone.

The lodger at the carpenter's, three doors down the street, was performing her usual afternoon solo on the piano, "*Connais-tu le pays?*" from *Mignon*. And whenever I hear it now, seldom enough in days contemptuous of harmony, it brings Jim and Betty back through a broad sunbeam full of dancing motes of dust; it epitomizes for me all the *Drang*—as the Germans call it—of those horrible years, when marriage, birth, death and every human activity were speeded up to their limit, and we did from year's end to year's end all that an enlightened humanity should not be doing, and left undone most of what it should have done.

"What time is it, sir?" Jim asked me suddenly.

"Five o'clock."

"Lord! I must run for it. My kit's at the station. Could I leave her here, sir?"

I nodded and walked into the little room beyond. When I came back she was sitting where she used to sit in school, bowed over her arms spread out on the inky desk. Her dark bobbed hair was all I could see, and the quivering jerky movement of her young shoulders. Jim had gone. Well! That was the normal state of Europe, then! I went back into the little room to give her time, but when I returned once more she, too, had gone.

The second winter passed, more muddy, more bloody even than the first, and less shot through with hopes of an ending. Betty showed me three or four of Jim's letters, simple screeds with a phrase here and there of awkward and half-smothered feeling, and signed always "Your loving hubby, Jim." Her marriage was accepted in the village. Child-marriage was quite common then. In April it began to be obvious that their union was to be "blessed", as they call it.

One day early in May I was passing Mrs. Roofe's when I saw that lady in her patch of garden, and stopped to ask after Betty.

"Nearin' her time. I've written to Jim Beckett. Happen he'll get leave."

"I think that was a mistake, Mrs. Roofe. I would have waited till it was over."

"Maybe you're right, sir; but Betty's that fidgety about him not knowin'. She's dreadful young, you know, t' 'ave a child. I didn't 'ave my first till I was twenty-one."

"Everything goes fast these days, Mrs. Roofe."

"Not my washin'. I can't get the help, with Betty like this. It's a sad business this about the baby comin'. If he does get killed I suppose she'll get a pension, sir?"

Pension? Married in the wrong age, with the boy still under service age, if they came to look into it. I really didn't know.

"Oh, surely, Mrs. Roofe! But we won't think about his being killed. Jim's a fine boy."

Mrs. Roofe's worn face darkened.

"He was a fool to join up before his time; plenty of chance after, seemingly; and then to marry my girl like this! Well, young folk *are* fools!"

I was sitting over my Pensions work one evening, a month later, for it had now fallen to me to keep things listed in the village, when someone knocked at my door, and who should be standing there but Jim Beckett!

"Why! Jim! Got leave?"

"Ah! I had to come and see her. I haven't been there yet; didn' dare. How is she, sir?"

Pale and dusty, as if from a hard journey, his uniform all muddy and unbrushed, and his reddish hair standing up any-how—he looked wretched, poor boy!

"She's all right, Jim. But it must be very near, from what her mother says."

"I haven't had any sleep for nights, thinking of her—such a kid, she is!"

"Does she know you're coming?"

"No, I haven't said nothing."

"Better be careful. I wouldn't risk a shock. Have you anywhere to sleep?"

"No, sir."

"Well, you can stay here if you like. They won't have room for you there." He seemed to back away from me.

"Thank ye, sir. I wouldn' like to put you out."

"Not a bit, Jim; delighted to have you and hear your adventures."

He shook his head. "I don't want to talk of them," he said darkly. "Don't you think I could see 'er to-night, sir? I've come a long way for it, my God! I have!"

"Well, try! But see her mother first."

"Yes, sir," and he touched his forehead. His face, so young a face, already had that look in the eyes of men who stare death down.

He went away and I didn't see him again that night. They had managed, apparently, to screw him into their tiny cottage. He was only just in time, for two days later Betty had a boy-child. He came to me the same evening, after dark, very excited.

"She's a wonder," he said; "but if I'd known I'd never ha' done it, sir, I never would. You can't tell what you're doing till it's too late, it seems."

Strange saying from that young father, till afterwards it was made too clear!

Betty recovered quickly and was out within three weeks.

Jim seemed to have long leave, for he was still about, but I had little talk with him, for, though always friendly, he seemed shy of me, and as to talking of the war—not a word! One evening I passed him and Betty leaning on a gate, close to the river—a warm evening of early July, when the Somme battle was at its height. Out there hell incarnate; and here intense peace, the quietly flowing river, the willows, and unstirring aspens, the light slowly dying, and those two young things, with their arms round each other and their heads close together—her bobbed dark hair and Jim's reddish mop, getting quite long! I took good care not to disturb them. His last night, perhaps, before he went back into the furnace!

It was no business of mine to have my doubts, but I had been having them long before that very dreadful night when, just as I was going to bed, something rattled on my window, and going down I found Betty outside, distracted.

"Oh, sir, come quick! They've 'rested Jim."

As we went over she told me:

"Oh, sir, I was afraid there was some mistake about his leave—it was so long; I thought he'd get into trouble over it, so I asked Bill Pateman"—(the village constable)—"and now they've come and 'rested him for deserting. Oh! What have I done? What have I done?"

Outside the Roofes' cottage Jim was standing between a corporal's guard, and Betty flung herself into his arms. Inside I could hear Mrs. Roofe expostulating with the corporal, and the baby crying. In the sleeping quiet of the village street, smelling of hay just harvested, it was atrocious.

I spoke to Jim. He answered quietly, in her arms:

"I asked for leave, but they wouldn't give it. I had to come. I couldn't stick it, knowing how it was with her."

"Where was your regiment?"

"In the line."

"Good God!"

Just then the corporal came out. I took him apart.

"I was his schoolmaster, Corporal," I said. "The poor chap joined up when he was just sixteen—he's still under age, you see; and now he's got this child-wife and a newborn baby!"

The corporal nodded; his face was twitching, a lined, decent face with a moustache.

"I know, sir," he muttered. "I know. Cruel work, but I've got to take him. He'll have to go back to France."

"What does it mean?"

He lifted his arms from his sides and let them drop, and that gesture was somehow the most expressive and dreadful I ever saw.

"Deserting in face of the enemy," he whispered hoarsely. "Bad business! Can you get that girl away, sir?"

But Jim himself undid the grip of her arms and held her from him. Bending, he kissed her hair and face, then, with a groan, he literally pushed her into my arms and marched straight off between the guard.

And I was left in the dark, sweet-scented street with that distracted child struggling in my grasp.

"Oh, my God! My God! My God!" Over and over and over. And what could one say or do?

All the rest of that night, after Mrs. Roofe had got Betty back into the cottage, I sat up writing in duplicate the facts about Jim Beckett. I sent one copy to his regimental headquarters, the other to the chaplain of his regiment in France. I sent fresh copies two days later with duplicates of his birth certificates to make quite sure. It was all I could do. Then came a fortnight of waiting for news. Betty was still distracted. The thought that, through her anxiety, she herself had delivered him into their hands nearly sent her off her head. Probably her baby alone kept her from insanity, or suicide. And all that time the battle of the Somme raged and hundreds of thousands of women in England and France and Germany were in daily terror for their menfolk. Yet none, I think, could have had quite the feeling of that child. Her mother, poor woman, would come over to me at the schoolhouse and ask if I had heard anything.

"Better for the poor girl to know the worst," she said, "if it is the worst. The anxiety's killin' 'er."

But I had no news and could not get any at Headquarters. The thing was being dealt with in France. Never was the scale and pitch of the world's horror more brought home to me. This deadly little tragedy was as nothing—just a fragment of straw whirling round in that terrible wind.

And then one day I did get news—a letter from the chaplain—and seeing what it was I stuck it in my pocket and sneaked down to the river—literally afraid to open it till I was alone. Crouched up there, with my back to a haystack, I took it out with trembling fingers.

DEAR SIR,
The boy Jim Beckett was shot to-day at dawn. I am distressed at having to tell you and the poor child his wife. War is a cruel thing indeed.

I had known it. Poor Jim! Poor Betty! Poor, poor Betty! I read on:

I did all I could; the facts you sent were put before the Court Martial and the point of his age considered. But all leave had been stopped; his request had been definitely refused; the regiment was actually in the line, with fighting going on—and the situation extremely critical in that sector. Private considerations count for nothing in such circumstances—the rule is adamant. Perhaps it has to be—I cannot say. But I have been greatly distressed by the whole thing, and the Court itself was much moved. The poor boy seemed dazed; he wouldn't talk; didn't seem to take in anything; indeed, they tell me that all he said after the verdict, certainly all I heard him say, was: "My poor wife! My poor wife!" over and over again. He stood up well at the end.

He stood up well at the end! I can see him yet, poor impulsive Jim. Desertion, but not cowardice, by the Lord! No one who looked into those straight, blue eyes could believe that. But they bandaged them, I suppose. Well! a bullet in a billet more or less; what was it in that wholesale slaughter? As a raindrop on a willow tree drips into the river and away to sea—so that boy, like a million others, dripped to dust. A little ironical though, that his own side should shoot him, who went to fight for them two years before he need, to shoot him who wouldn't be legal food for powder for another month! A little ironical, perhaps, that he had left this son—legacy to such an implacable world! But there's no moral to a true tale like this—unless it be that the rhythm of life and death cares not a jot for any of us!

ENGLAND

by Edward John Moreton Drax Plunkett
(Lord Dunsany)

A prolific author who was known for his many books of fantasy, Plunkett (1878–1957) served as a captain in the British army and was wounded in 1916.

[From Plunkett's *Tales of War*. Boston: Little, Brown and Company, 1918.]

"AND THEN WE used to have sausages," said the Sergeant.

"And mashed?" said the Private.

"Yes," said the Sergeant, "and beer. And then we used to go home. It was grand in the evenings. We used to go along a lane that was full of them wild roses. And then we come to the road where the houses were. They all had their bit of a garden, every house."

"Nice, I calls it, a garden," the Private said.

"Yes," said the Sergeant, "they all had their garden. It came right down to the road. Wooden palings: none of that there wire."

"I hates wire," said the Private.

"They didn't have none of it," the N. C. O. went on. "The gardens came right down to the road, looking lovely. Old Billy Weeks he had them tall pale-blue flowers in his garden nearly as high as a man."

"Hollyhocks?" said the Private.

"No, they wasn't hollyhocks. Lovely they were. We used to stop and look at them, going by every evening. He had a path up the middle of his garden paved with red tiles, Billy Weeks had; and these tall blue flowers growing the whole way along it, both sides like. They was a wonder. Twenty gardens there must have been, counting them all; but none to touch Billy Weeks with his pale-blue flowers. There was an old windmill away to the left. Then there were the swifts sailing by overhead and screeching: just about as high again as the houses. Lord, how them birds did fly. And there was the other young fellows, what were not out walking, standing about by the roadside, just doing nothing at all. One of them had a flute: Jim Booker, he was. Those were great days. The bats used to come out, flutter, flutter, flutter; and then there'd be a star or two; and the smoke from the chimneys going all grey; and a little cold wind going up and down like the bats; and all the colour going out of things; and the woods looking all strange, and a wonderful quiet in them, and a mist coming up from the stream. It's a queer time that. It's always about that time, the way I see it: the end of the evening in the long days, and a star or two, and me and my girl going home.

"Wouldn't you like to talk about things for a bit the way you remember them?"

"Oh, no, Sergeant," said the other, "you go on. You do bring it all back so."

"I used to bring her home," the Sergeant said, "to her father's house. Her father was keeper there, and they had a house in the wood. A fine house with queer old tiles on it, and a lot of large friendly dogs. I knew them all by name, same as they knew me. I used to walk home then along the side of the wood. The owls would be about; you could hear them yelling. They'd float out of the wood like, sometimes: all large and white."

"I knows them," said the Private.

"I saw a fox once so close I could nearly touch him, walking like he was on velvet. He just slipped out of the wood."

"Cunning old brute," said the Private.

"That's the time to be out," said the Sergeant. "Ten o'clock on a summer's night, and the night full of noises, not many of them, but what there is, strange, and coming from a great way off, through the quiet, with nothing to stop them. Dogs barking, owls hooting, an old cart; and then just once a sound that you couldn't account for at all, not anyhow. I've heard sounds on nights like that that nobody 'ud think you'd heard, nothing like the flute that young Booker had, nothing like anything on earth."

"I know," said the Private.

"I never told any one before, because they wouldn't believe you. But it doesn't matter now. There'd be a light in the window to guide me when I got home. I'd walk up through the flowers of our garden. We had a lovely garden. Wonderful white and strange the flowers looked of a night-time."

"You bring it all back wonderful," said the Private.

"It's a great thing to have lived," said the Sergeant.

"Yes, Sergeant," said the other, "I wouldn't have missed it, not for anything."

For five days the barrage had rained down behind them: they were utterly cut off and had no hope of rescue: their food was done, and they did not know where they were.

INTRODUCTION TO THE TRENCHES

by Richard Aldington

Aldington (1892–1962) was already an important young British writer and poet when he enlisted in 1916. He had helped the American poet Ezra Pound describe and create the Imagist Movement, had promoted the work of his friend D. H. Lawrence, and had married the American poet Hilda Doolittle in 1913. When he wrote of his war experiences in the episodic novel Death of a Hero *(1929), sections of it were published as short stories, including this one about a soldier's first night in the "No Man's Land" trenches of Belgium in 1916: "It was like living in the graveyard of the world—dead trees, dead houses, dead mines, dead villages, and dead men."*

[From Aldington's *Death of a Hero*. London: Chatto & Windus, 1929.]

WINTERBOURNE HAD AN easy initiation into trench warfare. The cold was so intense that the troops on both sides were chiefly occupied in having pneumonia and trying to keep warm. He found himself in a quiet sector, which had been fought over by the French in 1914 and had been the scene of a fierce and prolonged battle in 1915, after the British took over the sector. During 1916, when the main fighting shifted to the Somme, the sector had settled down to ordinary trench warfare. Trench raids had not then been much developed, but constant local attacks were made on battalion or brigade fronts. A little later the sector atoned for this calm.

To Winterbourne, as to so many others, the time element was of extreme importance during the war years. The hour goddesses who had danced along so gaily before, and have fled from us since with such mocking swiftness, then paced by in a slow, monotonous file as if intolerably burdened. People at a distance thought of the fighting as heroic and exciting, in terms of cheering bayonet charges or little knots of determined men holding out to the last Lewis gun. That is rather like counting life by its champagne suppers and forgetting all the rest. The qualities needed were determination and endurance, inhuman endurance. It would be much more practical to fight modern wars with mechanical robots than with men. But then, men are cheaper, although in a long war the initial outlay on the robots might be compensated by the fact that the quality of men deteriorates while they cost more in upkeep. But that is a question for the War Departments. From the point of view of efficiency in war, the trouble is that men have feelings; to attain the perfect soldier we must eliminate feelings. To the human robots of the last war, time seemed indefinitely and most unpleasantly prolonged. The dimension then measured as a "day" in its apparent duration approached what we now call a "month." And the long series of violent stalemates on the Western front made any decision seem impossible. In 1916 it looked as if no line could be broken, because so long as enough new troops were hurried to threatened points the attacker was bound to be held up; and the supplies of new troops seemed endless. It became a matter of which side could wear down the other's man-power and moral endurance. So there also was the interminable. The only alternatives seemed an indefinite prolongation of misery, or death, or mutilation, or collapse of some sort. Even a wound was a doubtful blessing, a mere holiday, for wounded men had to be returned again and again to the line.

For the first six or eight "weeks," Winterbourne, like all his companions, was occupied in fighting the cold. The Pioneer company to which he was attached were digging a sap out into No Man's Land and making trench-mortar emplacements just behind the front line. They worked on these most of the night and slept during the day. But the ground was frozen so hard that progress was tediously slow.

The company were billeted in the ruins of a village behind the reserve trenches, over a mile from the front line. The landscape was flat, almost treeless except for a few shell-blasted stumps, and covered with snow frozen hard. Every building in sight had been smashed, in many cases almost level with the ground. It was a mining country, with great queer hills of slag and strange pit-head machinery in steel, reduced by shell-fire to huge masses of twisted rusting metal. They were in a salient, with the half-destroyed, evacuated town of M— in the elbow-crook on the extreme right. The village churchyard was filled with graves of French soldiers; there were graves inside any of the houses which had no cellars, and graves flourished over the bare landscape. In all directions were crosses, little wooden crosses, in ones and twos and threes, emerging blackly from the frozen snow. Some were already askew; one just outside the ruined village had been snapped short by a shell-burst. The dead men's caps, mouldering and falling to pieces, were hooked on to the tops of the crosses—the grey

German round cap, the French blue and red kepi, the English khaki. There were also two large British cemeteries in sight—rectangular plantations of wooden crosses. It was like living in the graveyard of the world—dead trees, dead houses, dead mines, dead villages, and dead men. Only the long steel guns and the transport waggons seemed alive. There were no civilians, but one of the mines was still worked about a mile and a half further from the line.

Behind Winterbourne's billet were hidden two large howitzers. They fired with a reverberating crash which shook the ruined houses, and the diminishing scream of the departing shells was strangely melancholy in the frost-silent air. The Germans rarely returned the fire—they were saving their ammunition. Occasionally a shell screamed over and crashed sharply among the ruins; the huge detonation spouted up black earth or rattling bricks and tiles. Fragments of the burst shell-case hummed through the air.

But it was the cold that mattered. In his efforts to defend himself against it, Winterbourne, like the other men, was strangely and wonderfully garbed. Round his belly, next the skin, he wore a flannel belt. Over that, a thick woollen vest, grey flannel shirt, knitted cardigan jacket, long woollen under-pants, and thick socks. Over that, service jacket, trousers, puttees, and boots; then a sheep-skin coat, two mufflers round his neck, two pairs of woollen gloves, and over them trench gloves. In addition came equipment—box respirator on the chest, steel helmet, rifle, and bayonet. The only clothes he took off at night were his boots. With his legs wrapped in a greatcoat, his body in a grey blanket, a ground-sheet underneath, pack for pillow, and a dixie of hot tea and rum inside him, he just got warm enough to fall asleep when very tired.

Through the broken roof of his billet Winterbourne could see the frosty glitter of the stars and the white rime. In the morning, when he awoke, he found his breath frozen on the blanket. In the line his short moustache formed icicles. The boots beside him froze hard, and it was agony to struggle into them. The bread in his haversack froze greyly; and the taste of frozen bread is horrid. Little spikes of ice formed in the cheese. The tins of jam froze and had to be thawed before they could be eaten. The bully beef froze in the tins and came out like chunks of reddish ice. Washing was a torment. They had three tubs of water between about forty of them each day. With this they shaved and washed—about ten or fifteen to a tub. Since Winterbourne was a late-comer to the battalion, he had to wait until the others had finished. The water was cold and utterly filthy. He plunged his dirty hands into it with disgust, and shut his eyes when he washed his face. This humiliation, too, he accepted.

He always remembered his first night in the line. They paraded in the ruined village street about four o'clock. The air seemed crackling with frost, and the now familiar bloody smear of red sunset was dying away in the south-west. The men were muffled up to the ears, and looked grotesquely bulky in their sheep or goat skin coats, with the hump of box respirators on their chests. Most of them had sacking covers on their steel helmets to prevent reflection, and sacks tied round their legs for warmth. The muffled officer came shivering from his billet as the men stamped their feet on the hard, frost-bound road. They drew picks and shovels from a dump, and filed silently through the ruined street behind the officer. Their bayonets were silhouetted against the cold sky. The man in front of Winterbourne turned abruptly left into a ruined house. Winterbourne followed, descended four rough steps, and found himself in a trench. A notice said:

HINTON ALLEY
To the Front Line.

To be out of the piercing cold wind in the shelter of walls of earth was an immediate relief. Overhead shone the beautiful ironic stars.

A field-gun behind them started to crash out shells. Winterbourne listened to the long-drawn wail as they sped away and finally crashed faintly in the distance. He followed the man ahead of him blindly. Word kept coming down: "Hole here; look out." "Wire overhead." "Mind your head—bridge." He passed the messages on, after tripping in the holes, catching his bayonet in the field telephone wires, and knocking his helmet on the low bridge. They passed the reserve line, then the support, with the motionless sentries on the fire-step, and the peculiar smell of burnt wood and foul air coming from the dug-outs. A minute later came the sharp message: "Stop talking; don't clink your shovels." They were now only a few hundred yards from the German front line. A few guns were firing in a desultory way. A shell crashed outside the parapet about five yards from Winterbourne's head. It was only a whizz-bang, but to his unpractised ears it sounded like a heavy. The shells came in fours—Crump, CRUMP, CRRUMP; the Boche was bracketing. Every minute or so came a sharp ping!—fixed rifles firing at a latrine or an unprotected piece of trench. The duck-boards were more broken. Winterbourne stumbled over an unexploded shell, then had to clamber over a heap of earth where the side of the trench had been smashed in a few minutes earlier. The trench made another sharp turn, and he saw the bayonet and helmet of a sentry silhouetted against the sky. They were in the front line.

They turned sharp left. To their right were the fire-steps, with a sentry about every fifty yards. In between came traverses and dug-out entrances, with their rolled-up blanket gas-curtains. Winterbourne peered down them—there was a faint glow of light, a distant mutter of talk, and a heavy stench of wood and foul air. The man in front stopped and turned to Winterbourne:

"Halt! Password to-night's 'Lantern.'" Winterbourne halted, and passed the message on. They waited. He was standing almost immediately behind a sentry, and got on the fire-step beside the man to take his first look at No Man's Land.

"'Oo are you?" asked the sentry in low tones.

"Pioneers."

"Got a bit o' candle to give us, chum?"

"Awfully sorry, chum, I haven't."

"Them muckin' R.E.s gets 'em all."

"I've got a packet of chocolate, if you'd like it."

"Ah! Thanks, chum."

The sentry broke a bit of chocolate and began to munch.

"Muckin' cold up here, it is. Me feet's fair froze. Muckin' dreary, too. I can 'ear ole Fritz coughin' over there in 'is listenin' post—don't 'arf sound 'ollow. Listen."

Winterbourne listened, and heard a dull, hollow sound of coughing.

"Fritz's sentry," whispered the man. "Pore ole ——. Needs some liquorice."

"Move on," came the word from the man in front. Winterbourne jumped down from the fire-step and passed on the word.

"Good-night, chum," said the sentry.

"Good-night, chum."

Winterbourne was put on the party digging the sap out into No Man's Land. The officer stopped him as he was entering the sap.

"You're one of the new draft, aren't you?"

"Yes, sir."

"Wait a minute."

"Very good, sir."

The other men filed into the sap. The officer spoke in low tones:

"You can take sentry for the first hour. Come along, and don't stand up."

The young crescent moon had risen and poured down cold, faint light. Every now and then a Verey light was fired from the German or English lines, brilliantly illuminating the desolate landscape of torn, irregular wire and jagged shell-holes. They climbed over the parapet and crawled over the broken ground past the end of the sap. The officer made for a shell-hole just inside the English wire, and Winterbourne followed him.

"Lie here," whispered the officer, "and keep a sharp lookout for German patrols. Fire if you see them and give the alarm. There's a patrol of our own out on the right, so make sure before you fire. There's a couple of bombs somewhere in the shell-hole. You'll be relieved in an hour."

"Very good, sir."

The officer crawled away, and Winterbourne remained alone in No Man's Land, about twenty-five yards in front of the British line. He could hear the soft, dull thuds of picks and shovels from the men working the sap, and a very faint murmur as they talked in whispers. A Verey light hissed up from the English lines, and he strained his eyes for the possible enemy patrol. In the brief light he saw nothing but the irregular masses of German wire, the broken line of their parapet, shell-holes and debris, and the large stump of a dead tree. Just as the bright magnesium turned in its luminous parabola, a hidden machine-gun, not thirty yards from Winterbourne, went off with a loud crackle of bullets like the engine of a motor-bicycle. He started, and nearly pulled the trigger of his rifle. Then silence. A British sentry coughed with a deep hacking sound; then from the distance came the hollow coughing of a German sentry. Eerie sounds in the pallid moonlight. "Ping!" went a sniper's rifle. It was horribly cold. Winterbourne was shivering, partly from cold, partly from excitement.

Interminable minutes passed. He grew colder and colder. Occasionally a few shells from one side or the other went wailing overhead and crashed somewhere in the back areas. About four hundred yards away to his left began a series of loud, shattering detonations. He strained his eyes, and could just see the flash of the explosion and the dark column of smoke and debris. These were the German trench-mortars, the dreaded "minnies," although he did not know it.

Nothing different happened until about three-quarters of an hour had passed. Winterbourne got colder and colder, felt he had been out there at least three hours, and thought he must have been forgotten. He shivered with cold. Suddenly he thought he saw something move to his right, just outside the wire. He gazed intently, all tense and alert. Yes, a dark something was moving. It stopped, and seemed to vanish. Then near it another dark figure moved, and then a third. It was a patrol, making for the gap in the wire in front of Winterbourne. Were they Germans or British? He pointed his rifle towards them, got the bombs ready, and waited. They came nearer and nearer. Just before they got to the wire, Winterbourne challenged in a loud whisper:

"Halt, who are you?"

All three figures instantly disappeared.

"Halt, who are you?"

"Friend," came a low answer.

"Give the word or I fire."

"Lantern."

"All right."

One of the men crawled through the wire to Winterbourne, followed by the other two. They wore balaclava helmets and carried revolvers.

"Are you the patrol?" whispered Winterbourne.

"Who the muckin' 'ell d'you think we are? Father Christmas? What are you doin' out here?"

"Pioneers digging a sap about fifteen yards behind."

"Are you Pioneers?"

"Yes."

"Got a bit o' candle, chum?"

"Sorry, I haven't; we don't get them issued."

The patrol crawled off, and Winterbourne heard an alarmed challenge from the men working in the sap and the word "Lantern." A Verey light went up from the German lines just as the patrol were crawling over the parapet. A German sentry fired his rifle and a machine-gun started up. The patrol dropped hastily into the trench. The machine-gun bullets whistled cruelly past Winterbourne's head—zwiss, zwiss, zwiss. He crouched down in the hole. Zwiss, zwiss, zwiss. Then silence. He lifted his head and continued to watch. For two or three minutes there was complete silence. The men in the sap seemed to have knocked off work, and made no sound. Winterbourne listened intently. No sound. It was the most ghostly, desolate, deathly silence he had ever experienced. He had never imagined that death could be so deathly. The feeling of annihilation, of the end of existence, of a dead planet of the dead arrested in a dead time and space, penetrated his flesh along with the cold. He shuddered. So frozen, so desolate, so dead a world—everything smashed and lying inertly broken. Then "crack—ping!" went a sniper's rifle, and a battery of field-guns opened with salvoes about half a mile to his right. The machine-guns began again. The noise was a relief after that ghastly dead silence.

At last the N.C.O. came crawling out from the sap with another man to relieve him. A Verey light shot up from the German line in their direction just as the two men reached him. All three crouched motionless as the accurate German machine-gun fire swept the British trench parapet. Zwiss, zwiss, zwiss, the flights of bullets went over them. Winterbourne saw a strand of wire just in front of him suddenly flip up in the air where a low bullet had struck it. Quite near enough—not six inches above his head.

They crawled back to the sap, and Winterbourne tumbled in. He found himself face to face with the platoon officer, Lieutenant Evans. Winterbourne was shivering uncontrollably; he felt utterly chilled. His whole body was numb, his hands stiff, his legs one ache of cold from the knees down. He realised the cogency of the Adjutant's fare-well hint about looking after feet, and decided to drop his indiffer-ence to goose grease and neat's-foot oil.

"Cold?" asked the officer.

"It's bitterly cold out there, sir," said Winterbourne through chat-tering teeth.

"Here, take a drink of this"; and Evans held out a small flask.

Winterbourne took the flask in his cold-shaken hand. It chinked roughly against his teeth as he took a gulp of the terrifically potent army rum. The strong liquor half choked him, burned his throat, and made his eyes water. Almost immediately he felt the deadly chill beginning to lessen. But he still shivered.

"Good Lord, man! you're frozen," said Evans. "I thought it was colder than ever to-night. It's no weather for lying in No Man's Land. Corporal, you'll have to change that sentry every half hour—an hour's too long in this frost."

"Very good, sir."

"Have some more rum?" asked Evans.

"No, thanks, sir," replied Winterbourne; "I'm quite all right now. I can warm up with some digging."

"No; get your rifle and come with me."

Evans started off briskly down the trench to visit the other working parties. About a hundred yards from the sap he climbed out of the trench over the parados; Winterbourne scrambled after, more impeded by his chilled limbs, his rifle, and heavier equipment. Evans gave him a hand up. They walked about another hundred yards over the top, and then reached the place where several parties were digging trench-mortar emplacements. The N.C.O. saw them coming, and climbed out of one of the holes to meet them.

"Getting on all right, sergeant?"

"Ground's very hard, sir."

"I know, but—"

Zwiss, zwiss, zwiss, zwiss, came a rush of bullets, following the rapid tat-tat-tat-tat-tat-tat-tat of a machine gun. The sergeant ducked double. Evans remained calmly standing. Seeing his unconcern, Winterbourne also remained upright.

"I know the ground's hard," said Evans, "but those emplacements are urgently needed. Headquarters were at us again to-day about them. I'll see how you're getting on."

The sergeant hastily scuttled into one of the deep emplacements, followed in a more leisurely way by the officer. Winterbourne remained standing on top, and listened to Evans as he urged the men to get a move on. Tat-tat-tat-tat-tat. Zwiss, zwiss, zwiss, very close this time. Winterbourne felt a slight creep in his spine; but since Evans had not moved before, he decided that the right thing was to stand still. Evans visited each of the four emplacements, and then made straight for the front line. He paused at the parados.

"We're pretty close to the Boche front line here. He's got a machine-gun post about a hundred and fifty yards over there."

Tat-tat-tat-tat-tat-tat. Zwiss, zwiss, zwiss.

"Look! Over there."

Winterbourne just caught a glimpse of the quick flashes.

"Damn!" said Evans. "I forgot to bring my prismatic compass to-night. We might have taken a bearing on them, and got the artillery to turf them out."

He jumped carelessly into the trench, and Winterbourne dutifully followed. About fifty yards further on he stopped.

"I see from your paybook that you're an artist in civil life."

"Yes, sir."

"Paint pictures and draw?"

"Yes, sir."

"Why don't you apply for a draughtsman's job at Division? They need them."

"Well, sir, I don't particularly covet a hero's grave, but I feel very strongly I ought to take my chance in the line along with the rest."

"Ah! Of course. Are you a pretty good walker?"

"I used to go on walking tours in peace time, sir."

"Well, there's an order that every officer is to have a runner. Would you like the job of platoon runner? You'd have to accompany me, and you're supposed to take my last dying orders! You'd have to learn the lie of the trenches, so as to act as guide, take my orders to N.C.O.s, know enough about what's going on to help them if I'm knocked out, and carry messages. It's perhaps a bit more dangerous than the ordinary work, and you may have to turn out at odd hours, but it'll get you off a certain amount of digging."

"I'd like it very much, sir."

"All right; I'll speak to the Major about it."

"It's very good of you, sir."

"Can you find your way back to the sap? It's about two hundred yards along this trench."

"I'm sure I can, sir."

"All right. Go back and report to the corporal, and carry on."

"Very good, sir."

"You haven't forgotten the password?"

"No, sir—'Lantern.'"

About thirty yards along the trench there was a rattle of equipment, and Winterbourne found a bayonet about two feet from his chest. It was a gas sentry outside a company H.Q. dug-out.

"Halt! Who are yer?"

"Lantern."

The sentry languidly lowered his rifle.

"Muckin' cold to-night, mate."

"Bloody cold."

"What are you—Bedfords or Essex?"

"No; Pioneers."

"Got a bit of candle to give us, mate? It's muckin' dark in them dug-outs."

"Very sorry, chum, I haven't."

Rather trying, this constant demand for candle-ends from the Pioneers, who were popularly supposed by the infantry to receive immense "issues" of candles. But without candles the dug-outs were merely black holes, even in the daytime, if they were of any depth. They were deep on this front, since the line was a captured German trench reorganised. Hence the dug-outs faced the enemy instead of being turned away from them.

"Oh, all right; good-night."

"Good-night."

Winterbourne returned to the sap, and did two more half-hour turns as sentry, and for the rest of the time picked or shovelled the hard clods of earth into sandbags. The sandbags were then carried back to the front line and piled there to raise the parapet. It was a slow business. The sap itself was camouflaged to avoid observation. Winterbourne hadn't the slightest idea what its object was. He was very weary and sleepy when they finally knocked off work about one in the morning. An eight-hour shift, exclusive of time taken in getting to and from the work. The men filed wearily along the trench, rifles slung on the left shoulder, picks and shovels carried on the right. Winterbourne stumbled along, half asleep with the cold and the fatigue of unaccustomed labour. He felt he didn't mind how dangerous it was—if it was dangerous—to be a runner, provided he got some change from the dreariness of digging and filling and carrying sandbags.

After they passed the support line, the hitherto silent men began to talk incessantly. At reserve they got permission to smoke. Each grabbed in his pockets for a fag, and lighted it as he stumbled along the uneven duck-boards. After what seemed an endless journey to Winterbourne, they reached the four steps, climbed up, and emerged into the now familiar ruined street. It was silent and rather ghostly in the very pale light of the new moon. They dumped their picks and shovels, went to the cook to draw their ration of hot tea, which was served from a large black dixie and tasted unpleasantly of stew. They filed past the officer, who gave each of them a rum ration.

Winterbourne drank some of the tea in his billet, then took off his boots, wrapped himself up, and drank the rest. Some real warmth flushed into his chilled body. He was angry with himself for being so tired, after a cushy night on a cushy front. He wondered what Elizabeth and Fanny would say if they saw his animal gratitude for tea and rum. Fanny? Elizabeth? They had receded far from him; not so far as all the other people he knew, who had receded to several light years, but very far. "Elizabeth" and "Fanny" were now memories and names at the foot of sympathetic but rather remote letters. Drowsiness came rapidly upon him, and he fell asleep as he was thinking of the curious zwiss, zwiss made by machine-gun bullets passing overhead. He did not hear the two howitzers when they fired a dozen rounds before dawn.

THE INDOMITABLE TWEEDY

by A. P. (Alan Patrick) Herbert

Herbert (1890–1971) served in the British Royal Navy and became a lawyer and renowned author after the war. The hero of the piece is a hard-drinking "character."

[The story was first published in *Great Short Stories of the War: England, France, Germany, America*. London: Eyre & Spottiswoode, 1930.]

LATE ON THE second night they reached the Estaminet Rouge at Neuvillette, Kenneth tired and sober now, Geoffrey full of uneasy reflections. Even that village and that estaminet had their special history, tragic, comic, unforgettable. Here the transport had been quartered that December; here old Knight, the Quartermaster, had had his billet; and here was enacted, in this very room, that final scene in the ancient legend of Tweedy.

Madeleine remembered Tweedy—Madeleine the pink, the patient, the for ever agreeable genius of the house. Madeleine was still there, just the same age—and Madame, a little older, with all those nameless bottles behind her. Only Monsieur was not there. Monsieur had been a *prisonnier* in those old days, and always just about to come back. But he was not there.

Madeleine remembered Tweedy; and "Oh, la, la!" she said, with a shrug and a twinkle, very eloquent. It had happened after Kenneth's time, and Geoffrey in low tones recounted the legend again; his voice rambled in ghostly echoes about the bare and empty room.

Tweedy was a veteran of the War. He went out with the Regiment to the East in the early spring of 1915, a mature business man of thirty-five, a married man, and a capable company commander. Though racked with dysentery, he survived nine months of the East. Too ill to eat, to useful to be sent away, and too stubborn to "go sick" himself, he took to drink. The drink carried him through that campaign and destroyed him in the next. Arrived in

108

France, he found himself almost the sole survivor of those old cronies with whom he had begun the War. Within a few weeks the few veterans who remained had gone wounded or dead. They gave place to prim, distrustful senior officers with whom he had no sympathy, and young boys who did not drink. Tweedy felt himself alone. He consoled himself. Consolation, in France, was easily obtained. Always, till now, he had somehow managed to keep himself and his company efficient; but now, too generously consoled, the breaking-up of Tweedy began. He grew hazy about orders; his company, the best in the battalion, became slack and discontented. Over and over again he was on the verge of disaster; miraculously he escaped. Junior officers, because of his kindly good humour, his known courage and capacity, and the regimental tradition of "the old Tweedy," screened him from detection; and still he managed to keep a hold on himself in the line. He reserved his worst bouts for the villages behind; but so soon as his men were settled in their billets, then you would find Tweedy settled in his estaminet, bandying fuddled jokes with the French interpreter. It could not go on. But it was difficult to stop. He was seldom positively drunk, though it could never be said that he was positively sober; he simply lived in a fog. Senior officers and courts-martial require something more tangible than fog to act upon.

It would have been easier to dispose of a less resolute character. He was tucked away in the rear, in odd posts, as Town Major, as Salvage Officer, as this and that. But Tweedy was a fighter; he insisted on remaining with the fighting troops, however uncongenial. Sooner or later he managed to get himself returned to the battalion. And at last he was drunk—and detected—in the line.

Characteristically, his delinquency took the form of a flat refusal to leave the line when his company was relieved by troops of another regiment; and he was under the delusion, often and violently expressed, that the relieving officer, a complete stranger, was inefficient and unfit to take over the line. That having been formally conceded, and not till then, he was induced by two young officers of his own company to return to billets and placed under arrest.

Justice rubbed her hands. Tweedy had delivered himself at last. The heavy wheels of court-martial machinery slowly began to move. No more miracles.

But that Bacchic genius which had watched over Tweedy so long had not forgotten him yet. The evidence against him was strong—the company commander of the relieving regiment and his sergeant-major, and Tweedy's two young officers. It was strong; but it was mortal. The sergeant-major was sent to England for a protracted course of instruction in a cadet corps. A few days later his commander was killed.

There remained the two young officers, boys both of them, and gallant fellows. Murray and Foster were their names, and they were firm friends.

Six weeks passed, and during that time the division was moved many miles to the south, marching the whole way. Tweedy marched every day with the transport, like some great exhibition ox, silent and lowering; and at the end of every day was formally shut up under a sentry. Nothing could be done during that march, and at the end of it the wheels of Justice seemed to have ceased from moving. There was a long inexplicable delay. Perhaps the papers had been lost during the move; perhaps the Colonel had interceded on Tweedy's behalf; perhaps there had been a change in the Divisional Staff; perhaps there was a flaw in the case; perhaps the authorities had forgotten all about it. . . . No one knew.

But, because of the delay, the rigour of his confinement was relaxed; he was able to mix with his fellow-officers, to walk abroad. But he had no duties, and he was able to obtain a certain amount of consolation, though at this stage he kept a careful hand on himself.

Those two boys would stroll into some estaminet and greet him with respectful "sirs"; and he would give them a genial growl, a wave of the hand, and they would talk together about the company. He was courageous, he was a legendary figure, with a past behind him; and perhaps, young as they were, they recognised and admired in him the imperviousness, the Titanic solidity with which he confronted this last assault of Retribution. Seeing them altogether, you would never have believed that those two were the chosen instruments of his disgrace. And, for his part, it is certain that he bore them nothing but a kind of fatherly affection.

There followed for the battalion a period of hard work and heavy fighting. In and out, in and out—for a month the rests were few and very brief: sometimes a day, sometimes two. No one had the time to deal with Tweedy; no officer could be spared from the fighting-line to give evidence against a drunkard; he was indeed forgotten. His confinement became a mere form; practically he was free—free of the village, free of the Estaminet Rouge. . . . At the end of the first week young Foster was shot dead by a sniper.

After that the battalion came out for a brief rest. The legend ran that, just before they went back, young Murray came into that estaminet, that very room, and said a special good-bye to Tweedy. A fine young fellow, brown face, hazel eyes, and all the freshness of a schoolboy, he was feeling bitterly the loss of his friend; and he came in there to say good-bye because he had had "a presentiment" about

himself. They said he stood and looked at Tweedy in a kind of superstitious awe. He had determined now in his own mind that nothing
could touch Tweedy; Tweedy was immune, miraculously immune.
And by that immunity he, young Murray, was doomed, as Foster had
been doomed before him. They were meant to be the instruments of
a miracle, not of a disgrace—one of Tweedy's miracles.

Yet, in that conviction, he held out his hand to Tweedy and said
his good-bye without scorn, without resentment, even with warmth—
as if he realised that Tweedy, too, was in his way the miserable pawn
of circumstance. And Tweedy put down his glass and said: "Good-
bye, old boy. . . . I wish I could come with you." Which was perfectly
true. He waved a vague, encouraging hand as the lad went out, certain
that he was going to his death. Then he picked up his glass again.

What were his thoughts? Had he any thoughts? If the significance of
that parting penetrated at all that stolid ox-like mask, he gave no sign.
He spoke seldom. No man knew what was in his mind. Indeed, in the
ten days which followed few men saw him. Knight, the Quartermaster,
harassed and overworked, had his hasty meals with him, and saw him
occasionally as he passed through to his billet, sitting at that corner
table, utterly alone, heavy-jawed, robust, impassive, his thick legs
crossed, his head thrust forward, the little disc of baldness glowing
faintly at the back like the rising of the moon. Only the French interpreter bore him regular company, and drank him glass for glass, a sal-
low, wicked little man. Knight hated that, for M—— was a cheap soul,
and Tweedy was still a giant in his way. He puzzled Knight. Then, of
all times, he should have been a figure of contempt, but he remained a
pathetic figure. He regarded himself so obviously as a victim, misun-
derstood, misused, abandoned. No man had seen him ashamed.

He heard the guns all day; from Knight, with interest, he heard a
little news of the battalion's doings—casualties, successes; and when
his old company had done some notable thing, he sat up with conscious pride, and called for some more of the cheap champagne. He
heard that young Murray was in command of the company, had
shown great bravery, was certain of distinction; but one must suppose
that he gave no special thought to the fate of that young officer.

Yet it was odd that from the day of that good-bye he began to
drink heavily again; the control he had painfully regained during his
captivity collapsed; the old fuddle returned. He seemed to dwell now
continually in the past, Knight said; with that vague wave of the hand,
in scraps of sentences which had no verb, no end, and no beginning,
he mumbled reminiscences of "the old days," the old cronies—
Richards, Mortimer, Wallace. . . . All gone. And one night, when a
terrible din broke out up the line, he remembered suddenly his old

valour, and, lurching determinedly to the door, he shouted thickly that he was going up to join his company. The French interpreter sniggered in a corner; and halfway to the door Tweedy had forgotten his purpose. He sank abruptly into a chair and resumed his long vigil—waiting, waiting for the evidence to die.

But young Murray rode back into the village with the battalion; he rode back at the head of the company, in Tweedy's place, on Tweedy's horse—proud of himself, ashamed of himself. He knew that he had done well, but he had gone out with a fixed presentiment of death, as many other men have gone—Geoffrey paused there, thinking of the Stout Heart—he had spoken of that certitude to others; and no doubt, like Geoffrey, he was conscious of an uneasy, irrational disquiet, as if Fate had made a fool of him, as if he had failed to keep a promise. But, after all, he was alive.

They marched past the Estaminet Rouge on their way to billets, and Tweedy, blear-eyed and unashamed, stood in the doorway to see them go by. Young Murray rode erect on Tweedy's black horse, and some imp of mischief made him give the order "Eyes left!" as they trudged past their old commander. And Knight said that when the boy gravely made his own salute there was a mocking gleam in his eyes that seemed to say, "At any rate, I have cheated *you*, old monster! I have scotched the miracle. . . ."

For they were going out of the line for a long rest. There was no escape for Tweedy now.

But while young Murray rode back from the scattered billets of his men a German aeroplane flew over the village. The British guns opened fire, and the heavy fuse of a British shell hit him on the temple. He was killed instantly. And Tweedy was released from arrest without a stain on his character.

"What happened to him afterwards?" said Kenneth at the end.

"A few days later he fell off that same black horse and broke his leg. That saved him. . . . He's back at his business now, and leads, I believe, a perfectly blameless and sober life. . . . At Sydenham. As soon as he got away from the War he was all right. . . ."

The lamp had fallen low. It seemed cold in that room—the place where Tweedy had kept his unholy vigil. In some corner a mouse made stealthy noises. They shivered a little, while they peered about them into the deep shadows, as if the young ghost of Murray might steal out into the light, dumbly demanding the meaning of his end.

And, pondering the unspeakable irony of that story, they lit their candles and went silently to bed.

PINK FLANNEL

by Ford Madox Ford

Ford Madox Ford (1873–1939), born Ford Hermann Hueffer, was one of the most well-known British writers who went to war; he served on the French Front in a Welsh infantry battalion. Before the war he wrote his famous novel The Good Soldier. *This story centers around a soldier's all-consuming preoccupation with the loss of a personal letter amid a bombardment of the trenches.*

[Ford Madox Ford. *War Prose*. Carcanet Press, 1999.
Originally published in the magazine *Land and Water*, 72, May 8, 1919.]

W. L. JAMES waved his penny candle round the dark tent and the shadow of the pole moved in queer angles on the canvas sides.

It was a great worry—it was more than a worry! to have lost Mrs. Wilkinson's letter. There was very little in the tent—and still less that the letter could be in. When Caradoc Morris had brought him the letter in the front line, W. L. James had had with him, of what the tent now contained, only his trench coat, his tunic, and his shirts, of things that could contain letters. It could not be in the dirty collection of straps and old clothes that were in his valise; it could not be in his wash-basin or in his flea-bag. And he had not even read Mrs. Wilkinson's letter! Caradoc Morris had come down from the first Line Transport, and had given it to him at the very beginning of the strafe that had lasted two days. The sentry on the right had called out: "Rum Jar, left," and he and Morris had bolted up the communication trench at the very moment when, holding in his hand the longed-for envelope, he had recognised the hand-writing of the address. He knew he had put it somewhere for safety.

But where? Where the devil *could* you put a letter for safety in a beastly trench? In your trench coat—in your tunic—in your breeches pocket. There *was* not anywhere else.

He was tired: he was dog-tired. He was always dog-tired, anyhow, when he came out of the Front Line. Now he felt relaxed all over: dropping, for next morning he was going on ninety-six hours' leave and, for the moment, that seemed like an eternity of slackness. So that he could let himself go.

He could have let himself go altogether if he had not lost Mrs. Wilkinson's letter—or even if he had known what it contained. . . . He did not suppose, even if he had dropped it in the trench, that any-one would who picked it up would make evil use of it—forward it to Mrs. Wilkinson's husband, say? On the other hand, they might? . . .

He took off his tunic, his boots, and his puttees, and let himself, feet forward into his flea-bag. He blew out the candle that he had stuck on to the top of his tin hat. A triangle of stars became important before his eyes. The night was full of the babble of voices. He heard one voice call: "The major wants: *Mr. Britling Sees It Through.*" . . . The machine-guns said: "Wukka! Wukka!" under the pale stars, as if their voices were part of the stillness. The stars rose swiftly in the triangle of sky; they hung for a long time, then descended or went out. Much noise existed for a moment. He said to himself that the Hun had got the wind up, and, whilst he began to worry once more about the letter, as it were, with nearly all his brain, one spot of it said: "That insistent 'Wukka! Wukka!' to the right is from Wytschaete: the intermittent one is our 'G' trenches . . . There's an HE going to the top of Kemmel Hill. . . ."

So his mind made before his eyes pictures of the Flanders plain; the fact that the Germans were alarmed at the idea of a sudden raid—that our machine-guns were answering theirs—that their gunners were putting over some random shells from 4.2s. Presently our own 99-pounders or naval guns or something would shut them up. Then they would all be quiet. . . . A sense of deep and voluptuous security had descended on him. Out there, when you have nothing else to worry you, you calculate the chances: rifle fire 20 to 1 against MGs 30: Rum Jars 40; FA 70 against a shot of flying iron. Now his mind registered the fact that the chances of direct hits was nil, or bits of flying iron, 250 to 1 against—and his mind put the idea to sleep, as it were . . . He was in support. . . .

The noise continued—there were some big thumps away to the right. Our artillery was waking up. But the voices from the tents were audible: tranquil conversations about strafes, about Cardiff, about ship owners' profits, about the Divisional "Follies" . . . The Divisional "Follies"!

He would be going to the "Ambassadors"—with Mrs. Wilkinson—within twenty-four hours if he had any luck . . . GSO II had

promised to run him from Bailleul to Boulogne: he would catch the
one-o'clock leave boat; he would be in Town—Town—Town!—by
six. Mrs. Wilkinson would meet him on the platform. He would
keep her waiting twenty minutes in the vestibule of his hotel while
he had a quick bath. By 6.45 they would be dining together; she
would be looking at him across the table with her exciting eyes that
had dark pupils and yellow-brown iris! Her chin would be upon her
hands with the fingers interlocked. Then they would be in the dress
circle of the theatre—looking down on the nearly darkened stage
from which, nevertheless, a warm light would well upwards upon
her face. . . . And she would be warm, beside him, her hand touching
his hand amongst her furs. . . . And her white shoulders. . . . And
they would whisper, her hair just touching his ear. . . . And be warm.
. . . Warm!

And then. . . . Damn! Damn! Oh, damnation! . . . He had lost her
letter. . . . He did not know if she would meet him. . . . If she cared.
. . . If she cared still—or had ever cared. . . . He rolled over and
writhed in the long grass in which his flea-bag was laid. . . . The
pounding outside grew furious. . . . There seemed to be hundreds of
stars—and more and more and more shooting up into the triangle of
the tent-flap. He could see a pallid light shining down the blanket that
covered his legs. . . . And then, like a piece of madness, the earth
moved beneath him as if his bed had been kicked, and a hard sound
seemed to hammer his skull. . . . An immense, familiar sound—august
as if a God had spoken benevolently, the echoes going away among
the woodlands. And the immense shell whined over his head, as if a
railway train or the Yeth hounds were going on a long journey. . . .

The Very lights died down, the shell whined further and further
towards the plains; it seemed as if a dead silence fell. A voice said:
"Somebody's ducking out there!" and the voices began to talk again
in the dead silence that fell on the battle-field.

But his thoughts raged blackly. He was certain that Mrs. Wilkinson
would not meet him. . . . Then all his leave would be mucked up.
He imagined himself—he felt himself—arriving at Victoria, in the
half-light of the great barn, in the jostling crowd, with all the black
shadows, all sweeping up towards the barrier. And there would be a
beastly business with three coppers in a cramped telephone box. And
the voice of her maid saying that her mistress was out. . . . Where, in
God's name, had he put the letter? . . .

He tried to memorise exactly what had happened—but it ended at
that. . . . Caradoc Morris who had come back from a course, had
brought the letter down to the trench from the 1st Line Transport.
He had just looked at the envelope. Then the sentry had yelled out.

And he remembered distinctly that he had done something with the letter. But what? What?

The rum jar had bumped off: then gas had come over: then a Hun raid. They had got into the front line and it had taken hours to bomb and bayonet them out, and to work the beastly sandbags of that God-forsaken line into some semblance of a parapet again—a period of sweating and swearing, and the stink of gas, and shoving corpses out of the way. . . . His mind considered with horror what he could do if Mrs. Wilkinson refused to see him altogether. And it went on and on. . . .

He couldn't sleep. Then he said a prayer to St. Anthony—a thing he had not done since he had been a little boy in the Benedictine School at Ramsgate. The pale stars surveyed him from their triangle. One Very light ascended slowly over the dark plain. . . .

He was standing in Piccadilly, looking into a window from which there welled a blaze of light. Skirts brushed him then receded. An elderly, fat man in a brown cassock, with a bald head, a rope around the waist and a crook from which depended a gourd, was gazing into the window beside him. This saint remarked:

"You perceive? Pink flannel!"

The whole window, the whole shop—which was certainly Swan and Edgar's—was a deluge of pink—a rather odious pink with bluey suggestions. A pink that was unmistakable if ever you had seen any-thing like it. . . .

"Pink!" the saint said: "Bluey pink!"

Yes: there were pink monticules, pink watersheds, cascades of pink flannel, deserts, wild crevasses, perspectives. . . .

W. L. James looked at St. Anthony with deep anxiety: he was excited, he was bewildered. The saint continued to point a plump finger, and the crowd all around tittered.

The saint slowly ascended towards a black heaven that was filled with the beams from searchlights. . . .

And W. L. James found himself running madly in his stockinged feet, in the long grass beside the ditch to the tent at the head of the line. "Caradoc!" he was calling out "Caradoc Morris! Where the hell is my Field Service Pocket-Book?"

He got it out of the tunic pocket of his friend, who was in a dead sleep. He pulled a letter from the pocket that is under the pink flannel intended to hold a supply of pins. Holding the letter towards the candle that was at Caradoc's head, he read—as a man drinks after long hours on a hot road. . . .

And, as he stumbled slowly among tent ropes, he remembered that forgotten moment of his life. He remembered saying to himself— even as the sentry shouted "Rum jar: left," in the harsh Welsh accent that is like the croak of a raven—saying to himself: "I *must* put this letter safely away." And, before he had run, he had pulled out the FSPB, had undone the rubber bands, and had placed the unopened envelope in the little pocket that is under the pink flannel, "intended," as the inscription says, "to hold a supply of pins" . . .

He stood still beside his fleabag for a minute as the full remembrance came back to him. And a queer, as it were clean and professional satisfaction crept over him. Before, he had remembered only the, as it were, panic of running—though it was perfectly correct to run—up the communication trench. Now he saw that, even under that panic, he had been capable of a collected—ordered, and as it were, generous action. For he had tried to shield to the best of his ability the woman he loved at the cost of quite great danger to himself.

For the rum jar had flattened out the wretched sandbags of the trench exactly where he had been standing.

Later, of course, he had lent the pocket-book to Caradoc Morris— who was the sort of chap who never would have a pocket-book—for the purpose of writing a report to BHQ. . . . But he had certainly behaved well. . . .

He said to himself:

"By jove, I may be worthy of her even yet," and getting back into his fleabag, after he had pulled off his socks, which had been wetted by the dewy grass, he fell into pleasurable fancies of softly lighted restaurants, of small orchestras, of gentle contacts of hands and the soft glances of eyes that had dark pupils and brown iris. . . .

That is, mostly, the way war goes!

BLIND

by Mary Borden

The American author Mary Borden (1886–1968) was a millionaire's daughter who served as a nurse in a field hospital she paid for and established in France. This short story is based on her experience of the dazing horrors a nurse had to steel herself against; the narrator continually notes how "It didn't do to think." Although Borden wrote of her experiences during the war, she did not publish the writings until more than ten years later.

[From Borden's *The Forbidden Zone*. London: Heinemann, 1929.]

THE DOOR AT the end of the *baraque* kept opening and shutting to let in the stretcher-bearers. As soon as it opened a crack the wind scurried in and came hopping toward me across the bodies of the men that covered the floor, nosing under the blankets, lifting the flaps of heavy coats, and burrowing among the loose heaps of clothing and soiled bandages. Then the grizzled head of a stretcher-bearer would appear, butting its way in, and he would emerge out of the black storm into the bright fog that seemed to fill the place, dragging the stretcher after him, and then the old one at the other end of the load would follow, and they would come slowly down the centre of the hut looking for a clear place on the floor.

The men were laid out in three rows on either side of the central alley way. It was a big hut, and there were about sixty stretchers in each row. There was space between the heads of one row and the feet of another row, but no space to pass between the stretchers in the same row; they touched. The old territorials who worked with me passed up and down between the heads and feet. I had a squad of thirty of these old orderlies and two sergeants and two priests, who were expert dressers. Wooden screens screened off the end of the hut opposite the entrance. Behind these were the two dressing tables where the priests dressed the wounds of the new arrivals and got them

118

ready for the surgeons, after the old men had undressed them and washed their feet. In one corner was my kitchen where I kept all my syringes and hypodermic needles and stimulants.

It was just before midnight when the stretcher-bearers brought in the blind man, and there was no space on the floor anywhere; so they stood waiting, not knowing what to do with him.

I said from the floor in the second row: "Just a minute, old ones. You can put him here in a minute." So they waited with the blind man suspended in the bright, hot, misty air between them, like a pair of old horses in shafts with their heads down, while the little boy who had been crying for his mother died with his head on my breast. Perhaps he thought the arms holding him when he jerked back and died belonged to some woman I had never seen, some woman waiting somewhere for news of him in some village, somewhere in France. How many women, I wondered, were waiting out there in the distance for news of these men who were lying on the floor? But I stopped thinking about this the minute the boy was dead. It didn't do to think. I didn't as a rule, but the boy's very young voice had startled me. It had come through to me as a real voice will sound sometimes through a dream, almost waking you, but now it had stopped, and the dream was thick round me again, and I laid him down, covered his face with the brown blanket, and called two other old ones.

"Put this one in the corridor to make more room here," I said; and I saw them lift him up. When they had taken him away, the stretcher-bearers who had been waiting brought the blind one and put him down in the cleared space. They had to come round to the end of the front row and down between the row of feet and row of heads; they had to be very careful where they stepped; they had to lower the stretcher cautiously so as not to jostle the men on either side (there was just room), but these paid no attention. None of the men lying packed together on the floor noticed each other in this curious dream-place.

I had watched this out of the corner of my eye, busy with something that was not very like a man. The limbs seemed to be held together only by the strong stuff of the uniform. The head was unrecognisable. It was a monstrous thing, and a dreadful rattling sound came from it. I looked up and saw the chief surgeon standing over me. I don't know how he got there. His small shrunken face was wet and white; his eyes were brilliant and feverish; his incredible hands that saved so many men so exquisitely, so quickly, were in the pockets of his white coat.

"Give him morphine," he said, "a double dose. As much as you like." He pulled a cigarette out of his pocket. "In cases like this, if I am not about, give morphine; enough, you understand." Then he vanished like a ghost. He went back to his operating room, a small white figure with round shoulders, a magician, who performed miracles with knives. He went away through the dream.

I gave the morphine, then crawled over and looked at the blind man's ticket. I did not know, of course, that he was blind until I read his ticket. A large round white helmet covered the top half of his head and face; only his nostrils and mouth and chin were uncovered. The surgeon in the dressing station behind the trenches had written on his ticket, "Shot through the eyes. Blind."

Did he know? I asked myself. No, he couldn't know yet. He would still be wondering, waiting, hoping, down there in that deep, dark silence of his, in his own dark personal world. He didn't know he was blind; no one would have told him. I felt his pulse. It was strong and steady. He was a long, thin man, but his body was not very cold and the pale lower half of his clear-cut face was not very pale. There was something beautiful about him. In his case there was no hurry, no necessity to rush him through to the operating room. There was plenty of time. He would always be blind.

One of the orderlies was going up and down with hot tea in a bucket. I beckoned to him.

I said to the blind one: "Here is a drink." He didn't hear me, so I said it more loudly against the bandage, and helped him lift his head, and held the tin cup to his mouth below the thick edge of the bandage. I did not think then of what was hidden under the bandage. I think of it now. Another head case across the hut had thrown off his blanket and risen from his stretcher. He was standing stark naked except for his head bandage, in the middle of the hut, and was haranguing the crowd in a loud voice with the gestures of a political orator. But the crowd, lying on the floor, paid no attention to him. They did not notice him. I called to Gustave and Pierre to go to him.

The blind man said to me: "Thank you, sister, you are very kind. That is good. I thank you." He had a beautiful voice. I noticed the great courtesy of his speech. But they were all courteous. Their courtesy when they died, their reluctance to cause me any trouble by dying or suffering, was one of the things it didn't do to think about.

Then I left him, and presently forgot that he was there waiting in the second row of stretchers on the left side of the long crowded floor.

Gustave and Pierre had got the naked orator back onto his stretcher and were wrapping him up again in his blankets. I let them deal with him and went back to my kitchen at the other end of the hut, where my syringes and hypodermic needles were boiling in saucepans. I had received by post that same morning a dozen beautiful new platinum needles. I was very pleased with them. I said to one of the dressers as

I fixed a needle on my syringe and held it up, squirting the liquid through it: "Look. I've some lovely new needles." He said: "Come and help me a moment. Just cut this bandage, please." I went over to his dressing-table. He darted off to a voice that was shrieking somewhere. There was a man stretched on the table. His brain came off in my hands when I lifted the bandage from his head.

When the dresser came back I said: "His brain came off on the bandage."

"Where have you put it?"

"I put it in the pail under the table."

"It's only one half of his brain," he said, looking into the man's skull. "The rest is here."

I left him to finish the dressing and went about my own business. I had much to do.

It was my business to sort out the wounded as they were brought in from the ambulances and to keep them from dying before they got to the operating rooms: it was my business to sort out the nearly dying from the dying. I was there to sort them out and tell how fast life was ebbing in them. Life was leaking away from all of them; but with some there was no hurry, with others it was a case of minutes. It was my business to create a counter-wave of life, to create the flow against the ebb. It was like a tug of war with the tide. The ebb of life was cold. When life was ebbing the man was cold; when it began to flow back he grew warm. It was all, you see, like a dream. The dying men on the floor were drowned men cast up on the beach, and there was the ebb of life pouring away over them, sucking them away, an invisible tide; and my old orderlies, like old sea-salts out of a lifeboat, were working to save them. I had to watch, to see if they were slipping, being dragged away. If a man were slipping quickly, being sucked down rapidly, I sent runners to the operating rooms. There were six operating rooms on either side of my hut. Medical students in white coats hurried back and forth along the covered corridors between us. It was my business to know which of the wounded could wait and which could not. I had to decide for myself. There was no one to tell me. If I made any mistakes, some would die on their stretchers on the floor under my eyes who need not have died. I didn't worry. I didn't think. I was too busy, too absorbed in what I was doing. I had to judge from what was written on their tickets and from the way they looked and the way they felt to my hand. My hand could tell of itself one kind of cold from another. They were all half-frozen when they arrived, but the chill of their icy flesh wasn't the same as the cold inside them when life was almost ebbed away. My hands could instantly tell the difference between the cold of the harsh bitter night and the stealthy cold of death. Then there was another thing, a small fluttering thing. I didn't think about it or count it. My fingers felt it. I was in a dream, led this way and that by my cute eyes and hands that did many things, and seemed to know what to do.

Sometimes there was no time to read the ticket or touch the pulse. The door kept opening and shutting to let in the stretcher-bearers whatever I was doing. I could not watch when I was giving *piqûres*; but, standing by my table filling a syringe, I could look down over the rough forms that covered the floor and pick out at a distance this one and that one. I had been doing this for two years, and had learned to read the signs. I could tell from the way they twitched, from the peculiar shade of a pallid face, from the look of tight pinched-in nostrils, and in other ways which I could not have explained, that this or that one was slipping over the edge of the beach of life. Then I would go quickly with my long saline needles, or short thick camphor oil needles, and send one of the old ones hurrying along the corridor to the operating rooms. But sometimes there was no need to hurry; sometimes I was too late; with some there was no longer any question of the ebb and flow of life and death; there was nothing to do.

The hospital throbbed and hummed that night like a dynamo. The operating rooms were ablaze; twelve surgical *équipes* were at work; boilers steamed and whistled; nurses hurried in and out of the sterilising rooms carrying big shining metal boxes and enamelled trays; feet were running, slower feet shuffling. The hospital was going full steam ahead. I had a sense of great power, exhilaration and excitement. A loud wind was howling. It was throwing itself like a pack of wolves against the flimsy wooden walls, and the guns were growling. Their voices were dying away. I thought of them as a pack of beaten dogs, slinking away across the dark waste where the dead were lying and the wounded who had not yet been picked up, their only cover the windy blanket of the bitter November night.

And I was happy. It seemed to me that the crazy crowded bright hot shelter was a beautiful place. I thought, "This is the second battlefield. The battle now is going on over the helpless bodies of these men. It is we who are doing the fighting now, with their real enemies." And I thought of the chief surgeon, the wizard working like lightning through the night, and all the others wielding their flashing knives against the invisible enemy. The wounded had begun to arrive at noon. It was now past midnight, and the door kept opening and shutting to let in the stretcher-bearers, and the ambulances kept lurching in at the gate. Lanterns were moving through the windy dark from shed to shed. The nurses were out there in the scattered huts, putting the men to bed when they came over the dark ground, asleep, from the operating rooms. They would wake up in clean warm beds—those who did wake up.

"We will send you the dying, the desperate, the moribund," the Inspector General had said. "You must expect a thirty per cent mortality." So we had got ready for it; we had organised to dispute that figure.

We had built brick ovens, four of them, down the centre of the hut, and on top of these, galvanised iron cauldrons of boiling water were steaming. We had driven nails all the way down the wooden posts that held up the roof and festooned the posts with red rubber hot-water bottles. In the corner near to my kitchen we had partitioned off a cubicle, where we built a light bed, a rough wooden frame lined with electric light bulbs, where a man could be cooked back to life again. My own kitchen was an arrangement of shelves for saucepans and syringes and needles of different sizes, and cardboard boxes full of ampoules of camphor oil and strychnine and caffeine and morphine, and large ampoules of sterilized salt and water, and dozens of beautiful sharp shining needles were always on the boil.

It wasn't much to look at, this reception hut. It was about as attractive as a goods yard in a railway station, but we were very proud of it, my old ones and I. We had got it ready, and it was good enough for us. We could revive the cold dead there; snatch back the men who were slipping over the edge; hoist them out of the dark abyss into life again. And because our mortality at the end of three months was only nineteen per cent, not thirty, well, it was the most beautiful place in the world to me and my old grizzled *pépères*, Gaston and Pierre and Leroux and the others were to me like shining archangels. But I didn't think about this. I think of it now. I only knew it then, and was happy. Yes, I was happy there.

Looking back, I do not understand that woman—myself—standing in that confused goods yard filled with bundles of broken human flesh. The place by one o'clock in the morning was a shambles. The air was thick with steaming sweat, with the effluvia of mud, dirt, blood. The men lay in their stiff uniforms that were caked with mud and dried blood, their great boots on their feet; stained bandages showing where a trouser leg or a sleeve had been cut away. Their faces gleamed faintly, with a faint phosphorescence. Some who could not breathe lying down were propped up on their stretchers against the wall, but most were prone on their backs, staring at the steep iron roof.

The old orderlies moved from one stretcher to another, carefully, among the piles of clothing, boots and blood-soaked bandages—careful not to step on a hand or a sprawling twisted foot. They carried zinc pails of hot water and slabs of yellow soap and scrubbing brushes.

They gathered up the heaps of clothing, and made little bundles of the small things out of pockets, or knelt humbly, washing the big yellow stinking feet that protruded from under the brown blankets. It was the business of these old ones to undress the wounded, wash them, wrap them in blankets, and put hot-water bottles at their feet and sides. It was a difficult business peeling the stiff uniform from a man whose hip or shoulder was fractured, but the old ones were careful. Their big peasant hands were gentle—very, very gentle and careful. They handled the wounded men as if they were children. Now, looking back, I see their rough powerful visages, their shaggy eyebrows, their big clumsy, gentle hands. I see them go down on their stiff knees; I hear their shuffling feet and their soft gruff voices answering the voices of the wounded, who are calling to them for drinks, or to God for mercy.

The old ones had orders from the commandant not to cut the good cloth of the uniforms if they could help it, but they had orders from me not to hurt the men, and they obeyed me. They slit up the heavy trousers and slashed across the stiff tunics with long scissors, and pulled very slowly, very carefully at the heavy boots, and the wounded men did not groan or cry out very much. They were mostly very quiet. When they did cry out they usually apologised for the annoyance of their agony. Only now and then a wind of pain would sweep over the floor, tossing the legs and arms, then subside again.

I think that woman, myself, must have been in a trance, or under some horrid spell. Her feet are lumps of fire, her face is clammy, her apron is splashed with blood; but she moves ceaselessly about with bright burning eyes and handles the dreadful wreckage of men as if in a dream. She does not seem to notice the wounds or the blood. Her eyes seem to be watching something that comes and goes and darts in and out among the prone bodies. Her eyes and her hands and her ears are alert, intent on the unseen thing that scurries and hides and jumps out of the corner on to the face of a man when she's not looking. But quick, something makes her turn. Quick, she is over there, on her knees fighting the thing off, driving it away, and now it's got another victim. It's like a dreadful game of hide and seek among the wounded. All her faculties are intent on it. The other things that are going on, she deals with automatically.

There is a constant coming and going. Medical students run in and out.

"What have you got ready?"

"I've got three knees, two spines, five abdomens, twelve heads. Here's a lung case—haemorrhage. He can't wait." She is binding the man's chest; she doesn't look up.

"Send him along."

"Pierre! Gaston! Call the stretcher-bearers to take the lung to Monsieur D——." She fastens the tight bandage, tucks the blanket quickly round the thin shoulders. The old men lift him. She hurries back to her saucepans to get a new needle.

A surgeon appears.

"Where's that knee of mine? I left it in the saucepan on the window ledge. I had boiled it up for an experiment."

"One of the orderlies must have taken it," she says, putting her old needle on to boil.

"Good God! Did he mistake it?"

"Jean, did you take a saucepan you found on the windowsill?"

"Yes, sister, I took it. I thought it was for the *casse-croûte*; it looked like a *ragoût* of *mouton*. I have it here."

"Well, it was lucky he didn't eat it. It was a knee I had cut out, you know."

It is time for the old ones' *casse-croûte*. It is after one o'clock. At one o'clock the orderlies have cups of coffee and chunks of bread and meat. They eat their supper gathered round the stoves where the iron cauldrons are boiling. The surgeons and the sisters attached to the operating rooms are drinking coffee too in the sterilising rooms. I do not want any supper. I am not hungry. I am not tired. I am busy. My eyes are busy and my fingers. I am conscious of nothing about myself but my eyes, hands and feet. My feet are a nuisance, they are swollen, hurting lumps, but my fingers are perfectly satisfactory. They are expert in the handling of frail glass ampoules and syringes and needles. I go from one man to another jabbing the sharp needles into their sides, rubbing their skins with iodine, and each time I pick my way back across their bodies to fetch a fresh needle I scan the surface of the floor where the men are spread like a carpet, for signs, for my special secret signals of death.

"Aha! I'll catch you out again," Quick, to that one. That jerking! That sudden livid hue spreading over his form. "Quick, Emile! Pierre!" I have lifted the blanket. The blood is pouring out on the floor under the stretcher. "Get the tourniquet. Hold his leg up. Now then, tight—tighter. Now call the stretcher-bearers."

Someone near is having a fit. Is it epilepsy? I don't know. His mouth is frothy. His eyes are rolling. He tries to fling himself on the floor. He falls with a thud across his neighbour, who does not notice. The man just beyond propped up against the wall, watches as if from a great distance. He has a gentle patient face; this spectacle does not concern him.

The door keeps opening and shutting to let in the stretcher-bearers. The wounded are carried in at the end door and are carried out to the operating rooms at either side. The sergeant is counting the treasures out of a dead man's pockets. He is tying his little things, his letters and *briquet*, etc., up in a handkerchief. Some of the old ones are munching their bread and meat in the centre of the hut under the electric light. The others are busy with their pails and scissors. They shuffle about, kneeling, scrubbing, filling hot-water bottles. I see it all through a mist. It is misty but eternal. It is a scene in eternity, in some strange dream-hell where I am glad to be employed, where I belong, where I am happy. How crowded together we are here. How close we are in this nightmare. The wounded are packed into this place like sardines, and we are so close to them, my old ones and I. I've never been so close before to human beings. We are locked together, the old ones and I, and the wounded men; we are bound together. We all feel it. We all know it. The same thing is throbbing in us, the single thing, the one life. We are one body, suffering and bleeding. It is a kind of bliss to me to feel this. I am a little delirious, but my head is cool enough, it seems to me.

"No, not that one. He can wait. Take the next one to Monsieur D——, and this one to Monsieur Guy, and this one to Monsieur Robert. We will put this one on the electric light bed; he has no pulse. More hot-water bottles here, Gaston."

"Do you feel cold, *mon vieux*?"

"Yes, I think so, but pray do not trouble."

I go with him into the little cubicle, turn on the light bulbs, leave him to cook there; and as I come out again to face the strange heaving dream, I suddenly hear a voice calling me, a new far-away hollow voice.

"Sister! My sister! Where are you?"

I am startled. It sounds so faraway, so hollow and so sweet. It sounds like a bell high up in the mountains. I do not know where it comes from. I look down over the rows of men lying on their backs, one close to the other, packed together on the floor, and I cannot tell where the voice comes from. Then I hear it again.

"Sister! Oh, my sister, where are you?"

A lost voice. The voice of a lost man, wandering in the mountains, in the night. It is the blind man calling. I had forgotten him. I had forgotten that he was there. He could wait. The others could not wait. So I had left him and forgotten him.

Something in his voice made me run, made my heart miss a beat. I ran down the centre alleyway, round and up again, between the two rows, quickly, carefully stepping across to him over the stretchers that separated us. He was in the second row. I could just squeeze through to him.

"I am coming," I called to him. "I am coming."

I knelt beside him. "I am here," I said; but he lay quite still on his back; he didn't move at all; he hadn't heard me. So I took his hand and put my mouth close to his bandaged head and called to him with desperate entreaty.

"I am here. What is it? What is the matter?"

He didn't move even then, but he gave a long shuddering sigh of relief.

"I thought I had been abandoned here, all alone," he said softly in his faraway voice.

I seemed to awake then. I looked round me and began to tremble, as one would tremble if one awoke with one's head over the edge of a precipice. I saw the wounded packed round us, hemming us in. I saw his comrades, thick round him, and the old ones shuffling about, working and munching their hunks of bread, and the door opening to let in the stretcher-bearers. The light poured down on the rows of faces. They gleamed faintly. Four hundred faces were staring up at the roof, side by side. The blind man didn't know. He thought he was alone, out in the dark. That was the precipice, that reality.

"You are not alone," I lied. "There are many of your comrades here, and I am here, and there are doctors and nurses. You are with friends here, not alone."

"I thought," he murmured in that faraway voice, "that you had gone away and forgotten me, and that I was abandoned here alone."

My body rattled and jerked like a machine out of order. I was awake now, and I seemed to be breaking to pieces.

"No," I managed to lie again. "I had not forgotten you, nor left you alone." And I looked down again at the visible half of his face and saw that his lips were smiling.

At that I fled from him. I ran down the long, dreadful hut and hid behind my screen and cowered, sobbing, in a corner, hiding my face.

The old ones were very troubled. They didn't know what to do. Presently I heard them whispering:

"She is tired," one said.

"Yes, she is tired."

"She should go off to bed," another said.

"We will manage somehow without her," they said.

Then one of them timidly stuck a grizzled head round the corner of the screen. He held his tin cup in his hands. It was full of hot coffee. He held it out, offering it to me. He didn't know of anything else that he could do for me.

MARY POSTGATE

by Rudyard Kipling

Rudyard Kipling (1865–1936) did not serve in the war, but lent his fame and talent as a writer to Britain's War Propaganda Bureau. His son John, meanwhile, enlisted in the British Army's Irish Guards and was killed in France in 1915. The Germans began bombing England by air at the end of 1914; they used zeppelins in 1915 and 1916, and then made greater use of bomber planes in 1917 and early 1918.

[From Kipling's *A Diversity of Creatures*. Garden City, New York:
Doubleday, Page and Company, 1917.]

OF MISS MARY POSTGATE, Lady McCausland wrote that she was "thoroughly conscientious, tidy, companionable, and ladylike. I am very sorry to part with her, and shall always be interested in her welfare."

Miss Fowler engaged her on this recommendation, and to her surprise, for she had had experience of companions, found that it was true. Miss Fowler was nearer sixty than fifty at the time, but though she needed care she did not exhaust her attendant's vitality. On the contrary, she gave out, stimulatingly and with reminiscences. Her father had been a minor Court official in the days when the Great Exhibition of 1851 had just set its seal on Civilisation made perfect. Some of Miss Fowler's tales, none the less, were not always for the young. Mary was not young, and though her speech was as colourless as her eyes or her hair, she was never shocked. She listened unflinchingly to every one; said at the end, "How interesting!" or "How shocking!" as the case might be, and never again referred to it, for she prided herself on a trained mind, which "did not dwell on these things." She was, too, a treasure at domestic accounts, for which the village tradesmen, with their weekly books, loved her not. Otherwise she had no enemies; provoked no jealousy even among the plainest; neither gossip nor slander had ever been traced to her; she supplied the odd place at the Rector's or the Doctor's table at half an hour's notice; she was a sort of public aunt to very many small children of the village street, whose parents, while accepting everything, would have been swift to resent what they called "patronage"; she served on the Village Nursing Committee as Miss Fowler's nominee when Miss Fowler was crippled by rheumatoid arthritis, and came out of six months' fort-nightly meetings equally respected by all the cliques.

And when Fate threw Miss Fowler's nephew, an unlovely orphan of eleven, on Miss Fowler's hands, Mary Postgate stood to her share of the business of education as practiced in private and public schools. She checked printed clothes-lists, and unitemised bills of extras; wrote to Head and House masters, matrons, nurses, and doctors, and grieved or rejoiced over half-term reports. Young Wyndham Fowler repaid her in his holidays by calling her "Gatepost," "Postey," or "Packthread," by thumping her between her narrow shoulders or by chasing her bleating, round the garden, her large mouth open, her large nose high in air at a stiff-necked shamble very like a camel's. Later on he filled the house with clamour, argument, and harangues as to his personal needs, likes and dislikes, and the limitations of "you women," reducing Mary to tears of physical fatigue, or, when he chose to be humorous, of helpless laughter. At crises, which multiplied as he grew older, she was his ambassadress and his interpretress to Miss Fowler, who had no large sympathy with the young; a vote in his interest at the councils on his future; his sewing-woman, strictly accountable for mislaid boots and garments; always his butt and his slave.

And when he decided to become a solicitor, and had entered an office in London; when his greeting had changed from "Hullo, Postey, you old beast," to "Mornin', Packthread," there came a war which, unlike all wars that Mary could remember, did not stay decently outside England and in the newspapers, but intruded on the lives of people whom she knew. As she said to Miss Fowler, it was "most vexatious." It took the Rector's son who was going into business with his elder brother; it took the Colonel's nephew on the eve of fruit-farming in Canada; it took Mrs. Grant's son who, his mother said, was devoted to the ministry; and, very early indeed, it took Wynn Fowler, who announced on a postcard that he had joined the Flying Corps and wanted a cardigan waistcoat.

"He must go, and he must have the waistcoat," said Miss Fowler. So Mary got the proper-sized needles and wool, while Miss Fowler told the men of her establishment—two gardeners and an odd man, aged sixty—that those who could join the Army had better do so. The gardeners left. Cheape, the odd man, stayed on, and was promoted to the gardener's cottage. The cook, scorning to be limited in luxuries, also left, after a spirited scene with Miss Fowler, and took the house-maid with her. Miss Fowler gazetted Nellie, Cheape's seventeen-year-old daughter, to the vacant post; Mrs. Cheape to the rank of cook with occasional cleaning bouts; and the reduced establishment moved forward smoothly.

Wynn demanded an increase in his allowance. Miss Fowler, who always looked facts in the face, said, "He must have it. The chances are he won't live long to draw it, and if three hundred makes him happy—".

Wynn was grateful, and came over, in his tight-buttoned uniform, to say so. His training centre was not thirty miles away, and his talk was so technical that it had to be explained by charts of the various types of machines. He gave Mary such a chart.

"And you'd better study it, Postey," he said. "You'll be seeing a lot of 'em soon." So Mary studied the chart, but when Wynn next arrived to swell and exalt himself before his womenfolk, she failed badly in cross-examination, and he rated her as in the old days.

"You *look* more or less like a human being," he said in his new Service voice. "You *must* have had a brain at some time in your past. What have you done with it? Where'd you keep it? A sheep would know more than you do, Postey. You're lamentable. You are less use than an empty tin can, you dowey old cassowary."

"I suppose that's how your superior officer talks to *you*?" said Miss Fowler from her chair.

"But Postey doesn't mind," Wynn replied. "Do you, Packthread?"

"Why? Was Wynn saying anything? I shall get this right next time you come," she muttered, and knitted her pale brows again over the diagrams of Taubes, Farmans, and Zeppelins.

In a few weeks the mere land and sea battles which she read to Miss Fowler after breakfast passed her like idle breath. Her heart and her interest were high in the air with Wynn, who had finished "rolling" (whatever that might be) and gone on from a "taxi" to a machine more or less his own. One morning it circled over their very chimneys, alighted on Vegg's Heath, almost outside the garden gate, and Wynn came in, blue with cold, shouting for food. He and she drew Miss Fowler's bath-chair, as they had often done, along the Heath foot-path to look at the biplane. Mary observed that "it smelt very badly."

"Postey, I believe you think with your nose," said Wynn. "I know you don't with your mind. Now, what type's that?"

"I'll go and get the chart," said Mary.

"You're hopeless! You haven't the mental capacity of a white mouse," he cried, and explained the dials and the sockets for bomb-dropping till it was time to mount and ride the wet clouds once more.

"Ah!" said Mary, as the stinking thing flared upward. "Wait till our Flying Corps gets to work! Wynn says it's much safer than in the trenches."

"I wonder," said Miss Fowler. "Tell Cheape to come and tow me home again."

"It's all downhill. I can do it," said Mary, "if you put the brake on." She laid her lean self against the pushing-bar and home they trundled.

"Now, be careful you aren't heated and catch a chill," said over-dressed Miss Fowler.

"Nothing makes me perspire," said Mary. As she bumped the chair under the porch she straightened her long back. The exertion had given her a colour, and the wind had loosened a wisp of hair across her forehead. Miss Fowler glanced at her.

"What do you ever think of, Mary?" she demanded suddenly.

"Oh, Wynn says he wants another three pairs of stockings—as thick as we can make them."

"Yes. But I mean the things that women think about. Here you are, more than forty—"

"Forty-four," said truthful Mary.

"Well?"

"Well?" Mary offered Miss Fowler her shoulder as usual.

"And you've been with me ten years now."

"Let's see," said Mary. "Wynn was eleven when he came. He's twenty now, and I came two years before that. It must be eleven."

"Eleven! And you've never told me anything that matters in all that while. Looking back, it seems to me that *I've* done all the talking."

"I'm afraid I'm not much of a conversationalist. As Wynn says, I haven't the mind. Let me take your hat."

Miss Fowler, moving stiffly from the hip, stamped her rubber-tipped stick on the tiled hall floor. "Mary, aren't you *anything* except a companion? Would you *ever* have been anything except a companion?"

Mary hung up the garden hat on its proper peg. "No," she said after consideration. "I don't imagine I ever should. But I've no imagination, I'm afraid."

She fetched Miss Fowler her eleven-o'clock glass of Contrexéville.

That was the wet December when it rained six inches to the month, and the women went abroad as little as might be. Wynn's flying chariot visited them several times, and for two mornings (he had warned her by postcard) Mary heard the thresh of his propellers at dawn. The second time she ran to the window, and stared at the whitening sky. A little blur passed overhead. She lifted her lean arms towards it.

That evening at six o'clock there came an announcement in an official envelope that Second Lieutenant W. Fowler had been killed during a trial flight. Death was instantaneous. She read it and carried it to Miss Fowler.

"I never expected anything else," said Miss Fowler; "but I'm sorry it happened before he had done anything."

The room was whirling round Mary Postgate, but she found herself quite steady in the midst of it.

"Yes," she said. "It's a great pity he didn't die in action after he had killed somebody."

"He was killed instantly. That's one comfort," Miss Fowler went on.

"But Wynn says the shock of a fall kills a man at once—whatever happens to the tanks," quoted Mary.

The room was coming to rest now. She heard Miss Fowler say impatiently, "But why can't we cry, Mary?" and herself replying, "There's nothing to cry for. He has done his duty as much as Mrs. Grant's son did."

"And when he died, *she* came and cried all the morning," said Miss Fowler. "This only makes me feel tired—terribly tired. Will you help me to bed, please, Mary?—And I think I'd like the hot-water bottle."

So Mary helped her and sat beside, talking of Wynn in his riotous youth.

"I believe," said Miss Fowler suddenly, "that old people and young people slip from under a stroke like this. The middle-aged feel it most."

"I expect that's true," said Mary, rising. "I'm going to put away the things in his room now. Shall we wear mourning?"

"Certainly not," said Miss Fowler. "Except, of course, at the funeral. I can't go. You will. I want you to arrange about his being buried here. What a blessing it didn't happen at Salisbury!"

Every one, from the Authorities of the Flying Corps to the Rector, was most kind and sympathetic. Mary found herself for the moment in a world where bodies were in the habit of being despatched by all sorts of conveyances to all sorts of places. And at the funeral two young men in buttoned-up uniforms stood beside the grave and spoke to her afterwards.

"You're Miss Postgate, aren't you?" said one. "Fowler told me about you. He was a good chap—a first-class fellow—a great loss."

"Great loss!" growled his companion. "We're all awfully sorry."

"How high did he fall from?" Mary whispered.

"Pretty nearly four thousand feet, I should think, didn't he? You were up that day, Monkey?"

"All of that," the other child replied. "My bar made three thousand, and I wasn't as high as him by a lot."

"Then *that's* all right," said Mary. "Thank you very much."

They moved away as Mrs. Grant flung herself weeping on Mary's flat chest, under the lych-gate, and cried, "*I* know how it feels! *I* know how it feels!"

"But both his parents are dead," Mary returned, as she fended her off. "Perhaps they've all met by now," she added vaguely as she escaped towards the coach.

"I've thought of that too," wailed Mrs. Grant; "but then he'll be practically a stranger to them. Quite embarrassing!"

Mary faithfully reported every detail of the ceremony to Miss Fowler, who, when she described Mrs. Grant's outburst, laughed aloud.

"Oh, how Wynn would have enjoyed it! He was always utterly unreliable at funerals. D'you remember——" And they talked of him again, each piecing out the other's gaps. "And now," said Miss Fowler, "we'll pull up the blinds and we'll have a general tidy. That always does us good. Have you seen to Wynn's things?"

"Everything—since he first came," said Mary, "He was never destructive—even with his toys."

They faced that neat room.

"It can't be natural not to cry," Mary said at last. "I'm so afraid you'll have a reaction."

"As I told you, we old people slip from under the stroke. It's you I'm afraid for. Have you cried yet?"

"I can't. It only makes me angry with the Germans."

"That's sheer waste of vitality," said Miss Fowler. "We must live till the war's finished." She opened a full wardrobe. "Now, I've been thinking things over. This is my plan. All his civilian clothes can be given away—Belgian refugees, and so on."

Mary nodded, "Boots, collars, and gloves?"

"Yes. We don't need to keep anything except his cap and belt."

"They came back yesterday with his Flying Corps clothes"——Mary pointed to a roll on the little iron bed.

"Ah, but keep his Service things. Some one may be glad of them later. Do you remember his sizes?"

"Five feet eight and a half; thirty-six inches round the chest. But he told me he's just put on an inch and a half. I'll mark it on a label and tie it on his sleeping-bag."

"So that disposes of *that*," said Miss Fowler, tapping the palm of one hand with the ringed third finger of the other. "What waste it all is! We'll get his old school trunk to-morrow and pack his civilian clothes."

"And the rest?" said Mary. "His books and pictures and the games and the toys—and—and the rest?"

"My plan is to burn every single thing," said Miss Fowler. "Then we shall know where they are and no one can handle them afterwards. What do you think?"

"I think that would be much the best," said Mary. "But there's such a lot of them."

"We'll burn them in the destructor," said Miss Fowler.

This was an open-air furnace for the consumption of refuse; a little circular four-foot tower of pierced brick over an iron grating. Miss Fowler had noticed the design in a gardening journal years ago, and had had it built at the bottom of the garden. It suited her tidy soul, for it saved unsightly rubbish-heaps, and the ashes lightened the stiff clay soil.

Mary considered for a moment, saw her way clear, and nodded again. They spent the evening putting away well-remembered civilian suits, underclothes that Mary had marked, and the regiments of very gaudy socks and ties. A second trunk was needed, and, after that, a little packing case, and it was late next day when Cheape and the local carrier lifted them to the cart. The Rector luckily knew of a friend's son, about five feet eight and a half inches high, to whom a complete Flying Corps outfit would be most acceptable, and sent his gardener's son down with a barrow to take delivery of it. The cap was hung up in Miss Fowler's bedroom, the belt in Miss Postgate's; for, as Miss Fowler said, they had no desire to make tea-party talk of them.

"That disposes of *that*," said Miss Fowler. "I'll leave the rest to you, Mary. I can't run up and down in the garden. You'd better take the big clothes-basket and get Nellie to help you."

"I shall take the wheel-barrow and do it myself," said Mary, and for once in her life closed her mouth.

Miss Fowler, in moments of irritation, had called Mary deadly methodical. She put on her oldest water-proof and gardening-hat and her ever-slipping goloshes, for the weather was on the edge of more rain. She gathered firelighters from the kitchen, a half-scuttle of coals, and a faggot of brushwood. These she wheeled in the barrow down the mossed paths to the dank little laurel shrubbery where the destructor stood under the drip of three oaks. She climbed the wire fence into the Rector's glebe just behind, and from his tenant's rick pulled two large armfuls of good hay, which she spread neatly on the fire-bars. Next, journey by journey, passing Miss Fowler's white face at the morning-room window each time, she brought down in the towel-covered clothes-basket, on the wheel-barrow, thumbed and used Hentys, Marrayats, Levers, Stevensons, Baroness Orczys, Garvices, schoolbooks, and atlases, unrelated piles of the *Motor Cyclist*, the *Light Car*, and catalogues of Olympia Exhibitions; the remnants of a fleet of sailing-ships from nine-penney cutters to a three-guinea yacht; a prep-school dressing-gown; bats from three-and-sixpence to twenty-four shillings; cricket and tennis balls; disintegrated steam and clockwork locomotives with their twisted rails; a grey and red tin model of a submarine; a dumb gramophone and cracked records; golf-clubs that had to be broken across the knee, like his walking-sticks, and an assegai; photographs of private and public school cricket and football elevens, and his O.T.C. on the line of march; kodaks, and film-rolls; some pewters, and one real silver cup, for boxing competitions and Junior Hurdles; sheaves of school photographs; Miss Fowler's photograph; her own which he had borne off in fun and (good care she took not to ask!) had never returned; a playbox with a secret drawer; a load of flannels, belts, and jerseys, and a pair of spiked shoes unearthed in the attic; a packet of all the letters that Miss Fowler and she had ever written to him, kept for some absurd reason through all these years; a five-day attempt at a diary; framed pictures of racing motors in full Brooklands career, and load upon load of undistinguishable wreckage of tool-boxes, rabbit-hutches, electric batteries, tin soldiers, fret-saw outfits, and jig-saw puzzles.

Miss Fowler at the window watched her come and go, and said to herself, "Mary's an old woman. I never realised it before."

After lunch she recommended her to rest.

"I'm not in the least tired," said Mary. "I've got it all arranged. I'm going to the village at two o'clock for some paraffin. Nellie hasn't enough, and the walk will do me good."

She made one last quest round the house before she started, and found that she had overlooked nothing. It began to mist as soon as she had skirted Vegg's Heath, where Wynn used to descend—it seemed to her that she could almost hear the beat of his propellers overhead, but there was nothing to see. She hoisted her umbrella and lunged into the blind wet till she had reached the shelter of the empty village. As she came out of Mr. Kidd's shop with a bottle full of paraffin in her string shopping-bag, she met Nurse Eden, the village nurse, and fell into talk with her, as usual, about the village children. They were parting opposite the "Royal Oak," when a gun, they fancied, was fired immediately behind the house. It was followed by a child's shriek dying into a wail.

"Accident!" said Nurse Eden promptly, and dashed through the empty bar, followed by Mary. They found Mrs. Gerritt, the publican's wife, who could only gasp and point to the yard, where a little cart-lodge was sliding sideways amid a clatter of tiles. Nurse Eden snatched up a sheet drying before the fire, ran out, lifted something from the ground, and flung the sheet round it. The sheet turned scarlet and half her uniform too, as she bore the load into the kitchen. It was little Edna Gerritt, aged nine, whom Mary had known since her perambulator days.

"Am I hurted bad?" Edna asked, and died between Nurse Eden's dripping hands. The sheet fell aside and for an instant, before she could shut her eyes, Mary saw the ripped and shredded body.

"It's a wonder she spoke at all," said Nurse Eden. "What in God's name was it?"

"A bomb," said Mary.

"One o' the Zeppelins?"

"No. An aeroplane. I thought I heard it on the Heath but I fancied it was one of ours. It must have shut off its engines as it came down. That's why we didn't notice it."

"The filthy pigs!" said Nurse Eden, all white and shaken. "See the pickle I'm in! Go and tell Dr. Hennis, Miss Postgate." Nurse looked at the mother, who had dropped face down on the floor. "She's only in a fit. Turn her over."

Mary heaved Mrs. Gerritt right side up, and hurried off for the doctor. When she told her tale, he asked her to sit down in the surgery till he got her something.

"But I don't need it, I assure you," said she. "I don't think it would be wise to tell Miss Fowler about it, do you? Her heart is so irritable in this weather."

Dr. Hennis looked at her admiringly as he packed up his bag.

"No. Don't tell anybody till we're sure," he said, and hastened to the "Royal Oak," while Mary went on with the paraffin. The village behind her was as quiet as usual, for the news had not yet spread. She frowned a little to herself, her large nostrils expanded uglily, and from time to time she muttered a phrase which Wynn, who had never restrained himself before his women-folk, had applied to the enemy. "Bloody pagans! They are bloody pagans. But," she continued, falling back on the teaching that had made her what she was, "one mustn't let one's mind dwell on these things."

Before she reached the house Dr. Hennis, who was also a special constable, overtook her in his car.

"Oh, Miss Postgate," he said, "I wanted to tell you that that accident at the 'Royal Oak' was due to Gerritt's stable tumbling down. It's been dangerous for a long time. It ought to have been condemned."

"I thought I heard an explosion too," said Mary.

"You might have been misled by the beams snapping. I've been looking at 'em. They were dry-rotted through and through. Of course, as they broke, they would make a noise just like a gun."

"Yes?" said Mary politely.

"Poor little Edna was playing underneath it," he went on, still holding her with his eyes, "and that and the tiles cut her to pieces, you see?"

"I saw it," said Mary, shaking her head. "I heard it too."

"Well, we cannot be sure." Dr. Hennis changed his tone completely. "I know both you and Nurse Eden (I've been speaking to her) are perfectly trustworthy, and I can rely on you not to say anything—yet at least. It is no good to stir up people unless—"

"Oh, I never do—anyhow," said Mary, and Dr. Hennis went on to the country town.

After all, she told herself, it might, just possibly, have been the collapse of the old stable that had done all those things to poor little Edna. She was sorry she had even hinted at other things, but Nurse Eden was discretion itself. By the time she reached home the affair seemed increasingly remote by its very monstrosity. As she came in, Miss Fowler told her that a couple of aeroplanes had passed half an hour ago.

"I though I heard them," she replied, "I'm going down to the garden now. I've got the paraffin."

"Yes, but—what *have* you got on your boots? They're soaking wet. Change them at once."

Not only did Mary obey, but she wrapped the boots in a newspaper, and put them into the string bag with the bottles. So, armed with the longest kitchen poker, she left.

"It's raining again," was Miss Fowler's last word, "but—I know you won't be happy till that's disposed of."

"It won't take long. I've got everything down there, and I've put the lid on the destructor to keep the wet out."

The shrubbery was filling with twilight by the same time she had completed her arrangements and sprinkled the sacrificial oil. As she lit the match that would burn her heart to ashes, she heard a groan or a grunt behind the dense Portugal laurels.

"Cheape?" she called impatiently, but Cheape, with his ancient lumbago, in his comfortable cottage would be the last man to profane the sanctuary. "Sheep," she concluded, and threw in the fusee. The pyre went up in a roar, and the immediate flame hastened the night around her.

"How Wynn would have loved this!" she thought, stepping back from the blaze.

By its light she saw, half hidden behind a laurel not five paces away, a bare-headed man sitting very stiffly at the foot of one of the oaks. A broken branch lay across his lap—one booted leg protruding from beneath it. His head moved ceaselessly from side to side, but his body was as still as the tree's trunk. He was dressed—she moved sideways to look more closely—in a uniform something like Wynn's, with a flap buttoned across the chest. For an instant she had some idea that it might be one of the young flying men she had met at the funeral. But their heads were dark and glossy. This man's was as pale as a baby's, and so closely cropped that she could see the disgusting pink skin beneath. His lips moved.

"What do you say?" Mary moved towards him and stooped.

"Laty! Laty! Laty!" he muttered, while his hands picked at the dead wet leaves. There was no doubt as to his nationality. It made her so angry that she strode back to the destructor, though it was still too hot to use the poker there. Wynn's books seemed to be catching well. She looked up at the oak behind the man; several of the light upper and two or three rotten lower branches had broken and scattered their rubbish on the shrubbery path. On the lowest fork a helmet with dependent strings, showed like a bird's-nest in the light of a long-tongued flame. Evidently this person had fallen through the trees. Wynn had told her that it was quite possible for people to fall out of aeroplanes. Wynn told her, too, that trees were useful things to break an aviator's fall, but in this case the aviator must have been broken or he would have moved from his queer position. He seemed helpless except for his belt—and Mary loathed pistols. Months ago, after reading certain Belgian reports together, she and Miss Fowler had had dealings with one—a huge revolver with flat-nosed bullets, which later, Wynn said, were forbidden by the rules of war to be used against civilised enemies. "They're good enough for us," Miss Fowler had replied. "Show Mary how it works." And Wynn, laughing at the mere possibility of any such need, had led the craven winking Mary into the Rector's disused quarry, and had shown her how to fire the terrible machine. It lay now in the top-left-hand drawer of her toilet-table—a memento not included in the burning. Wynn would be pleased to see how she was not afraid.

She slipped up to the house to get it. When she came through the rain, the eyes in the head were alive with expectation. The mouth even tried to smile. But at sight of the revolver its corners went down just like Edna Gerritt's. A tear trickled from one eye, and the head rolled from shoulder to shoulder as though trying to point out something.

"*Cassée. Tout cassée,*"[1] it whimpered.

"What do you say?" said Mary disgustedly, keeping well to one side, though only the head moved.

"*Cassée,*" it repeated. "*Che me rends. Le médicin!*[2] *Toctor!*"

"Nein!" said she, bringing all her small German to bear with the big pistol. "*Ich haben der todt Kinder gesehn.*"[3]

The head was still. Mary's hand dropped. She had been careful to keep her finger off the trigger for fear of accidents. After a few moments' waiting, she returned to the destructor, where the flames were falling, and churned up Wynn's charring books with the poker. Again the head groaned for the doctor.

"Stop that!" said Mary, and stamped her foot. "Stop that, you bloody pagan!"

The words came quite smoothly and naturally. They were Wynn's own words, and Wynn was a gentleman who for no consideration on earth would have torn little Edna into those vividly coloured strips and strings. But this thing hunched under the oak-tree had done that thing. It was no question of reading horrors out of newspapers to Miss Fowler. Mary had seen it with her own eyes on the "Royal Oak" kitchen table. She must not allow her mind to dwell upon it. Now Wynn was dead, and everything connected with him was lumping and rustling and tinkling under her busy poker into red black dust and grey leaves of ash. The thing beneath the oak would die too. Mary had seen death more than once. She came of a family that had a knack of dying under, as she told Miss Fowler, "most distressing circumstances." She would stay where she was till she was entirely satisfied that It was dead—dead as dear papa in the late 'eighties; aunt Mary in 'eighty-nine; mamma in 'ninety-one; cousin Dick in 'ninety-five; Lady McCausland's housemaid in 'ninety-nine; Lady McCausland's sister in nineteen hundred and one; Wynn buried five days ago; and Edna Gerritt still waiting for decent earth to hide her. As she thought—her underlip caught up by one faded canine, brows knit and nostrils wide—she wielded the poker with lunges that jarred the grating at the bottom, and careful scrapes round the brick-work above. She looked at her wrist-watch. It was getting on to half-past four, and the rain was coming down in earnest. Tea would be at five. If It did not die before that time, she would be soaked and would have to change. Meantime, and this occupied her, Wynn's things

---

1. "Broken. It's all broken" [*French*]
2. "I'm hurt. The doctor!" [*French*]
3. "I've seen the dead children." [*German*]

were burning well in spite of the hissing wet, though now and again a book-back with a quite distinguishable title would be heaved up out of the mass. The exercise of stoking had given her a glow which seemed to reach to the marrow of her bones. She hummed—Mary never had a voice—to herself. She had never believed in all those advanced views—though Miss Fowler herself leaned a little that way—of woman's work in the world; but now she saw there was much to be said for them. This, for instance, was *her* work—work which no man, least of all Dr. Hennis, would ever have done. A man, at such a crisis, would be what Wynn called a "sportsman"; would leave everything to fetch help, and would certainly bring It into the house. Now a woman's business was to make a happy home for—for a husband and children. Failing these—it was not a thing one should allow one's mind to dwell upon—but—

"Stop it!" Mary cried once more across the shadows. "*Nein*, I tell you! *Ich haben der todt Kinder gesehn*."

But it was a fact. A woman who had missed these things could still be useful—more useful than a man in certain respects. She thumped like a paviour through the settling ashes at the secret thrill of it. The rain was damping the fire, but she could feel—it was too dark to see—that her work was done. There was a dull red glow at the bottom of the destructor, not enough to char the wooden lid if she slipped it half over against the driving wet. This arranged, she leaned on the poker and waited, while an increasing rapture laid hold on her. She ceased to think. She gave herself up to feel. Her long pleasure was broken by a sound that she had waited for in agony several times in her life. She leaned forward and listened, smiling. There could be no mistake. She closed her eyes and drank it in. Once it ceased abruptly.

"Go on," she murmured, half aloud. "That isn't the end."

Then the end came very distinctly in a lull between two rain-gusts. Mary Postgate drew her breath short between her teeth and shivered from head to foot. "*That's* all right," said she contentedly, and went up to the house, where she scandalised the whole routine by taking a luxurious hot bath before tea, and came down looking, as Miss Fowler said when she saw her lying all relaxed on the other sofa, "quite handsome!"

THE BLIND ONES

by Isaak Babel

Born in Odessa, Russia, Babel (1894–1940) became—with Maxim Gorky's encouragement—a master of the short story. He had a distinctly bold and clear style, and was so frank that the Soviet authorities eventually suppressed his writing and then murdered him while he was under arrest. Although Babel went to the Romanian Front with the Russian Army in 1917, this story takes place in the aftermath of the new Bolshevik government's withdrawal from the war, but before Germany's treaty agreement with Russia in 1918. The narrator visits blind soldiers in a makeshift nursing facility in Petrograd.

[From the magazine *Novaya Zhizn*, May 19, 1918.
Translated from the Russian by Bob Blaisdell.]

THE SIGNBOARD READ: "Shelter for Blind Soldiers." I rang at the tall oak doors. No one answered. The door seemed open. I went in and saw this:

Down a wide staircase walked a big black-haired fellow in dark glasses. He waved a reed cane before him. After he had successfully conquered the staircase, there lay in front of the blind man multiple ways—blind alleys, dark alleys, steps, side-rooms. His cane quietly tapped the smooth, dimly shining walls. His still head was tilted up. He moved slowly, felt for the step with his foot, stumbled and fell. A streak of blood cut his prominent white forehead, ran down around his temple, and disappeared under his dark glasses. The black-haired fellow lifted up and wetting his finger in the blood, softly called, "Kablukov." The door of the neighboring room opened soundlessly. Before me flitted more reed canes. The blind ones went to help their fallen comrade. Some did not find him, pressing themselves to the walls and looking up with unseeing eyes, while others took him by the arm, lifted him from the floor and, their heads drooping, awaited a nurse or orderly.

A nurse came. She led the soldiers to their rooms, then explained to me:

"Every day such things happen. This house doesn't suit us, really doesn't suit. We need a level, one-floor house with long corridors. Our shelter—it's a booby trap. All the stairs, stairs! . . . The men fall every day."

Our government, as is known, exhibits an administrative energy in only two events—when it is necessary to flee or whine. In the periods of all of our evacuations and disastrous mass-resettlements, the government's work takes on an attitude of busy, creative liveliness and efficient passion.

I was told about the process of evacuating the blind from the shelter.

The initiative for the transfer came from the wounded themselves. The Germans were closely approaching, and their fear of this occupation drove them into complete agitation. The reasons for their agitation were many. The first of them is that any kind of alarm is sweet for the blind. The excitement seizes them quickly and irresistibly, and their nervous anxiety to reach an imaginary goal overwhelms their despondent bodies for a while.

The second reason for fleeing was a particular fear of the Germans.

The majority of the men in the wards had been sent back from captivity. They were firmly convinced that if the Germans came they would again be forced to serve, forced to work, forced to starve.

The nurses told them: "You're blind—no one needs you, there's nothing they'll make you do."

They answered: "A German doesn't let up, a German gives everyone work. We lived among the Germans, nurse."

This alarm was touching and was apparent in the psychology of all the returning prisoners.

The blind ones asked to be led into the depths of Russia. As evacuations were already anticipated, the decision was quickly given. And here began the main thing.

With the imprint of decisiveness on their thin faces, the wrapped-up blind ones stretched themselves along to the train station.

The guides then told the story of their adventures.

The whole day it rained. Clumped in a heap, the downcast men waited the whole night under a landing. Then in cold, dark boxcars, they made their way across the face of our motherland. They went to councils, into the dirty reception halls, then awaited the distribution of rations. Dismayed, direct, silent, they submissively walked after the tired, vexed guards. Some pushed on into villages. The villages had no use of them. No one did. The worthless particles of human dust, needed by no one, wandered like blind puppies through the empty stations and looked for a home. No home turned up. Everyone returned to Petrograd. In Petrograd, it was quiet, so quiet.

Beside the main building crouched a one-story hovel. In it lived the particular people of a particular time—the families of blind ones.

I chatted with one of the women—a fleshy young woman in a housecoat with Kavkazi slippers. There sat her husband—an old, bony Pole with an orange face from the poison gas.

I asked and quickly took it in: she was a Russian woman of our time, sent spinning by the whirlwind of war, by shock, by migration.

In the beginning of the war she joined the nurses "out of patriotism."

She had gone through a lot: mutilated "soldier-boys," German air-strikes, evening dances at officers' gatherings, officers in jodhpurs, a female disease, love for some kind of man in authority, then—the Revolution, the campaign, another love, evacuation and subcommittees.

Somewhere, at some point, her parents had been in Simbirsk along with her sister Varya, and her cousin was in the rail service . . . But for a year and a half her parents hadn't written, her sister Varya was far away, so her warm memories of home had evaporated.

All she had now was weariness, a body falling apart, a seat by a window, a fondness for lethargy, a dull gaze idly shifting from one object to another, and her husband—the blind Pole with an orange face.

There were several such women at the shelter. They did not leave because there was nowhere to go and no reason to. The supervising nurse often said to them:

"I don't understand what we have here . . . Everyone piled in a heap and so we live, but you're not supposed to be living here. . . . I can't refer to this as a shelter anymore, because we're a public establishment, but now . . . nothing now can be understood."

In a dark cramped room sat two pale bearded peasants across from each other on narrow beds. Their glassy eyes did not move. With quiet voices they spoke about the land, about wheat, about the going price for piglets.

In another room a creaky and apathetic old man was teaching a tall strong soldier to play the fiddle. The pathetic screechy sounds wavered from the bow on the trembling strings.

I went on further.

In one of the rooms a woman was moaning. I looked and saw a girl about seventeen years old with a crimson little face who was writhing from pain on a wide bed. Her dark husband sat in the corner on a small stool, his hand plaiting a basket in wide motions while he attentively but coldly listened to her moans.

The girl married him half a year ago.

Soon in a particular hovel for particular people a little one will be born.

This child will be, truly, a child of our times.

MISAPPLIED ENERGY

by William T. Scanlon

Who was the author William T. Scanlon? He may have been a Harvard graduate, as a Harvard magazine notes the book's publication; or a University of Toronto graduate, as its alumni magazine also notes the publication; he was a U.S. Marine in the 97th Company according to a contemporary review of the book or the 6th Marines according to a recent history. This story, about American soldiers in France, is an episode from his novel.

[From Scanlon's *God Have Mercy on Us!: A Story of 1918*.
Boston: Houghton Mifflin Company, 1929]

I WAS SITTING in my hole reading by a home-made candle made out of bacon grease and old rag wick. Murphy was lying on his back not far away.

Murphy said: "What are you reading?"

"The Bible. Did you ever read it?" (I had a pocket-size Testament.)

Murphy said: "I looked at one back in Tours when Hancock was shooting his head off about the Kaiser being the whore that sat on seven hills and caused the war. . . ."

"That was a lot of cheap stuff," I said. "Hancock read it in some paper. . . ."

Murphy: "Well, if it's in the Bible I suppose it's true. . . . Still I leave all that up to the priests. . . . That's what they get paid for. . . ."

I said: "Remember how we used to argue with Hancock up in the old trenches about 'He that kills by the sword shall perish by the sword'? . . ."

Murphy: Yes, and I still stick to what I always said—we haven't got any swords . . . and it doesn't say anything about machine-guns and rifles. . . ."

Just then one of the fellows came up and said Captain Ladd wanted to see me, so I went over to his dug-out.

He said: "Corporal, I have here some very important documents that the Intelligence Section just sent up." He pointed to a bundle of papers on the ground. He picked up a sheet and passed it to me. It was written in German.

He said: "Can you read it?"

"No, sir."

He said: "Well, it doesn't make any difference. . . . Neither can I, but here is what I want you to do with them. Pick out a detail of men—five or six—and to-night, about eleven o'clock, take these papers and distribute them inside the German lines in as open a space as you can find. We want the Germans to find them. Come in later and I'll give you the papers."

I picked out six men—Young, Dale, White, Quinn, Bretherton, and Carney. I told them to be ready at ten-forty-five. No equipment was to be worn, I told them, except gas-masks, and they were to be tied on securely so they wouldn't make a noise. No weapons were to be carried except an automatic revolver. Revolvers were furnished only to corporals and sergeants, so I had to dig around to borrow six of them, but I did. Extra clips would be carried in the pocket, as no belts could be worn. We were not a combat group or patrol and it was up to us to avoid any encounter.

A little before eleven I called in at the Captain's hole and he gave me a bundle of papers. They were about the size of a regular book leaf, and were cheap paper, like newspaper stock.

The Captain told us to go down the ravine to where the last man was posted and then cut across the field until we hit a main road which ran between Soissons and Château-Thierry. We would have to be careful along that road, as the Germans used it at night and our artillery usually shelled it at regular intervals, but to-night they would not shell this part of the road in front of our positions between the hour of eleven-thirty and twelve-thirty. The Captain suggested that along this road and the sides of the road would be a good place to distribute the papers.

It was about eleven-fifteen when I left and close to eleven-thirty by the time I reached the last man in the ravine. This was Hancock. I left my gas-mask with him. It was always a bother, as no matter how you tied it down it would flop up, and, besides, it would hinder me crawling on my belly through the grass. The other men wanted to keep their masks, so I let them. I knew the lines were too close together to use gas.

We started across the field toward the road on our hands and knees, and as we got farther out we dropped flat and wriggled the rest of the way on our bellies. I was leading, the rest following fairly close behind.

The German lines seemed restless. Star shells were going up right along; also signal lights for batteries—green and red. The artillery on both sides were firing away, trying to bust each other up.

We were snaking through grass which was about six or eight inches high and heavy with dew. We were soaking wet. It was slow work, as we had to stop crawling when the star shells were up.

I was looking straight ahead through the grass when all at once I found my head sticking out over a small embankment. About ten feet ahead was a road. I stopped. This road was inside the German lines and they had outposts in back of us, although their main line was on the other side of the road in a wood similar to ours. I could hear a waggon creaking in the distance and soon a French two-wheeled waggon went by drawn by one horse. It was off the road on the grassy part alongside. It was headed north.

I gradually lowered myself down over the embankment. I told the next man to crawl along about ten feet and then come over. I sent one man one way and the next man the other and told them to get about ten feet apart before letting themselves down on the side of the road. Each one had some of the papers. I told them to keep down and scatter the papers out in front. Two of us crept out to the road and distributed the stuff as best we could for about two hundred feet along the road.

It did not take very long and we were soon crawling back. The path was easy to pick out, as the grass was all flattened out. It was about twelve-fifteen when we got back. I got my gas-mask from Hancock and reported back to the Captain.

I had saved one of the sheets, and the next day I got Eberle to translate it. It went something like this:

To the German Soldier

The people of the United States are still friends of the people of Germany. The United States did not enter the War to fight the German people. We are at war with the German Military Power which is trying to murder the people of the world the way they are murdering you. You are being deceived by them. Here is an offer that we make to you. Every German soldier who will lay down his arms and enter our lines of his own free will will be furnished free transportation to the United States and will be given a large piece of rich farm land that he can work for himself. We have plenty of good land and can take care of you all.

I can't remember how it was signed.

That night I heard Murphy getting a patrol together. He came to borrow my automatic for one of his men. I told him I would be on guard from 1 to 3 a.m. and would need the gun, so he said he would have it back to me by that time.

About a quarter to one I went down to the top sergeant's hole to see if he had any orders. His hole was right next to the Captain's and there was an opening between them just as between Murphy's and mine. I was just about to go when I heard somebody slide into the hole next to me and start to talk in an excited voice. It was Murphy.

He said: "Lookit, Captain! . . . I picked up a whole bunch of German orders that somebody dropped along the road!"

There was a rattling of papers for a minute. I looked through the hole and saw Murphy pulling little papers out of all his pockets.

Then the Captain spoke. "German orders, hell! These are the papers I sent out last night to be distributed in the German lines. And you had to go out and pick them up again—!"

"Well, my orders were to pick up any information about the German lines I could, and as soon as I spotted these papers along the road and saw that they were written in German, I figured some despatch runner had dropped them."

"Did you get any information about the German positions?"

"No, sir, nothing but these papers. It took us quite a while to pick them up."

"I guess you got them all all right."

Murphy went out and I followed. When I caught up with him I started to bawl him out.

I said: "What did you want to go and pick up all those German papers for when I had such a hard time scattering them along the road?"

Murphy said: "So you're the guy that did it?"

"Yes, didn't we do a good job?"

"Too damned good! We crawled along that road for over an hour on our hands and knees picking them up. Next time put them all in one pile."

THE FLY

by Katherine Mansfield

New Zealand's great master of short stories, Mansfield (1888–1923) lived most of the last fifteen years of her life in Europe, where she died of tuberculosis. This story is about a London businessman shaken by memories of his son's death ("Time, he had declared then, he had told everybody, could make no difference. Other men perhaps might recover, might live their loss down, but not he. How was it possible? His boy was an only son"). Mansfield's brother, an army instructor, had been killed while demonstrating the use of grenades in France in October 1915.

[First published in *The Nation*, March 18, 1922]

"Y'ARE VERY SNUG in here," piped old Mr. Woodifield, and he peered out of the great, green-leather armchair by his friend the boss's desk as a baby peers out of its pram. His talk was over; it was time for him to be off. But he did not want to go. Since he had retired, since his . . . stroke, the wife and the girls kept him boxed up in the house every day of the week except Tuesday. On Tuesday he was dressed and brushed and allowed to cut back to the City for the day. Though what he did there the wife and girls couldn't imagine. Made a nuisance of himself to his friends, they supposed. . . . Well, perhaps so. All the same, we cling to our last pleasures as the tree clings to its last leaves. So there sat old Woodifield, smoking a cigar and staring almost greedily at the boss, who rolled in his office chair, stout, rosy, five years older than he, and still going strong, still at the helm. It did one good to see him.

Wistfully, admiringly, the old voice added, "It's snug in here, upon my word!"

"Yes, it's comfortable enough," agreed the boss, and he flipped the *Financial Times* with a paper-knife. As a matter of fact he was proud of his room; he liked to have it admired, especially by old

Woodifield. It gave him a feeling of deep, solid satisfaction to be planted there in the midst of it in full view of that frail old figure in the muffler.

"I've had it done up lately," he explained, as he had explained for the past—how many?—weeks. "New carpet," and he pointed to the bright red carpet with a pattern of large white rings. "New furniture," and he nodded towards the massive bookcase and the table with legs like twisted treacle. "Electric heating!" He waved almost exultantly towards the five transparent, pearly sausages glowing so softly in the tilted copper pan.

But he did not draw old Woodifield's attention to the photograph over the table of a grave-looking boy in uniform standing in one of those spectral photographers' parks with photographers' storm-clouds behind him. It was not new. It had been there for over six years.

"There was something I wanted to tell you," said old Woodifield, and his eyes grew dim remembering. "Now what was it? I had it in my mind when I started out this morning." His hands began to tremble, and patches of red showed above his beard.

Poor old chap, he's on his last pins, thought the boss. And, feeling kindly, he winked at the old man, and said jokingly, "I tell you what. I've got a little drop of something here that'll do you good before you go out into the cold again. It's beautiful stuff. It wouldn't hurt a child." He took a key off his watch-chain, unlocked a cupboard below his desk, and drew forth a dark, squat bottle. "That's the medicine," said he. "And the man from whom I got it told me on the strict Q.T. it came from the cellars at Windor Castle."

Old Woodifield's mouth fell open at the sight. He couldn't have looked more surprised if the boss had produced a rabbit.

"It's whisky, ain't it?" he piped feebly.

The boss turned the bottle and lovingly showed him the label. Whisky it was.

"D'you know," said he, peering up at the boss wonderingly, "they won't let me touch it at home." And he looked as though he was going to cry.

"Ah, that's where we know a bit more than the ladies," cried the boss, swooping across for two tumblers that stood on the table with the water-bottle, and pouring a generous finger into each. "Drink it down. It'll do you good. And don't put any water with it. It's sacrilege to tamper with stuff like this. Ah!" He tossed off his, pulled out his handkerchief, hastily wiped his moustaches, and cocked an eye at old Woodifield, who was rolling his in his chaps.

The old man swallowed, was silent a moment, and then said faintly, "It's nutty!"

But it warmed him; it crept into his chill old brain—he remembered.

"That was it," he said, heaving himself out of his chair. "I thought you'd like to know. The girls were in Belgium last week having a look at poor Reggie's grave, and they happened to come across your boy's. They're quite near each other, it seems."

Old Woodifield paused, but the boss made no reply. Only a quiver in his eyelids showed that he heard.

"The girls were delighted with the way the place is kept," piped the old voice. "Beautifully looked after. Couldn't be better if they were at home. You've not been across, have yer?"

"No, no!" For various reasons the boss had not been across.

"There's miles of it," quavered old Woodifield, "and it's all as neat as a garden. Flowers growing on all the graves. Nice broad paths." It was plain from his voice how much he liked a nice broad path.

The pause came again. Then the old man brightened wonderfully.

"D'you know what the hotel made the girls pay for a pot of jam?" he piped. "Ten francs! Robbery, I call it. It was a little pot, so Gertrude says, no bigger than a half-crown. And she hadn't taken more than a spoonful when they charged her ten francs. Gertrude brought the pot away with her to teach 'em a lesson. Quite right, too; it's trading on our feelings. They think because we're over there having a look round we're ready to pay anything. That's what it is." And he turned towards the door.

"Quite right, quite right!" cried the boss, though what was quite right he hadn't the least idea. He came round by his desk, followed the shuffling footsteps to the door, and saw the old fellow out. Woodifield was gone.

For a long moment the boss stayed, staring at nothing, while the grey-haired office messenger, watching him, dodged in and out of his cubby-hole like a dog that expects to be taken for a run. Then: "I'll see nobody for half an hour, Macey," said the boss. "Understand? Nobody at all."

"Very good, sir."

The door shut, the firm heavy steps recrossed the bright carpet, the fat body plumped down in the spring chair, and leaning forward, the boss covered his face with his hands. He wanted, he intended, he had arranged to weep . . .

It had been a terrible shock to him when old Woodifield sprang that remark upon him about the boy's grave. It was exactly as though the earth had opened and he had seen the boy lying there with Woodifield's girls staring down at him. For it was strange. Although over six years had passed away, the boss never thought of the boy except as lying unchanged, unblemished in his uniform, asleep for ever. "My son!" groaned the boss. But no tears came yet. In the past, in the first few months and even years after the boy's death, he had only to say those words to be overcome by such grief that nothing short of a violent fit of weeping could relieve him. Time, he had declared then, he had told everybody, could make no difference. Other men perhaps might recover, might live their loss down, but not he. How was it possible? His boy was an only son. Ever since his birth the boss had worked at building up this business for him; it had no other meaning if it was not for the boy. Life itself had come to have no other meaning. How on earth could he have slaved, denied himself, kept going all those years without the promise for ever before him of the boy's stepping into his shoes and carrying on where he left off?

And that promise had been so near being fulfilled. The boy had been in the office learning the ropes for a year before the war. Every morning they had started off together; they had come back by the same train. And what congratulations he had received as the boy's father! No wonder; he had taken to it marvellously. As to his popularity with the staff, every man jack of them down to old Macey couldn't make enough of the boy. And he wasn't the least spoilt. No, he was just his bright natural self, with the right word for everybody, with that boyish look and his habit of saying, "Simply splendid!"

But all that was over and done with as though it never had been. The day had come when Macey had handed him the telegram that brought the whole place crashing about his head. "Deeply regret to inform you . . ." And he had left the office a broken man, with his life in ruins.

Six years ago, six years. . . . How quickly time passed! It might have happened yesterday. The boss took his hands from his face; he was puzzled. Something seemed to be wrong with him. He wasn't feeling as he wanted to feel. He decided to get up and have a look at the boy's photograph. But it wasn't a favorite photograph of his; the expression was unnatural. It was cold, even stern-looking. The boy had never looked like that.

At that moment the boss noticed that a fly had fallen into his broad inkpot, and was trying feebly but desperately to clamber out again. Help! help! said those struggling legs. But the sides of the inkpot were wet and slippery; it fell back again and began to swim. The boss took up a pen, picked the fly out of the ink, and shook it on to a piece of blotting-paper. For a fraction of a second it lay still on the dark patch that oozed round it. Then the front legs waved, took hold, and, pulling its small, sodden body up, it began the immense task of cleaning the ink from its wings. Over and under, over and under, went a leg along a wing, as the stone goes over and under the scythe. Then there was a pause, while the fly, seeming to stand on the tips of its toes, tried to expand first one wing and then the other. It succeeded at last, and, sitting down, it began, like a minute cat, to clean its face. Now one could imagine that the little front legs rubbed against each other lightly, joyfully. The horrible danger was over; it had escaped; it was ready for life again.

But just then the boss had an idea. He plunged his pen back into the ink, leaned his thick wrist on the blotting-paper, and as the fly tried its wings down came a great heavy blot. What would it make of that? What indeed! The little beggar seemed absolutely cowed, stunned, and afraid to move because of what would happen next. But then, as if painfully, it dragged itself forward. The front legs waved, caught hold, and, more slowly this time, the task began from the beginning.

He's a plucky little devil, thought the boss, and he felt a real admiration for the fly's courage. That was the way to tackle things; that was the right spirit. Never say die; it was only a question of . . . But the fly had again finished its laborious task, and the boss had just time to refill his pen, to shake fair and square on the new-cleaned body yet another dark drop. What about it this time? A painful moment of suspense followed. But behold, the front legs were again waving; the boss felt a rush of relief. He leaned over the fly and said to it tenderly, "You artful little b . . ." And he actually had the brilliant notion of breathing on it to help the drying process. All the same, there was something timid and weak about its efforts now, and the boss decided that this time should be the last, as he dipped the pen deep into the inkpot.

It was. The last blot fell on the soaked blotting-paper, and the draggled fly lay in it and did not stir. The back legs were stuck to the body; the front legs were not to be seen.

"Come on," said the boss. "Look sharp!" And he stirred it with his pen—in vain. Nothing happened or was likely to happen. The fly was dead.

The boss lifted the corpse on the end of the paper-knife and flung it into the waste-paper basket. But such a grinding feeling of wretchedness seized him that he felt positively frightened. He started forward and pressed the bell for Macey.

"Bring me some fresh blotting-paper," he said sternly, "and look sharp about it." And while the old dog padded away he fell to wondering what it was he had been thinking about before. What was it? It was . . . He took out his handkerchief and passed it inside his collar. For the life of him he could not remember.

A CATALOG OF SELECTED
DOVER BOOKS
IN ALL FIELDS OF INTEREST

A CATALOG OF SELECTED DOVER
BOOKS IN ALL FIELDS OF INTEREST

100 BEST-LOVED POEMS, Edited by Philip Smith. "The Passionate Shepherd to His Love," "Shall I compare thee to a summer's day?" "Death, be not proud," "The Raven," "The Road Not Taken," plus works by Blake, Wordsworth, Byron, Shelley, Keats, many others. 96pp. 5 3/16 x 8 1/4. 0-486-28553-7

100 SMALL HOUSES OF THE THIRTIES, Brown-Blodgett Company. Exterior photographs and floor plans for 100 charming structures. Illustrations of models accompanied by descriptions of interiors, color schemes, closet space, and other amenities. 200 illustrations. 112pp. 8 3/8 x 11. 0-486-44131-8

1000 TURN-OF-THE-CENTURY HOUSES: With Illustrations and Floor Plans, Herbert C. Chivers. Reproduced from a rare edition, this showcase of homes ranges from cottages and bungalows to sprawling mansions. Each house is meticulously illustrated and accompanied by complete floor plans. 256pp. 9 3/8 x 12 1/4.

0-486-45596-3

101 GREAT AMERICAN POEMS, Edited by The American Poetry & Literacy Project. Rich treasury of verse from the 19th and 20th centuries includes works by Edgar Allan Poe, Robert Frost, Walt Whitman, Langston Hughes, Emily Dickinson, T. S. Eliot, other notables. 96pp. 5 3/16 x 8 1/4. 0-486-40158-8

101 GREAT SAMURAI PRINTS, Utagawa Kuniyoshi. Kuniyoshi was a master of the warrior woodblock print — and these 18th-century illustrations represent the pinnacle of his craft. Full-color portraits of renowned Japanese samurais pulse with movement, passion, and remarkably fine detail. 112pp. 8 3/8 x 11. 0-486-46523-3

ABC OF BALLET, Janet Grosser. Clearly worded, abundantly illustrated little guide defines basic ballet-related terms: arabesque, battement, pas de chat, relevé, sissonne, many others. Pronunciation guide included. Excellent primer. 48pp. 4 3/16 x 5 3/4.

0-486-40871-X

ACCESSORIES OF DRESS: An Illustrated Encyclopedia, Katherine Lester and Bess Viola Oerke. Illustrations of hats, veils, wigs, cravats, shawls, shoes, gloves, and other accessories enhance an engaging commentary that reveals the humor and charm of the many-sided story of accessorized apparel. 644 figures and 59 plates. 608pp. 6 1/8 x 9 1/4.

0-486-43378-1

ADVENTURES OF HUCKLEBERRY FINN, Mark Twain. Join Huck and Jim as their boyhood adventures along the Mississippi River lead them into a world of excitement, danger, and self-discovery. Humorous narrative, lyrical descriptions of the Mississippi valley, and memorable characters. 224pp. 5 3/16 x 8 1/4. 0-486-28061-6

ALICE STARMORE'S BOOK OF FAIR ISLE KNITTING, Alice Starmore. A noted designer from the region of Scotland's Fair Isle explores the history and techniques of this distinctive, stranded-color knitting style and provides copious illustrated instructions for 14 original knitwear designs. 208pp. 8 3/8 x 10 7/8. 0-486-47218-3

ALICE'S ADVENTURES IN WONDERLAND, Lewis Carroll. Beloved classic about a little girl lost in a topsy-turvy land and her encounters with the White Rabbit, March Hare, Mad Hatter, Cheshire Cat, and other delightfully improbable characters. 42 illustrations by Sir John Tenniel. 96pp. 5³⁄₁₆ x 8¼.   0-486-27543-4

AMERICA'S LIGHTHOUSES: An Illustrated History, Francis Ross Holland. Profusely illustrated fact-filled survey of American lighthouses since 1716. Over 200 stations — East, Gulf, and West coasts, Great Lakes, Hawaii, Alaska, Puerto Rico, the Virgin Islands, and the Mississippi and St. Lawrence Rivers. 240pp. 8 x 10¾.
0-486-25576-X

AN ENCYCLOPEDIA OF THE VIOLIN, Alberto Bachmann. Translated by Frederick H. Martens. Introduction by Eugene Ysaye. First published in 1925, this renowned reference remains unsurpassed as a source of essential information, from construction and evolution to repertoire and technique. Includes a glossary and 73 illustrations. 496pp. 6⅛ x 9¼.   0-486-46618-3

ANIMALS: 1,419 Copyright-Free Illustrations of Mammals, Birds, Fish, Insects, etc., Selected by Jim Harter. Selected for its visual impact and ease of use, this outstanding collection of wood engravings presents over 1,000 species of animals in extremely lifelike poses. Includes mammals, birds, reptiles, amphibians, fish, insects, and other invertebrates. 284pp. 9 x 12.   0-486-23766-4

THE ANNALS, Tacitus. Translated by Alfred John Church and William Jackson Brodribb. This vital chronicle of Imperial Rome, written by the era's great historian, spans A.D. 14-68 and paints incisive psychological portraits of major figures, from Tiberius to Nero. 416pp. 5³⁄₁₆ x 8¼.   0-486-45236-0

ANTIGONE, Sophocles. Filled with passionate speeches and sensitive probing of moral and philosophical issues, this powerful and often-performed Greek drama reveals the grim fate that befalls the children of Oedipus. Footnotes. 64pp. 5³⁄₁₆ x 8 ¼.   0-486-27804-2

ART DECO DECORATIVE PATTERNS IN FULL COLOR, Christian Stoll. Reprinted from a rare 1910 portfolio, 160 sensuous and exotic images depict a breathtaking array of florals, geometrics, and abstracts — all elegant in their stark simplicity. 64pp. 8⅜ x 11.   0-486-44862-2

THE ARTHUR RACKHAM TREASURY: 86 Full-Color Illustrations, Arthur Rackham. Selected and Edited by Jeff A. Menges. A stunning treasury of 86 full-page plates span the famed English artist's career, from *Rip Van Winkle* (1905) to masterworks such as *Undine, A Midsummer Night's Dream*, and *Wind in the Willows* (1939). 96pp. 8⅜ x 11.
0-486-44685-9

THE AUTHENTIC GILBERT & SULLIVAN SONGBOOK, W. S. Gilbert and A. S. Sullivan. The most comprehensive collection available, this songbook includes selections from every one of Gilbert and Sullivan's light operas. Ninety-two numbers are presented uncut and unedited, and in their original keys. 410pp. 9 x 12.
0-486-23482-7

THE AWAKENING, Kate Chopin. First published in 1899, this controversial novel of a New Orleans wife's search for love outside a stifling marriage shocked readers. Today, it remains a first-rate narrative with superb characterization. New introductory Note. 128pp. 5³⁄₁₆ x 8¼.   0-486-27786-0

BASIC DRAWING, Louis Priscilla. Beginning with perspective, this commonsense manual progresses to the figure in movement, light and shade, anatomy, drapery, composition, trees and landscape, and outdoor sketching. Black-and-white illustrations throughout. 128pp. 8⅜ x 11.   0-486-45815-6

THE BATTLES THAT CHANGED HISTORY, Fletcher Pratt. Historian profiles 16 crucial conflicts, ancient to modern, that changed the course of Western civilization. Gripping accounts of battles led by Alexander the Great, Joan of Arc, Ulysses S. Grant, other commanders. 27 maps. 352pp. 5⅜ x 8½. 0-486-41129-X

BEETHOVEN'S LETTERS, Ludwig van Beethoven. Edited by Dr. A. C. Kalischer. Features 457 letters to fellow musicians, friends, greats, patrons, and literary men. Reveals musical thoughts, quirks of personality, insights, and daily events. Includes 15 plates. 410pp. 5⅜ x 8½. 0-486-22769-3

BERNICE BOBS HER HAIR AND OTHER STORIES, F. Scott Fitzgerald. This brilliant anthology includes 6 of Fitzgerald's most popular stories: "The Diamond as Big as the Ritz," the title tale, "The Offshore Pirate," "The Ice Palace," "The Jelly Bean," and "May Day." 176pp. 5⅜ x 8½. 0-486-47049-0

BESLER'S BOOK OF FLOWERS AND PLANTS: 73 Full-Color Plates from Hortus Eystettensis, 1613, Basilius Besler. Here is a selection of magnificent plates from the Hortus Eystettensis, which vividly illustrated and identified the plants, flowers, and trees that thrived in the legendary German garden at Eichstätt. 80pp. 8⅜ x 11. 0-486-46005-3

THE BOOK OF KELLS, Edited by Blanche Cirker. Painstakingly reproduced from a rare facsimile edition, this volume contains full-page decorations, portraits, illustrations, plus a sampling of textual leaves with exquisite calligraphy and ornamentation. 32 full-color illustrations. 32pp. 9⅜ x 12¼. 0-486-24345-1

THE BOOK OF THE CROSSBOW: With an Additional Section on Catapults and Other Siege Engines, Ralph Payne-Gallwey. Fascinating study traces history and use of crossbow as military and sporting weapon, from Middle Ages to modern times. Also covers related weapons: balistas, catapults, Turkish bows, more. Over 240 illustrations. 400pp. 7¼ x 10⅛. 0-486-28720-3

THE BUNGALOW BOOK: Floor Plans and Photos of 112 Houses, 1910, Henry L. Wilson. Here are 112 of the most popular and economic blueprints of the early 20th century — plus an illustration or photograph of each completed house. A wonderful time capsule that still offers a wealth of valuable insights. 160pp. 8⅜ x 11. 0-486-45104-6

THE CALL OF THE WILD, Jack London. A classic novel of adventure, drawn from London's own experiences as a Klondike adventurer, relating the story of a heroic dog caught in the brutal life of the Alaska Gold Rush. Note. 64pp. 5³⁄₁₆ x 8¼. 0-486-26472-6

CANDIDE, Voltaire. Edited by Francois-Marie Arouet. One of the world's great satires since its first publication in 1759. Witty, caustic skewering of romance, science, philosophy, religion, government — nearly all human ideals and institutions. 112pp. 5³⁄₁₆ x 8¼. 0-486-26689-3

CELEBRATED IN THEIR TIME: Photographic Portraits from the George Grantham Bain Collection, Edited by Amy Pastan. With an Introduction by Michael Carlebach. Remarkable portrait gallery features 112 rare images of Albert Einstein, Charlie Chaplin, the Wright Brothers, Henry Ford, and other luminaries from the worlds of politics, art, entertainment, and industry. 128pp. 8⅜ x 11. 0-486-46754-6

CHARIOTS FOR APOLLO: The NASA History of Manned Lunar Spacecraft to 1969, Courtney G. Brooks, James M. Grimwood, and Loyd S. Swenson, Jr. This illustrated history by a trio of experts is the definitive reference on the Apollo spacecraft and lunar modules. It traces the vehicles' design, development, and operation in space. More than 100 photographs and illustrations. 576pp. 6¾ x 9¼. 0-486-46756-2

A CHRISTMAS CAROL, Charles Dickens. This engrossing tale relates Ebenezer Scrooge's ghostly journeys through Christmases past, present, and future and his ultimate transformation from a harsh and grasping old miser to a charitable and compassionate human being. 80pp. 5³⁄₁₆ x 8¼.　　　　　　　　　　0-486-26865-9

COMMON SENSE, Thomas Paine. First published in January of 1776, this highly influential landmark document clearly and persuasively argued for American separation from Great Britain and paved the way for the Declaration of Independence. 64pp. 5³⁄₁₆ x 8¼.　　　　　　　　　　　　　　　　　0-486-29602-4

THE COMPLETE SHORT STORIES OF OSCAR WILDE, Oscar Wilde. Complete texts of "The Happy Prince and Other Tales," "A House of Pomegranates," "Lord Arthur Savile's Crime and Other Stories," "Poems in Prose," and "The Portrait of Mr. W. H." 208pp. 5³⁄₁₆ x 8¼.　　　　　　　　　　0-486-45216-6

COMPLETE SONNETS, William Shakespeare. Over 150 exquisite poems deal with love, friendship, the tyranny of time, beauty's evanescence, death, and other themes in language of remarkable power, precision, and beauty. Glossary of archaic terms. 80pp. 5³⁄₁₆ x 8¼.　　　　　　　　　　　　　　　0-486-26686-9

THE COUNT OF MONTE CRISTO: Abridged Edition, Alexandre Dumas. Falsely accused of treason, Edmond Dantès is imprisoned in the bleak Chateau d'If. After a hair-raising escape, he launches an elaborate plot to extract a bitter revenge against those who betrayed him. 448pp. 5³⁄₁₆ x 8¼.　　　　　　0-486-45643-9

CRAFTSMAN BUNGALOWS: Designs from the Pacific Northwest, Yoho & Merritt. This reprint of a rare catalog, showcasing the charming simplicity and cozy style of Craftsman bungalows, is filled with photos of completed homes, plus floor plans and estimated costs. An indispensable resource for architects, historians, and illustrators. 112pp. 10 x 7.　　　　　　　　　　　　0-486-46875-5

CRAFTSMAN BUNGALOWS: 59 Homes from "The Craftsman," Edited by Gustav Stickley. Best and most attractive designs from Arts and Crafts Movement publication — 1903–1916 — includes sketches, photographs of homes, floor plans, descriptive text. 128pp. 8¼ x 11.　　　　　　　　　　　0-486-25829-7

CRIME AND PUNISHMENT, Fyodor Dostoyevsky. Translated by Constance Garnett. Supreme masterpiece tells the story of Raskolnikov, a student tormented by his own thoughts after he murders an old woman. Overwhelmed by guilt and terror, he confesses and goes to prison. 480pp. 5³⁄₁₆ x 8¼.　　　　0-486-41587-2

THE DECLARATION OF INDEPENDENCE AND OTHER GREAT DOCUMENTS OF AMERICAN HISTORY: 1775-1865, Edited by John Grafton. Thirteen compelling and influential documents: Henry's "Give Me Liberty or Give Me Death," Declaration of Independence, The Constitution, Washington's First Inaugural Address, The Monroe Doctrine, The Emancipation Proclamation, Gettysburg Address, more. 64pp. 5³⁄₁₆ x 8¼.　　　　　　　　0-486-41124-9

THE DESERT AND THE SOWN: Travels in Palestine and Syria, Gertrude Bell. "The female Lawrence of Arabia," Gertrude Bell wrote captivating, perceptive accounts of her travels in the Middle East. This intriguing narrative, accompanied by 160 photos, traces her 1905 sojourn in Lebanon, Syria, and Palestine. 368pp. 5⅜ x 8½.
0-486-46876-3

A DOLL'S HOUSE, Henrik Ibsen. Ibsen's best-known play displays his genius for realistic prose drama. An expression of women's rights, the play climaxes when the central character, Nora, rejects a smothering marriage and life in "a doll's house." 80pp. 5³⁄₁₆ x 8¼.　　　　　　　　　　　　　　　0-486-27062-9

DOOMED SHIPS: Great Ocean Liner Disasters, William H. Miller, Jr. Nearly 200 photographs, many from private collections, highlight tales of some of the vessels whose pleasure cruises ended in catastrophe: the *Morro Castle, Normandie, Andrea Doria, Europa,* and many others. 128pp. 8⅜ x 11¾.　0-486-45366-9

THE DORÉ BIBLE ILLUSTRATIONS, Gustave Doré. Detailed plates from the Bible: the Creation scenes, Adam and Eve, horrifying visions of the Flood, the battle sequences with their monumental crowds, depictions of the life of Jesus, 241 plates in all. 241pp. 9 x 12.　0-486-23004-X

DRAWING DRAPERY FROM HEAD TO TOE, Cliff Young. Expert guidance on how to draw shirts, pants, skirts, gloves, hats, and coats on the human figure, including folds in relation to the body, pull and crush, action folds, creases, more. Over 200 drawings. 48pp. 8¼ x 11.　0-486-45591-2

DUBLINERS, James Joyce. A fine and accessible introduction to the work of one of the 20th century's most influential writers, this collection features 15 tales, including a masterpiece of the short-story genre, "The Dead." 160pp. 5³⁄₁₆ x 8¼.

0-486-26870-5

EASY-TO-MAKE POP-UPS, Joan Irvine. Illustrated by Barbara Reid. Dozens of wonderful ideas for three-dimensional paper fun — from holiday greeting cards with moving parts to a pop-up menagerie. Easy-to-follow, illustrated instructions for more than 30 projects. 299 black-and-white illustrations. 96pp. 8⅜ x 11.

0-486-44622-0

EASY-TO-MAKE STORYBOOK DOLLS: A "Novel" Approach to Cloth Dollmaking, Sherralyn St. Clair. Favorite fictional characters come alive in this unique beginner's dollmaking guide. Includes patterns for Pollyanna, Dorothy from *The Wonderful Wizard of Oz,* Mary of *The Secret Garden,* plus easy-to-follow instructions, 263 black-and-white illustrations, and an 8-page color insert. 112pp. 8¼ x 11.　0-486-47360-0

EINSTEIN'S ESSAYS IN SCIENCE, Albert Einstein. Speeches and essays in accessible, everyday language profile influential physicists such as Niels Bohr and Isaac Newton. They also explore areas of physics to which the author made major contributions. 128pp. 5 x 8.　0-486-47011-3

EL DORADO: Further Adventures of the Scarlet Pimpernel, Baroness Orczy. A popular sequel to *The Scarlet Pimpernel,* this suspenseful story recounts the Pimpernel's attempts to rescue the Dauphin from imprisonment during the French Revolution. An irresistible blend of intrigue, period detail, and vibrant characterizations. 352pp. 5³⁄₁₆ x 8¼.　0-486-44026-5

ELEGANT SMALL HOMES OF THE TWENTIES: 99 Designs from a Competition, Chicago Tribune. Nearly 100 designs for five- and six-room houses feature New England and Southern colonials, Normandy cottages, stately Italianate dwellings, and other fascinating snapshots of American domestic architecture of the 1920s. 112pp. 9 x 12.　0-486-46910-7

THE ELEMENTS OF STYLE: The Original Edition, William Strunk, Jr. This is the book that generations of writers have relied upon for timeless advice on grammar, diction, syntax, and other essentials. In concise terms, it identifies the principal requirements of proper style and common errors. 64pp. 5⅜ x 8½.　0-486-44798-7

THE ELUSIVE PIMPERNEL, Baroness Orczy. Robespierre's revolutionaries find their wicked schemes thwarted by the heroic Pimpernel — Sir Percival Blakeney. In this thrilling sequel, Chauvelin devises a plot to eliminate the Pimpernel and his wife. 272pp. 5³⁄₁₆ x 8¼.　0-486-45464-9